Layers

Of The Past

LAYERS OF THE PAST
Copyright © 2014 AlTonya Washington

This is a work of fiction. Characters, names, incidents, organizations and dialogue in this novel are either products of the author's imagination or are used fictitiously.

ISBN: 978-0-9911814-0-7

Cover Art Design By: Carrie Enders
Cover Art From IStockphoto.com
Printed in The USA By CreateSpace LLC

To My Patient, Yet Insatiable Readers,
You Asked For This- Hope You're Ready For
Where It Takes You

~PROLOGUE~

Long Beach, California~ 2001

"That him?" Huron Base fixed his jade stare on the slender man across the store-front street. His expression was assessing as though he were taking inventory.

The tall, stout young man standing next to Huron stepped out from the shade of the burgundy shop canopy to take a closer look across the street. "Yeah…" he sneered the word, his thin lips curling up to partially bare his teeth. "That's the snitch muthafucka, alright."

Grinning, Huron eased his sunglasses back in place. "Gettin' a little swole about it, huh man? Not like the guy had you sent up to Folsom or some shit."

Theodore Sturgess rolled his eyes. "Trust me when I say my old man's wrath is worse than Folsom could ever be."

"Tell me again what kickin' this guy's ass is gonna solve?" Huron continued to study the man who strolled the sidewalk browsing merchant wares with the woman he held hands with.

"It'll solve a lot."

"A lot, huh?" Huron smirked. "All but putting you among the employed again. Don't sound like you'll get your job back either way."

Theodore gave an impatient snort. "Just my dad tryin' to be hard for a minute. I'll get it back but I want that big-mouth nigga to pay for some of it, alright?"

Bowing his head then, Huron chuckled over his friend's way of neglecting any wrongdoing on his own end. "And tell me why *I* need to be the one to fight this fool?"

Theodore finally pulled his steady hazel gaze away from his enemy across the street and studied Huron in disbelief. "Are you shittin' me, man? You're Huron Base," he grunted out a laugh. "Hell, man you even *named* yourself. You're your own badass entity. Nobody without colors got as much juice as you," he referred to his friend's lack of gang affiliation.

"Cats gonna think twice when they find out you got my back," Theodore nodded, looking pleased with himself, "not just personal-like friends and shit- but when it comes to handlin' business. Yeah," he shot the cuffs of the gray polo shirt he wore, "they gonna think twice 'bout snitching on my business to my pops or anybody else."

5

"Hmph," Huron's mouth curved down in an impressed smile. "You surprise me, Thee. Didn't know you had sense enough to strategize that deep."

Theodore grinned, but the gesture showed signs of wear. "I know this ain't your usual kind of job no more, B. 'Preciate it."

Huron's grin brought a more vibrant sparkle to his emerald gaze behind the shades. "We go back," he said and clapped the other man's shoulder.

"All the way back," Theodore added, reciprocating the shoulder clap.

"So lemme go teach this fool a lesson," Huron nudged Theodore's elbow with his own. "Been a while since I gave these a workout," he flexed his fingers before clenching them into two massive fists.

Theodore whistled to relay being impressed. "Thanks for lookin' out, man."

Huron's mouth tightened grimly so infinitesimally that it may have gone unnoticed. "Goin' way back or not, you'll owe me for this." He looked to Theodore over the tops of his sunglasses. "You know that, right?"

"Yeah man, cool," Theodore nodded. Everyone knew that his old friend did nothing for free. Huron Base always collected. One would do well to accept the fact that payment would be collected in one way or another.

"B," Theodore reached for Huron's arm when he looked ready to proceed. "I know that this is gonna cost me, so I want that punk bitch to remember this. Years from now when he's out livin' his goody two shoes life, I want him to remember this and know I was the one he should've never crossed."

Huron grinned, reaching into a back jean's pocket for the gloves there. "Never thought you liked workin' for Mr. Frank's finance company so much."

6

Theodore returned the grin. "Just make him hurt."

Again, Huron flexed his fingers. Spreading them wide, he inserted them into the black leather gloves he'd taken from his pocket. "That's a guarantee," he promised.

~1~

Kaanapali, Maui~13 years later...

Kamari Grade held the slim bottle of sunscreen to her chest as though it were a priceless artifact. "You're not serious," her lush brown gaze was wide and unwavering while she gawked at the woman seated a few feet away.

"Why do you think that?" Eliza Breck's thick blonde mane whipped wildly about her face thanks to a rejuvenating breeze.

Kam laughed at her friend's playfully stunned expression. "We're in Hawaii, remember? Top destination of sun worshipers around the world."

Eliza glanced across her shoulder and then leaned close to Kam as if she were about to impart with a guarded secret. "We sun worshipers only step out to pay homage when we *need* to- it isn't the most symbiotic relationship."

"Ah…" Still clutching the bottle, Kam reclined on the cushioned, waterproof lounge and tried to make sense of her friend's outlook. Quickly, she skimmed Eliza's already tanned skin. "So you're saying that you've come here to Maui where sun is practically pouring in along our own private little stretch of beach and you don't intend to pay even a *little* homage?"

Eliza shrugged, a prim yet teasing smile coming to her mouth. Leaning back into the lounge's pearl gray cushioning then too, she closed her eyes. "Cousteau appreciates me being the same tone all over. I'd like to keep myself that way."

"*Cousteau* appreciates, huh?" Kamari's expression harbored a bit more animation then. "And I guess when it comes to knowing whether you're the same tone all over, he'd know better than anyone, right?"

Eliza flushed, giving her tan a richer appearance. "Kam, that man has seen parts of me that I've never and *will* never see."

"I got it!" Kam laughed, but still held the bottle out of Eliza's grasp when she reached for it. "Not so fast...just what are you willing to do for this bottle?"

"Mmm Kam…" Eliza gave a decadent stretch and naughty smile. "I've done things during the last two weeks that have damn well earned me that bottle of sunscreen."

Kamari's laughter resurfaced. "Do tell!" She pushed up from the lounge.

9

"Don't play," Eliza ordered.

"Let's see how far you're willing to go!" Kam sprinted backwards away from the lounge area set along the shore. She turned toward the sea and looked back to see if her friend would give chase. She had.

Laughing wildly and taunting with devilish intent, Kam led Eliza on a merry chase along the beach until they were splashing in the foamy waves of the Pacific.

~~~

Huron Base arrived out on the massive stone lanai that faced the staggering beauty of sand, sky and ocean. For a moment, he allowed himself to dwell in a state of captivation. The sea never failed to do that and he appreciated that he could be so affected.

Huron headed over to a tall, sterling silver food cart that teemed with an array of treats. The three-tiered device held diverse offerings of fruit on the bottom tier with muffins, Danish and croissants in the middle. The level was fashioned with a mechanism to help the food maintain its fresh-baked warmth.

The top tier was dedicated to beverages. Huron bypassed the mixed offerings of teas and coffees and helped himself to a glass of apple juice. Glass in hand, he went to lean against one of the stone columns that supported the high ceiling roof which was constructed of the same rust-colored stone as the columns.

Huron grinned suddenly, noticing the man who relaxed on one of the four maplewood lounges across the patio. He cleared his throat.

"Wasn't it you who said that sleeping 'til four p.m. was on the menu everyday this week?" Huron called, walking toward the lounge area.

Cousteau Morgan's grin held the same roughish undertones as his friend's. "Any man would happily pass on sleep to enjoy this view."

"Agreed," Huron's opinion then had more to do with the lush environment. "No place like Hawaii," he sighed, settling to a lounge.

Cousteau arched a long, sleek brow in his old friend's direction and served up a half shrug. "Hawaii's got beauty- true. But right now, it's running a very distant second to that."

Huron tracked his brilliant stare in the direction Cousteau nodded and he released a slow whistle in response. Gaze fixed on the shore, he set his juice glass to the low polished maple table that stood between the lounges. He didn't care if the glass made it to the table's square surface or not.

Delighted as well, Cousteau followed Huron's whistle with a chuckle. "That was exactly my reaction," he shared.

Reclining on his lounge, Huron stared transfixed by the sight of the two beauties frolicking amidst the crashing early morning waves. He was riveted on Kamari and; at once, felt the tell-tale tightening below his waist. He muttered a curse. He'd just let her out of bed an hour ago after she'd nourished his 6am erection with a dose of her body.

The sight of her bouncing around and being doused by foamy currents of water, had his cock craving another healthy dose.

Cousteau, his turquoise stare then a passion-darkened cobalt, was focused on Eliza. "Count Elly and me out of any excursions today, will you? Takin' her back to bed when she's done with her playdate."

"Not a problem," Huron's response came out in a rumble. "Kam's day will turn out the same."

The men at last traded glances and shortly after the warm soft roar of male laughter lifted between them. Cousteau curbed his laughter on a playful groan and eased a leg off the lounge. The sole of a leather sandal hit the lanai's rose blush marble flooring with a resounding slap and he buried the heels of his hands into his eyes.

"She's gonna kill me, B. She's gonna kill me and I can't wait to let her."

"Hell man, is there a better way to go?" Huron's words were caught up in laughter.

"Hmph no," Cousteau seemed to sober a little. "No there isn't."

Following the intense Las Vegas meeting with former business associates Dutch and Sandra Breslin, Huron and Kamari set off to their Hawaii destination. The villa Huron kept in Kaanapali, Maui was a breathtaking work of art. Kam had wanted to explore every inch of the 10,000 square foot dwelling the moment they'd arrived.

The only room Huron was interested in was the bedroom suite of which there were eight. The couple spent four days alone before Kam noted that the place was too remarkable to enjoy on their own. Huron disagreed, but loved Kam's idea of inviting Cousteau and Eliza to share it with them. The couples had delighted in ten exquisite days at the retreat before ever venturing out to enjoy the rest of what the area had to offer.

"We don't deserve this, B," Cousteau's stare rivaled the ocean for vividness as it fixed once more upon the shore. Eliza stood near her lounge talking with Kam while they toweled off from their romp.

"Agreed, " Huron reached for his juice glass. "You'll forgive me if I don't feel guilty enough to talk myself out of enjoying every bit of it."

"Hell, I don't either," Cousteau could only manage half a smile though.

Huron pulled his eyes away from the beauty along the shore and back to his old friend. "What's up with the long face, Cous?"

"Men like us shouldn't count on enjoying this kind of ...goodness for long." Agitation registered when Cousteau heard the laugh Huron gave.

"I think that's *my* line," Huron teased, giving a bewildered shake of his head. "What the fuck, Cous? You second guessing everything you told Eliza?"

"Just what do you think that was?" Cousteau leaned forward on his lounge and eyed his friend curiously. "About my part in uncovering that story on her mom? That was nothing."

Instant realization stirred in Huron's eyes then and he shook his head more determinedly. "That's all there is."

"You know that's not true-"

"Then it's all that matters."

"It's not even *half* of what matters."

"Fuck Cous, what good does all the rest serve?" Huron's tone was a low growl then, impatience with his friend heightened. "It was all in another life- one that plays no part in who you are now."

Cousteau's laughter bellowed then. "Are you kidding? It has *everything* to do with it. Have you forgotten how I managed to uncover the dirt I had on Jessica Breck?"

Huron waved off the query involving Eliza's mother. "It's got nothing to do with you."

"B-"

"You know what I mean."

"Shit," Cousteau rested his elbows to his knees and used one hand to drag back the wealth of maple brown waves that tumbled into his eyes. "All I know is that the past- recent or long past- has a way of working itself into the present. You don't believe that, ask Jessica Breck."

Huron studied the juice in his glass. "Jessica was a grown woman who made her own decisions."

"Decisions that involved my family." Cousteau worked his fingers over the bridge of his aquiline nose. "I spent so much time talking to El about *her* people, I never got around to my own."

"And what do you think telling her any of that will solve?" Huron sat up a bit on his lounge. "All it'll do is make her worry more about her mother."

That much was true Cousteau realized. Jessica Breck was then a guest of the county. The socialite had admitted to the murder of her nephew in an attempt to hide damning proof of her...work in the porn industry.

"I believe what I have to say could do just the opposite since the rest of it involves the very thing her mother won't share. It's the very thing that could serve as Jessica Breck's very own, gold-embossed get out of jail free card."

~~~

Las Vegas, Nevada~

Jeffrey Kears stood and began to shuffle a sheaf of papers back into the silver briefcase he'd brought with him into the rather ostentatious penthouse office.

"I think it's best if I wasn't part of the rest of this conversation," Kears rapidly secured the locks on his case.

"Aw, sit on down Jeff," Dutch Breslin's hearty chuckle resounded in reaction to his attorney's unease. "We ain't doin' nothin' but shootin' the breeze um... hypothesizin'- *that's* the word."

Jeff Kears smiled, but continued to gather his belongings from the silver encased glass table that sat between red overstuffed leather sofas. "Understood Dutch, but I really need to be going."

"Jeff?" Sandra Breslin's voice coasted out like a fine brandy. "Are you sure there's nothing we can do to get Huron to change his mind?"

Weeks prior, Huron Base had paid a special visit to the Breslins where he informed them that he was giving up his interest in Fine Lines Studios. Huron made the couple a more than generous offer to divest himself of any ties to the adult film company.

Given the turn of events involving Jessica Breck's murder of Simon Breck, the Breslins were rather curious about the timing. There was also the matter of the woman Huron was seeing- a woman who was in the business of uncovering secrets.

"I'd advise against trying to change his mind," Jeff's tight smile turned into a bonafide grimace. "Huron Base isn't a man who takes kindly to his decisions being questioned." He gave his clients the benefit of a stern gaze then. "Base's offer for cutting his monetary ties is far more than he initially put in. You're coming out on top in this."

Dutch snorted something akin to a harsh laugh. "Only thing better than havin' Base money is Base involvement- even silent involvement is gold."

Jeff smiled as though he'd expected the outlook from his client and friend. "Listen Dutch, you don't want to go down this road."

"I didn't get where I am by not playin' every card in my hand."

15

Jeff nodded, familiar with the man's undying pride. "As a gambler, you should know some cards are better if held or left in the deck altogether."

A throat cleared from someone unseen. "Are you two going to trade card anthologies all day? If so, we can continue with more pressing matters later," the hidden voice chimed in.

Jeff made a faster attempt at shoving his two phones into his suitcoat pockets then. "I'll be saying 'goodbye' to you folks. Dutch?" he fixed the man with a cautionary look. "Think about what I said."

The door closed behind Jeff with a soft thud.

"Is that the sound of the upstanding attorney taking his leave?"

"He's gone," Dutch spoke to the triangular speaker box on the leather encased glass desk he sat behind.

"Good to hear. Now...when would you like it done?"

"Dutch?" Sandra Breslin's usually cool demeanor betrayed signs of disturbance. "Sweetheart, are you sure this is the only way?" She inched closer to the sofa cushions she clutched.

Dutch Breslin's sigh echoed the one from the speaker then. The emerging voice held a gruff edge when it resounded from the box that time.

"I don't have time for this, Breslin. Why don't you call me when your conscience shuts the fuck up?"

"Dammit Sandy!" Dutch growled to his wife when the phone line abruptly silenced.

"I'm sorry!" Sandra Breslin bolted from the sofa, clutching her arms about her middle as though she was experiencing pain. "There has to be another way! This will destroy us! I know it!"

16

"Do you like the way we live, Sugar?" Dutch asked, a calm suddenly radiating in his eyes. "Without Huron's backing, certain businesses we dabble in might start bein' a little trickier to handle without that silent yet formidable wall of protection he so effortlessly provides."

"I know," Sandra shuddered, raking her hands through her glossy whiskey brown tresses. "I just don't know what good this is for if *we're* the ones who wind up dead."

Dutch chortled. "Aw San-"

"No Dutch!" Sandra rounded on her husband. "You know we'd be the first ones he'd hunt down if anything happened to his latest acquisition."

"You're overreacting," Dutch drawled.

Sandra sauntered toward the desk, took a seat on one of the cushioned leather bound corners. "Think about it, D, *we* were the first he came to cut ties with. It's been over a month and he hasn't made any other major moves to back off any other holdings."

Dutch blinked, seeming to contemplate the validity in his wife's words. Leaning back in a gargantuan desk chair, he fiddled with the buttons along the front of his vest. "You think he's waiting to see if there'll be any backlash?" He brought his elbows to the desk. "See if we'd get others to rally against what he's trying to do?"

"I don't think he believes we'd have the nerve to go against him at all." Sandra eased off the desk and strolled the room. "I really think his plan was to show Ms. Grade that he'd do anything to make himself worthy of her." She tapped an index nail to the crescent shaped diamond nestled between her breasts. "We were first on his list because of Jessica- her daughter is good friends with Ms. Grade." Sandra paced the room with greater intent, worrying the silver chain securing her diamond. She came to a stop before the floor to ceiling windows that looked down on the street below.

The Las Vegas Strip was void of many bodies at that time of morning. Most likely, said bodies were recovering from nights they'd never forget in rooms they could scarcely afford.

"What 'cha thinkin' San?" Dutch inquired. While playing every card in his hand had gone a long way to ensure the success of his life, it didn't hold a candle to the support and counsel of a smart woman. His wife was that woman.

"Huron has interests far more lucrative and powerful than ours…" Sandra wedged her thumbnail between her teeth while she pondered. "We were special to Ms. Grade so that put distancing himself from us at the top of his list."

Dutch gave a mystified shrug. "Maybe that's it then, if it was about that."

Sandra was already shaking her head, her blue eyes narrowed by speculation. "He actually loves this one. A man like that…" she faced the windows as her words trailed away. She made a point of keeping her appreciative smile hidden from her husband as the image of Huron Base filled her mind. She collected herself before fantasizing got the better of her.

"I've seen that man with scores of women over the years," she slanted Dutch a bland look. "He didn't look at one of them with an ounce of the emotion that all but pours out of him when he looks at the little troubleshooter."

"What's your point, darlin?"

Sandra returned to the desk and reclaimed her perch along the corner. "He'll break every shady tie he's got. He's not a thug anymore, climbing the ranks and breaking bones to make a name for himself. Legitimately, he's worth

18

more than he could spend in twenty lifetimes. He'll cut anything else that's not above board."

She smoothed her hands over a pencil slim black satin skirt and propped them to her hips. "The problem with that is the more powerful-*upstanding* ones among us will see it as business and keep on trucking. Those of us who still very much depend on his backing for our own less than legitimate dealings will have a tougher time of it."

Sandra moved around to where her husband sat and leaned against the desk again. "Just wait before you make any outrageous moves. You'll need cover if you pull something like this. Once Huron cuts ties with the rest of his black sheep friends, you'll have all the cover you need."

Dutch reached for Sandra's hand, pressed a kiss to her wrist. "Forgive me for bein' impatient, Sugar."

"Well...we don't have to sit by twiddling our thumbs," she toyed with a lock of his salt and pepper hair, "not when there's so much to do."

Dutch Breslin grinned. "What you gettin' at, gal?"

Sandra settled down onto her husband's lap. "Ms. Grade finds such enjoyment uncovering other people's secrets, let's see what *she's* got to uncover."

~~~

"This is so beautiful," Eliza marveled while wringing a few last droplets of water from her hair. "So remote...the guy really adores his privacy."

"Yeah," Kam had finished with her towel and was folding it. "Yes, he does," she tossed down the towel.

"So..." Eliza folded her arms beneath ample breasts barely covered by a halter-style bikini top. "Does that tone mean that you're content not knowing what he does for a living?"

Kam studied the white sand she squished between her toes. "That trip to Vegas confirmed that he's got...involvements that could be a conflict of interest if he keeps them and I keep my job." She tucked a reddish lock behind her ear and smiled when a breeze dislodged it. "I don't think I want to know any more, El and that makes me feel guilty as hell. Like I- like I'm betraying my job for my man."

"And what a man..." Eliza raved, giggling when Kam rolled her eyes and smiled. "Ah girl, cheer up," she gave a little agitated dance. "At least the gesture's being reciprocated. You're betraying *your* job and in a way, he's betraying his."

"Fine Lines is a big money maker, El. I'm sure he walked away from a heavy cash flow when he broke his partnership with them."

"At least there's reciprocity there, Kam." Eliza slapped her hands to her thighs in a helpless fashion. "Not like me. I'm here, having a fantastic time in a fantastic place and trying not to feel guilty as hell over it because my mother's in jail. But she...she let me think I'd betrayed our family with Cousteau after his exposé on us. All the while, *she* was the one trying to hide her dirt. Hmph, I'll bet she never lost a night of sleep worrying over what that did to me."

"We're gonna get her out," Kam promised, knowing that, despite her attempts at being cold, Eliza was truly worried about her mom. "You've got me working on this and we're going to find something to get her out of there."

"I know Kam," Eliza's tone held a resolved quality.

"So? No more guilt, alright? Your mom wouldn't want you wasting time on that useless emotion."

Eliza nodded, deciding to accept Kam's words as fact when Cousteau came up behind her, scooped her against his wide chest and crushed her mouth beneath his for a quick, heated second.

"Playtime's over," he growled into her neck.

"Oh," Eliza groaned. "I thought it was just about to start."

"Mmm...I like the way you think, Ms. Breck," Cousteau looked up and slanted Kam a sly wink before carrying away his giggling burden.

Kam returned the wave Eliza tossed up. She took a step back, only to find the move impeded by a wall of solid muscle. Before she could turn, hands cupped her hips.

"Can't imagine you'd try to tan this body," Huron murmured against her nape and spanned one hand across her taut, honey brown skin until he hooked her inner thigh.

Weakened, Kam let her head rest against the unyielding plane of his chest. His thumb brushed the front of her bikini bottom and launched a slow assault on her clit which forced a small cry from her throat.

"Do you know anything better I...can do with it?" She gasped. The sound that met her question would've sent her to her knees had his hold on her hip and thigh been any lighter.

"Oh, I can think of a lot better things to do with this body," he spoke with certainty and commenced to proving it right there in the middle of paradise.

~2~

Sensation slammed her body in an unrelenting wave. Pleasure drunk, Kam was sure she could have crumpled to the fine sand beneath her feet. Huron's grip on her waist however, kept her right where she wanted to be. He'd taken her to climax with his ruthless manipulation of her clit, but he was by no means done with his captivating torture.

Kam rested her head back once more, pillowing it against a flexing pectoral that was partially bared by his open shirt. Her lips were parted, but no sound emerged. She was too aroused, stunned silent by the devastating delight of his hand inside her bikini- his middle finger caressing her silken folds.

Kam arched slightly, hoping to hint at her impatience for him to do more. He sensed her urgency without the subtle hints. Having barely curved his finger inside her, the pad of the digit was already coated by a substantial layer of her moisture.

Huron smiled when she left off the subtle hints and took his wrist in both her hands in an attempt to direct him to her satisfaction. He didn't disappoint her, yet his willingness to meet her demands was given with maddening slowness. His middle finger curved inside her a bit more and Kam finally regained use of her vocal chords.

She whimpered. Gradually, she moved to her toes, aching to gain as much pleasure as he would allow. Slowly, her body began to ride the wide finger he used to lightly stroke her. Kam's singular intention was divided when his hand at her hip moved upward to cradle a breast still hidden behind the baby blue fabric of her top.

The material was no barrier against the circular rubs from Huron's thumb. Kamari bit her lip, only *just* stifling the cry roused by his touch. Her nipple tensed, puckering to grab every ounce of sensation that his thumb met out.

Not to be outdone in the erotic gifts department, his middle finger; slightly curved into her sex, suddenly surged high. The sound Kam gave in reaction was between a gasp and a cry. His exploration was thorough and she welcomed it. Once again, her hands curved over his wrist. Her hold was a loose one. She was as stimulated by the stroking dips and rotations of his finger as she was by the light bumps of his wrist against her palm where she held onto him.

Huron had tired of caressing fabric and found his way inside the barely there bikini top. His middle finger encountered a nipple and mimicked the slow rotations its twin made inside Kam's moist center. The bare nub, already taut in response to his manipulations forced a low groan from the back of his throat.

The sound vibrating through his chest then, doused Kam in shivers that were thrilling instead of jarring. By then, he had resumed his task of thumbing her clit while claiming her obscenely with his middle and index fingers.

"Huron..." her tone was pleading.

"If you're about to ask me to stop-forget it."

"No...please..." she murmured, having no plans of doing anything so ridiculous.

His index finger had joined the seductive play at her breast. It and his thumb, gently tugged and twisted the beaded nipple before rounding out the heated play with soothing brushes from the thumb.

Kam found herself imagining that his tongue was there instead. "Put your mouth on me...please Huron..."

He did. Though not in the way she had intended, it was just as delectable. His tongue bathed her nape for a few more alluring moments. Then, his mouth grazed the curve of her ear before his lips closed over the lobe and suckled.

Kam felt her brain go into sensory overload in the midst of the triple caress. The way his tongue licked and sucked her earlobe while his fingers tormented her nipples, provided vivid sensations of how it'd feel if that part of her body were inside his mouth.

Moreover, the ravenous suckling and possessive fingering had her thoughts venturing to other oral treasures that tongue of his was capable of offering. She bucked her hips with more force then, intent on capturing the second climax that crept dangerously close.

Huron felt it- felt the telltale tensing of her vaginal walls that told him she'd be drowning his fingers in her cream very soon. He ceased his play mid-thrust and smiled

24

when he heard the sound she uttered. It carried a tone of infuriated disbelief.

Kam felt not an ounce of shame over her greed. She even reached for his wrist to put him back where she wanted him. Huron resisted, instead turning the tables to catch both *her* wrists in one of his hands. He made her walk with him, nudging her forward in spite of her whimpered protests. Along the way, they passed the folding lounge she'd relaxed in. Huron snagged the back of the chair and dragged it along.

He led them away from the shore in the direction of the house. Massive palm trees dotted the lengthy stretch of beach along the stone wall that sectioned it. Wide leaves swayed vibrantly amidst the breeze and offered healthy swatches of shade.

Kam tried to halt her steps several times in route to their destination. She even offered soft words of promised pleasure to Huron if he'd stop moving. He only chuckled and continued to nudge her forward.

They stopped beneath the shelter of three towering palms and he released her there. He took the beach towel and spread it across the cushioned seating of the lounge. Kam waited, watching him doff the white shirt that contrasted beautifully against the rich caramel of his skin. Once his magnificent chest was bared, he settled back on the lounge.

"You were saying?" he prompted.

Kam smiled and took a few steps closer to the chair. "I'm afraid you're still wearing too many clothes for 'what I was saying'," she eyed the army green cargo shorts he sported.

"So? Handle it then," he shrugged and captured the wrist nearest him. He tugged until she was straddling his lap.

25

The lounge was wide enough to accommodate Huron's wide body with Kam's knees on either side of his hips. "How long will it take for you to get me out of my clothes?" he asked.

"We'll just work around them," hastily, she unfastened the waistband and unbuttoned the fly.

"Hey? Don't I get any foreplay?" he whined.

"Payback for leaving me hanging back there," she grumbled.

"Doesn't seem fair."

"It doesn't?" Kam smiled, noticing his unfairly long lashes settling as sensation claimed him once she'd taken him out of the cargo shorts and boxers.

"Kam…" Huron let his head fall back against the lounge.

She cradled him loosely in her hand and enjoyed the chance to torture *him* a bit. She approved of his width and the way he filled her palm. Deliberately, she swiped her thumb along the length of his sex. She topped off the caress with a few slow swipes across the wide, mushroom-shaped tip.

Huron made a anguished sound and began to lightly thrust into her hand. Kam bent to nuzzle into his chest where she pulled a small, flat nipple between her lips and swirled her tongue around the small bud. She felt it pebble instantly beneath her manipulations. Gradually, she increased the pressure, moaning softly when his hand disappeared in her hair.

"Kam," her name on his tongue was practically a gasp.

She relished the taste of him. Beneath the soap, there was something distinctly male and heady. It motivated her to intensify her suckling at his chest. The mock thrusts Huron pushed into her hand also seemed to intensify.

"Kam...Kam wait," he urged and was soon trying to ease her back from his chest. "Babe..."

She refused to relinquish her hold on him. Gloving his cock, she continued the orgasm inducing strokes. All the while, her thumb luxuriated in the pre-cum glistening at the head of his caramel toned endowment. She'd have him exploding in her hand much too soon if she kept that up.

The realization sent a wicked triumph sparkling in the cocoa brown depths of Kamari's eyes. "What were you saying about no foreplay?"

Gently, he dragged her up over him. "You've done your job," he plied her with a seeking kiss then.

Kam got lost in the act. Cupping Huron's face, her nails grazed the silky whiskers that shaped his light beard and goatee. His kiss was possessive and devouring and Kam was so mesmerized by it that it didn't sink in that her bikini was missing until a strong, sudden breeze crossed her nipples and sex.

She had but a second to let the reality of being naked outdoors sink in before she was being filled by his wide erection. Her gasp carried in tune with a faint cry that dissolved into a moan as pleasure thrummed its way inside her like the slow ooze of warm syrup.

Huron kept his gaze fixed on Kam, studying the mix of emotions her lovely face revealed as she took him slow. As lovely as she was, it was difficult for Huron to keep watch. The feel of her body stretching to receive him, to envelop him in her tight depths, promised to lull him into a passion haze that weighed his eyelids, enticing them to close.

Kam brought her hands to his, squeezing for purchase while easing herself down over him. Pleasure and the mildest stab of pain surged. The pain was minor and in no way distracted from the stirring satisfaction that was consuming her. In truth, the 'pain' was merely a reminder of all the sweet ways the powerful male beneath her had possessed her body over the last several weeks.

Final remnants of discomfort vanished shortly with only the sweet pleasure remaining and cresting. Kam had taken Huron in a series of slow, circular moves that continued until she was fully seated.

Huron gave her the time he felt she needed to adjust. Then, his hold was tightening at her hips. He lifted her slightly, then settled her- repeating the move while his hips rose to gently slam against her, deepening his possession of her body with every thrust.

Kam's resulting moans held a wavering chord. The sounds were in sync to her rocking hips. She lifted her arms, tunneling her fingers through her hair which arched her breasts more prominently in the process. Huron couldn't resist the temptation. He raised his head from the lounge, one hand snaking over Kam's hip and up the front of her body to cup one of the pert mounds. He tormented himself for a while, growing progressively jealous of his fingers squeezing and caressing her nipple. He needed his mouth there.

Kam linked her arms around Huron's neck, nails grazing the crop of sleek hair tapered there while his mouth worked over her. Eventually, her fingers weakened and could no longer apply the raking caress to the back of his neck. The potent tugs of his lips and tongue sucking her nipple; as though the bud provided him with some necessary nourishment, had completely weakened her body.

Only her most intimate muscles seemed capable of any activity. They continued to massage and squeeze the
28

stiff muscle that stretched her. Huron maintained his task of orchestrating her moves. *That* endeavor was often to Kam's regret when sheathing himself inside her became too much and threatened to make him come before he was ready. In those moments, he'd tap her bottom to urge her to still for a second.

When Kam refused to comply, he'd simply lift her off until he'd tamped down the raging need to fill her with his seed. She refused to let him unseat her when he next made the attempt. She'd tired of the control she had allowed him to assert and clutched the back of the lounge in order to steady herself. Elation hummed and she surrendered wildly, clenching and releasing him.

The growl rumbling through his chest told her he'd soon be of a mind to make another play at tugging her off. While she appreciated the effort he made to make it last, to make it good for them both, Kam couldn't stand it. She needed him too much.

"Kam-"

"Shh…" She smiled at the broken tone of his voice. "Shh...let it happen, let it happen…I'm not going anywhere. You can have all you want later," she made the promise while squeezing him insatiably inside her walls. She was desperately attempting to keep her own climax at bay until he was right there with her.

"Kamari...fuck…" Huron rasped out and surrendered to the raging demands of his body.

Spasms rocked her when heavy jets of his semen splashed thickly, warming her womb. Huron kept her close, still molesting one nipple beneath his lips and tongue. The other, he treated to an expert fondling between his thumb and forefinger.

Kam treasured the rich breeze and the medley it drew from the mingle of swaying leaves, birdsong and the crash of the ocean. The brilliance of sky and clouds overhead was as much a treat for her mind as the climax was for her body.

The lovers stilled in their embrace. Breathing slowed and heart rates gradually assumed a steadier beat. Too depleted to think on their current state of dress, the two collapsed on the lounge and submitted to exhaustion.

***

The day passed in much the same manner as it had begun. The couples kept to themselves inside the palatial beachfront home. There were no complaints about enjoying a lazy day. The group met on one of the garden side terraces to enjoy a late lunch of jerk chicken, with snap peas, dirty rice and caramelized plantains.

The filling meal wooed everyone back to bed. It was intended, of course, given the group's high intensity plans for the evening. Before heading indoors, they made plans for a night out on the town.

Lahaina, also located in West Maui was a town known for its extraordinary array of shops and restaurants. The town was also known for the dozens of art galleries it boasted. On the National Register of Historic Places, Lahaina's perfect climate and oceanfront locale made it a great spot for an array of activities including energetic shows featuring traditional Polynesian dancers. Such entertainment was in store for that evening.

~~~

"B…" Cousteau greeted when Huron arrived in the billiards room that night.

Set just across from the lanai, the room was enormous with its open entryways. The entrances could be

30

sealed by sliding glass walls that didn't hinder the gorgeous beach views on three sides. On that particular evening, the glass walls were left disengaged allowing for the rejuvenating sea air to filter the room.

"Looks like my plan to spend the day in bed wasn't such a bad one after all," Cousteau bragged.

"I never said spending the day in bed was bad," Huron grinned, "I just didn't want to *sleep* through all of it." He nodded past his friend's shoulder. "So where's your prettier half?"

"Still getting dressed," Cousteau glanced back toward the main house. "And you? What about *your* prettier half?"

"Same."

Cousteau grinned. "Get you a drink, while you wait?" he offered.

"Sounds good. What are you havin'?"

Cousteau raised a distinctive stout bottle. "Red Stripe," he called.

Huron went to stare out over the view while Cousteau got the beer. The sun was just setting and the sky was an awesome blending of purples and blues with hints of orangish pink throughout.

"This place is incredible, man. When'd you get it?" Cousteau asked as he rounded the bar.

"While back," Huron explained, still looking out over the landscape. "Business associate asked me to consider taking it instead of the interest in his company. He brought me here and I told him he had a deal."

"Sounds right!" Cousteau laughed. "Only a place as outrageous as this could make you back off your top rule of engagement."

Anyone who did business with Huron or had only heard of him in passing, knew that he always demanded

31

controlling interest; from any company he helped out of financial stress, over monetary payment.

Huron smirked, accepting the beer from Cousteau. "It's a status thing-at least it was. When I brought Kam here and she loved it I um," he cleared his throat when emotion intervened. "I wanted to take her someplace no one knew about so we wouldn't be bothered and she actually fell in love with it and for the first time, it didn't feel like some shallow status symbol. It felt like...home because- she was here." He laughed suddenly as though his own words had surprised him. "I obviously need a drink, lots of 'em," he said.

"Understood, man," Cousteau grabbed his beer and came to join Huron near the window. "I felt the same when I took El to my place in Malibu. I didn't need it," he downed a swig of the beer, "way too big for one person. I was there for years and it hadn't felt like home 'til I had Elly there."

"What are your plans with El?"

"What else?" Cousteau shrugged, his manner playfully nonchalant. "Marry her and keep her barefoot and pregnant," soft laughter flooded and he shrugged again. "Barefoot and pregnant at least twice- hopefully three times."

"Makes sense," Huron smiled. "You've known each other long enough."

"And? You tryin' to tell me your plans with Kam aren't the same?"

Huron took a long drag from the bottle. "She doesn't know me the way El knows you."

"I think I asked about *your* ideas."

"Hmph," Huron's expression harbored a sadness when he studied the bottle. "I knew she was it almost from the minute I met her but I've got a long way to go before I can even *think* about making that happen."

Cousteau perched on the pool table's glossy pine frame. "You really think she cares about how far you've got to go?"

"I believe she cares about it more than she'll ever admit," Huron leaned against the window, juggling the beer bottle in his hand then. "I'm not a man she could give herself to like that. I'm not a man she *should* give herself to like that."

One last drag and Cousteau was done with his beer. "I won't even bother to go into why that's such bullshit since I got a feeling you know that already."

"Cous man..." Huron set aside the bottle and began to walk the room. "You know that job of hers has already bumped up against me once."

"Well maybe you should just tell her whatever's left before it makes another bump."

"I could do that..." Huron nodded, "or," he pointed a finger toward the ceiling as another idea hit, "I could get rid of it all and never have to tell her the rest."

~3~

Kam heard the soft chiming of her mobile as she was on her way out of the bedroom suite she'd shared with Huron since their arrival in Maui. Silently, she issued a reminder to shut the thing off for the rest of the night.

The ringing had gotten progressively louder, making the phone easier to fish out of the tote bag she'd planned to leave behind that night in preference of something daintier. Her agitation over the call changed when she noticed Tenille Yancey's name on the faceplate. Smiling then, she greeted her assistant.

"Don't you have a shred of wifely honor, woman? You *do* have a sexy war hero at home to take care of, don't you? Why are you still at the office?"

"And why do you just automatically assume that I'm still at the office?" Tenille feigned outrage. "You can't tell that from my cellphone."

"This is *you* I'm talking about," Kam rolled her eyes in amusement. "And weren't you the one complaining about sexual frustration not so long ago?"

Tenille's husband Blake had recently returned home from his latest tour of duty in the Middle East. Blake Yancey's homecoming had been bittersweet. The tour would probably be his last in light of the leg injury he had sustained. On the 'sweet' side of things, the decorated Marine captain was expected to make a full recovery.

"Actually… that's one of the things I'm calling to talk to you about."

"Uh oh," Kam let a playful cringe come through in her voice. "I opt to stay out of sexual frustration discussions from here on out."

Tenille laughed. "Got it! I only wanted to ask about taking a few days off next month. Me and Blake were talking about just getting lost for a while."

"Oh Tenille! Honey that sounds great-"

"Well nothing's set in stone, yet," Tenille piped up, caution clinging to her words. "We could easily reschedule if you and Huron aren't back."

"Don't you dare," Kam pointed toward the floor while giving the order. "I haven't forgotten that I have a business to take care of."

"You also have a man to take care of," Tenille had known her boss long enough and well enough to feel comfortable voicing the soft reminder. "Huron Base looks like a man with...large appetites. May take a lot of time to care for him properly."

"Mmm hmm and that's why it's convenient to live in the same town."

"Living in the same town is good… I was thinking you might return with an announcement of sorts...he *has* met your folks after all."

"Let's not forget who was responsible for that!" Kamari laughed.

"And I happily accept the blame, but since you never reamed me for sharing that info with him, I take it things are intense- jumping the broom- intense."

Kam laughed again. "Go home Tenille. Your romantic side's going full steam tonight. Huron and me are about as far off from commitment as anyone could get." Silently, Kam had to take stock of the fact that the man *had* recently pulled out of a lucrative business arrangement because of her.

"We're just having a good time together, you know?" She spoke to Tenille but wondered who she was really trying to convince. "*Anyway*, having a good time is something we can easily do in San Francisco. You and Blake can go on and dust off those passports."

"Passports? I doubt we'll go very far."

"Well just have fun with your guy wherever you go." Kam urged in a dreamy tone.

"Thanks," Tenille's response was equally dreamy and then she gasped. "I did have another reason for calling."

"Uh oh," Kam's cringe that time wasn't quite so playful.

Kamari always made a point of leaving her accounts in good standing whenever she took a break and left town- which didn't occur very often. The diligence gave her staff an easier time of dealing with the clients once she'd had an opportunity to check in on things before heading off to parts unknown. Rarely were there any flare-ups on that score. Of course, there was always a first time.

"It's not like that," Tenille soothed.

Kam wasn't convinced. "Are you sure?" She dropped to the arm of a chair near the walk in closet. "I can definitely come back early. It's not a problem," she ignored the part of her that shrieked disappointment over having to end the trip before its time.

"Kam? Stop. Everything's good." Tenille spoke the words as though she were talking to a child. "The Park brothers just called to find out about bumping up their quarterly meeting. They're all coming in on the eighth for some family event and thought they could work the meeting in then since everyone would be on hand."

Kam was already nodding in response to the request from the car repair entrepreneurs who ran a franchise of garages nationwide. The Parks, high on customer service, sent out sleepers three times per year, courtesy of Kam's organization. The sleepers tested the efficiency and attentiveness of Park retail stores and garages.

"Yeah Tenille, yes that's fine. Send me the dates and times the guys are requesting."

"Will do. This next item isn't about a client- not an official one, that is. I told them you were out of town and that I wasn't sure whether you were looking to add to your current workload."

"Okay, so tell me about 'em," Kam left her perch on the arm of the chair and went in search for the shoes she'd wear that evening.

"I'm not even sure it'll turn into an actual case, Kam. I got the feeling they were pretty edgy about moving forward. Looks like some kind of missing persons situation

37

and I think they aren't sure whether the disappearance was voluntary or not."

Kam paused over a pair of strappy see through pumps. "That sounds curious."

"Yeah...I told them it wasn't really the sort of job we did, and they said they had a lead on someone who could be responsible and that they knew *you* were the best at finding info on folks who wanted to hide."

"Well...they're smart and I do like smart clients," Kam teased, passing over the pumps in favor of a sexier pair of sandals. "Could be a great case to hand off to another team," she sighed. "If I *had* another team."

The women shared hearty laughter then. It was Tenille who sobered first.

"That's not such a bad idea, Kam. You know you've got enough agents to formulate a secondary tier. Those folks are used to taking instructions, but I think quite a few of them would serve you well in positions that'd require more client involvement."

Kam dropped her sandals to the bottom corner of the dresser and then leaned against the wide polished oak surface. "Have you got anyone in mind?"

"A few names come to mind."

"Well work me up a document then- names, cases worked, strengths, weaknesses... I'll give it a look."

"I'm shocked!" Tenille expressed a theatrical gasp. "Finally- I've penetrated the brick wall you've got around delegating responsibilities to the rest of your staff."

"That brick wall's been crumbling for the last couple of years," Kam admitted. "It's a big load for one person to carry. I'm starting to see that."

"You're right. It *is* a big load for one person, especially when that person has something else...big on their plate..."

38

"Have I told you that you're a rather crude employee?" Kam pretended to be unamused.

"Mmm...but I'm an employee who speaks the truth and is damn good at her job, right?"

"Damn right," Kam sighed, "so get me that document of names *after* you see to that gorgeous soldier of yours."

"Not a problem. Night, Kam."

"Night," Kam weighed the slender mobile in her palm once the connection broke.

The easy mood that held while she chatted with Tenille, drained a bit as thoughts then resurfaced about that *big* item on her plate and she and Huron not being at commitment's doorstep yet. Hell...was *she* at commitment's door? The man had most definitely come in and; for lack of better phrasing, swept her off her feet. She couldn't argue that it felt beyond great to have a man *that* incredible woo her the way he had, but what did she really know about him?

She knew he was powerful, self-made, attentive... she thought about them together... Oh yes, the son of a bitch was beyond attentive when it came to intimacy. In spite of all that, they were still no closer to revealing all the layers that made them who they were.

Yet Huron was making more headway in that department than she was. Kam knew he was setting the stage to completely divest himself of anything that could be categorized as illegal. The fact that he was making such moves for her, was sobering. She could admit that. Sobering yes, but it didn't spook her in the least.

The man was fast becoming a thing she craved and she loved what that did to her body. But this... this went beyond sex or at least it would very quickly if things continued to move along at the rate they were. Soon, she'd be confessing that she was in love with him- a thing she'd almost done many times over the course of the last several weeks.

Such a confession, especially if he reciprocated would put their...affair on a whole other level.

Kam leaned more fully into the dresser and thought about that word- reciprocated. A relationship required reciprocity, didn't it? If *he* was ready to shed those parts of himself that made him who he was, it was only fair and right that *she* do the same.

Shedding for her would mean more than getting rid of- it would mean confessing, *sharing* the darkest parts of herself. Those were parts she swore no one else would ever know.

There was a slight rap of knuckles to one of the double doors leading into the bedroom suite and then the rough, familiar baritone touched her ears.

"You decent?" Huron called.

Kam maintained her spot against the dresser. "Do you want me to be?" She smiled when he entered the room.

Huron closed the distance to her in a few, unhurried strides. He trapped her between his hands resting flat on either side of her on the dresser surface.

"That a trick question?" he asked.

Her response halted on a tiny moan when his hands were suddenly easing beneath her thighs. They slid upward until he was scooping her ample bottom into his palms. The move allowed him to tug her closer until he was snug in the cradle of her thighs. He captured the gasp she was about to utter when he kissed her, savaging her mouth with the ruthless thrusting of his hungry tongue.

Kamari moaned, wantonly rubbing her sex against the fly of his jeans. The skirt she wore, a short chic number, was crafted of some airy material that slid away to expose

40

her thighs the second he'd grabbed her. The fabric bunched at her waist to reveal black panties.

The lacy undergarment was hardly a barrier to the sensation roused when she rolled her hips and delighted in what his then raging erection did to her.

"Kam...goddammit..." Huron knew his restraint had snapped. He'd completely forgotten that he'd come up there to see what was keeping her.

Cousteau and Eliza were downstairs waiting on them so they could head out to begin their evening. Right then, Huron was *holding* his only plans for the evening.

Kam was arched up high against him, her breasts crushed into his chest. He could actually feel her nipples straining behind the push up bra beneath a black chiffon shirt.The garment made the plump, caramel toned mounds appear even more enticing. Her nails grazed his nape while she suckled his earlobe and whimpered her need.

That sound stripped Huron of the last flimsy ties that had been pitifully restraining the demands of his hormones. Seconds later, his face was inside her shirt and he was nuzzling into her deliciously fragrant cleavage.

He was working to delve beyond the constraints of her bra while strong fingers closed around the crotch of her panties. Kam fisted a bit of his shirt when she heard the scrap of lingerie rip and then give way completely as he pulled it from her body. His thumb took swift possession of her clit and a smile of sheer arrogance curved his mouth when she cried out her approval. Her hips bucked in sync with the circular strokes he made against the sensitive bud.

Kam threw back her head, her breathing coming in rapid pants. The effect made her breasts heave in a manner that was undeniably inviting to the hungry male who couldn't take his eyes off them. His thumb was still at work on her clit, though he applied the pressure intermittently then.

He didn't want her to come. He was too in love with the sounds she flooded into his ears, to deny himself the enjoyment of that. The hand still cupping her ass moved to wrench back one side of her blouse and cup a heaving breast. His fingers raked a straining nipple and his proud smile gained definition when she beat out her frustration with a weak fist to his chest.

Huron rubbed at the diamond hard nub so intently, he urged it from its spot inside the bra cup.

"Huron!" Her voice was barely a gasp she was so breathless from the satisfaction he instilled from his attention to that bared area of her anatomy. Shakily, she moved to cup his strong jaw.

Huron understood her intention and needed no persuasion. His mouth was on her, closing on the nipple puckered hard and sweet for his tongue. He whimpered when her taste drove him to suck the spot ravenously for endless moments. His breath escaped in ragged tufts when his tongue bathed the bud and then outlined it.

He replicated the action when his nose outlined the spot before sweeping the nub from side to side with adoring nudges.

Kam eased her fingers up through the close cut curls of his sleek, dark hair. She wanted to sob over being imprisoned on desire's edge and forbidden to tip over into orgasm. He was still torturing her clit and Kam could have screamed her pleasure when he finally put the pressure on heavily. She craved that he'd grant her the ecstasy he promised with no further teasing.

Huron still nursed a raging erection behind the jeans and feared he'd be coming inside them any minute. He felt her wetting his hand as his thumb molested her clit. He filled her with three thick fingers, imagining they were his famished cock. Slowly, he began to fuck her with them. Realization wove in amidst arousal when he felt her tense around them.

Instinctively, he began to withdraw but she captured his wrist and held him fast. "Give me this or what I really want," she breathed.

He knew what she really wanted and, as mind-blowingly sexy as she was, he could only focus on the pain he'd been causing her. He could feel her tense when his fingers moved inside her and he knew she was tender.

Was it any surprise? He'd been taking her every day- several times a day since they'd been there. She was such a little thing; the acknowledgement heightened his arousal instead of quelling it. His lashes fluttered, pleasure reigniting when his fingers thrust deeper inside her core.

A measure of self-loathing still weighed in though. Huron didn't know what jabbed at him more- the fact that he hadn't been more careful with her or the fact that she hadn't made him aware that he needed to be.

Her cries were coming in at a higher pitch and closer together. Kam braced her hands on either side of her hips atop the dresser to give herself greater leverage. She bucked against his fingers, riding them with impressive fervor and sobbing out her delight with every surge of her body.

The pressure was exquisite, but she wanted more. Every movement of her hips nudged her against the lengthy muscle along his thigh. *That* was what she wanted to be filled with.

Huron used his free hand to tug hers away from the front of his jeans when she tried to undo them.

"Huron plea-"

"No."

"Please…"

During her begging and his flat refusals however, she did manage to free him of his jeans. Huron cursed viciously when he felt her hand moving inside the front of his boxers to close over his dick. His legs promised to give way beneath him and he braced the hand; that wasn't knuckles deep in slick tightness, to the dresser.

He gave her free reign over his body. Not that he'd had much choice. She assaulted his erection with a few slow strokes, moving her hand up and down his length. Laughter mingled with her gasps when she heard his whimper. Her thumb spread pre-cum from the slit at the head of his shaft and caused him to emit the neediest sounds.

Huron wouldn't tolerate her teasing for long however. Brushing aside the hand she used to torment him, he cupped his sex and guided it home.

Kam sucked in a sharp breath when he breached her core. She made another fist and delighted in the captivating mix of pleasure and pain as he penetrated, stretching her to accept him. The pain was fleeting the instant he was fully seated and taking her with filling, slow plunges that hit the same perfect spot over and over again.

The move sent pinpricks of erotic elation to every nerve ending Kam possessed.

"Ready to come?" he murmured close to her ear.

Kam couldn't even respond verbally, she was so affected by the way the words rasped on his tongue. She heard him growl a curse then and knew he could feel her drenching his cock with her need. He returned the favor seconds later, spewing thick warm blasts of his semen as he pumped her with throbbing surges that rocked Kam as well as the dresser she sat on. Her inner muscles squeezed relentlessly, milking his cock for every last drop of his seed.

Vaguely, she noted that she'd need to change the outfit she had painstakingly selected for the evening. She didn't mind and could forego a night out altogether if it meant staying right where she was for more of the devastating sex Huron Base was fully capable of dishing out.

Afterwards, their mingled, heavy breathing filled the room. Huron set his handsome face in the crook of her neck to inhale her scent. Kam rested her head back on the dresser mirror and delighted in the aftershocks of sensation his then semi-hard arousal still provided her.

Stimulation mellowed into relaxation. The only thing that would've made the moment more incredible would've been if they were in the decadent bed across the room. Their friends had other ideas though.

"Hey?! What the hell are you guys doin'?!"

Cousteau's deep voice carried up from below and sent the lovers' unified laughter into the air.

~4~

"Thanks," Cousteau smiled at the subtly flirtatious waitress when she returned with his drink refill. He toasted Huron with his glass once the woman made her departure. "And thank *you* for not deckin' me in front of my girl, earlier," he said.

Huron grinned. "What the hell are you talkin' about?" he knew full well, but chose to deny it. "Did I look like I had any sinister intentions when I came downstairs with Kam?"

Cousteau almost choked on his Sam Adams. "We're friends, B. You can admit it. At least admit to bein' pissed."

"I'd have been pissed had I been interrupted before I got what I went up there for."

"What you went up there for..." Cousteau rubbed his jaw and appeared confused. "I thought you went up there to see if she was ready to go?"

"That was my intention," Huron slumped down a bit in the cushioned high-backed chair he occupied, "but that changed by the time I walked into the room..."

Cousteau eyed his friend while downing another swig of his drink. "Have you told her you love her yet?"

Huron tensed, appearing none too pleased by the fact that the man had read him so easily. "What for?" he snapped.

Cousteau barked a laugh. "Because she needs to know!"

"Again, I ask, 'what for?'" Huron finished off what remained of his Heineken, caught the waitress' attention and signaled for another. "You think that'll stop her from walking away once she puts all the pieces in place about her puzzle of me?"

Cousteau made a sour face. "I don't think anything you've said could accomplish that, unless you're ready to include the story of your past when you tell her you love her."

"Jesus Cous, what good will that do-"

"It'd do *her* a world of good to hear it from *you* instead of finding out another way."

"Is that what you told yourself about Eliza?" Huron asked blackly.

"Tell myself that every day," Cousteau shrugged. "Doesn't put me any closer to coming clean with her. In my defense though, Elly doesn't make her living by peeling back the ugly layers of a person's life."

Huron grunted an ill-humored laugh and pushed his chair back from the table. He went to stare down at the dance floor below.

Cousteau, Eliza, Huron and Kam had decided on a popular restaurant/dancehall for their night out. Huron watched Kam and Eliza down on the crowded floor. Following a hearty supper, the women decided to dance off some of the delicious meal.

Cousteau and Huron promised to join them, but had gotten caught up in conversation and drink instead. Teardrop was an extraordinary establishment. The place actually seemed to shimmer from its seaside locale along the shores of Lahaina, Maui.

The interior would have been completely darkened were it not for the sconces that dotted the walls. They emitted a captivating bluish-white light that seemed to mimic the shimmer of the moonlight off the ocean.

The strobe lighting on the dance floor offered a similar effect, but Huron had no trouble locating his tiny auburn-haired beauty and her blonde friend below.

"It won't be a wise move to wait on telling her what you need to, man," Cousteau chimed in.

Huron didn't turn to look at his friend. "You know like I do that we-*men*- rarely make the best decisions when love is the issue."

Cousteau took his drink and left the table to stare down at the dancefloor as well. "So you're tellin' me you're gonna wait to share your story once you burn all your black hats?"

"If I burn all my black hats, I may not have to tell her about any of them," Huron reasoned.

***

Theodore Sturgess wore a grim expression that evening. "How serious is this?" he asked the man standing before his desk.

"I don't think it's serious at all," Jonah Byrd seemed more interested in studying the links on the silver wristwatch he wore. "Just ramblings from a disgruntled former employee," he said.

"Shit," Theo shut the folder containing the report he hadn't expected. "Last time somebody ran to my dad about the way I was handling things, it cost me my job."

"Theo, man, your dad is a good guy, a tough guy and he's retired now. You've got the top spot."

"That might make me feel better Jonah it if wasn't for the fact that the son of a bitch flapping his gums has an entire board to listen to his theories now."

"Which doesn't matter since the coward's accusations are groundless," Jonah, still so enamored of his watch, didn't notice the blood draining from Theo's light honey-toned face.

"I need you to watch this guy, Jonah," Theo urged when Jonah finally looked his way. "See if he's got anymore tidbits he wants to share with the board."

"And if he does?"

"Let him," Theo studied the crease in his gray trousers, "but let me know the minute he does."

"What then?"

"No idea…" Theo smoothed a hand over his bald head. "I'll think of something. Thanks Joan," Theo said before Jonah could query further. "Shut the door on your way out, will you?"

Jonah lingered only a moment longer. When the door shut behind the man, Theo reached for the cordless on his desk and dialed out to his assistant.

"Rhonda? Call Base Holdings for me."

***

"Is there a reason why you're givin' me such a hard time?" Huron was asking when he and Cousteau returned to the table they shared in the private dining room of Teardrop Lounge.

"I like what you're trying to do for her," Cousteau replied simply, honesty alight in his striking gaze. "To win her love, respect, approval... I like the man it's turning you into."

"Damn," Huron's laughter roused appreciative smiles from the passing waitresses. "Apologies for not being more worthy before."

"Shut the fuck up," Cousteau muttered teasingly before he sobered. "I just think it's a good move, is all. Wish I could make some big, over the top gesture to win El that way-know for sure that I've got her once and for all."

"Yeah well," Huron didn't appear comforted by the idea. "Aside from that thing with Breslin, I don't want Kam knowing about any of my other 'over the top' gestures."

And you don't have to worry about winning over Eliza either," he said after finishing his drink. "You've already got her. Her mother trying to make you look bad to save her own ass, did a lot of the work there."

"And that might not sting so bad if the woman wasn't in a jail cell on a murder wrap right now."

"El doesn't blame you for that."

"Maybe she should."

"Dancing is the perfect way to remove those gloom and doom expressions!" Kamari declared as she and Eliza approached the table upon their return.

"Kam's right, get out there!" Eliza hitched a thumb over her shoulder.

Cousteau eyed the women in disbelief. "Don't you guys plan to take a breather after all that?"

Kam and Eliza exchanged looks. "We intend to!" They said.

"We're suggesting that *you two* go down to the dancefloor," Kam said.

"Together." Eliza clarified.

Huron and Cousteau burst into laughter amidst their dates' phony confusion.

"What's so funny?" Eliza asked, propping her fist to her chin.

"Yeah, me and El had a great time," Kam added.

The group was still laughing when Huron felt his phone vibrate in the front pocket of his jeans and he cursed. The oath cut through the laughter and everyone silenced to look his way.

"Business is calling," Cousteau noted when he saw Huron with the phone.

"They aren't supposed to bother me unless they need to," Huron studied the faceplate and let the call go to voicemail. The phone rang against almost instantly.

"Sounds like they need to," Cousteau mused.

Kam leaned over to stroke Huron's hand fisted around the phone. "Take care of it," she gave a defeated shrug. "I got a call today. Looks like I may have to head back soon for business, too."

Huron bristled, clearly not welcoming the news. "When?" He asked while the second call went to voicemail.

"Not too soon," she toyed with her hair and grimaced when the phone rang again. "Handle your business."

Huron waited a beat longer, then nodded once and left the table.

Cousteau nudged Eliza's elbow with his. "Is it just me or do you feel like a lazy bum next to those two?"

Laughter surged among the threesome then.

"Bum or not, I'm trying to soak up all the good times I can," Eliza sighed, some of the amusement leaving her pretty face. "I have a feeling it's gonna be hell on earth when we get back to California."

"Don't think like that, babe," Cousteau tugged the flaring sleeve of Eliza's black blouse.

"No choice," she shook her head. "My uncle Samuel already called me twice to tell me how blood thirsty the press was becoming. Hmph, the press is *always* blood thirsty when it comes to us, so for Sam to call 'specially to tell me that, must mean they've gotten *really* bad."

Cousteau's playfulness vanished like mist. "Why didn't you tell me, Elly?"

Sighing, she rested her forehead in her palm. "I didn't want to ruin everybody else's good time. There's nothing you can do, anyway."

Her assumption sent a muscle jumping fiercely along Cousteau's jawline. He felt it and dipped his head to keep either woman from noticing.

"Hey?" Kam reached for Eliza's hand and squeezed. "I'm still on this."

"But you've done enough," Eliza's smile was sad. "You've got your own stuff to handle."

"Jessica's my client, El. She deserves my attention like any other. The fact that she's the mother of my best friend in the world, entitles her to a little more attention."

Tears had gathered in Eliza's blue stare. She laughed through them while squeezing Kamari's hand.

"More drinks, folks?"

Cousteau smiled at his lovely companions and then up at the waitress who had inquired. "More drinks are definitely needed and keep 'em comin'."

~~~

"This better be damned good," Huron was almost snarling into the phone receiver.

"Calm down, B," Nevil Willis sighed as though he'd expected such a greeting. "I know I'm riskin' havin' my ass kicked for callin', but I just talked to Sturg."

Huron stilled, recognizing the name as the shortened version of the one belonging to his friend Theo Sturgess. "How'd he make contact?"

"Through Boris."

Huron hissed a curse and winced, hearing the name of his head of security. Long ago, he'd established the protocol for contacting him regarding anything having to do with his...outside interests. Such calls were routed through Boris Caswell as though they were any other business communication.

Boris then made contact with either Rave Grant or Nevil Willis, the men who kept up appearances by serving as Huron's personal security. Routing the calls in such a manner, told Huron two things: Theo Sturgess hadn't called about getting together for drinks or laughs and; whatever the matter was, it had the ability to send all hell breaking loose- if it hadn't already.

"What'd he say?" Huron was asking Nevil.

The man shared a condensed version of the conversation. Apparently, a recently terminated employee had stuck his nose into some of Theo's dealings and had taken what he knew to the board. That meant his old friend was up to his old tricks, Huron mused and then silently re-worked the notion.

Theo Sturgess had never learned from the mistakes of his past, he only tried to concoct new ways to play out the same mistakes. For the man to contact Huron meant this latest attempt had graduated to a new level of stupidity.

"Is that it?" Huron grated, peeved that there weren't more details.

"All, except that Sturg wants to meet in person to discuss our options."

"*Our* options?"

"That's what *I* said," easy laughter was evident in Nevil's voice, "but he wouldn't tell me anymore. I told him I'd call back when I had a date."

"Shit," Huron tried to work out the sudden tension in the middle of his brow.

"Sorry B, I know what a good time you're havin' out there."

Huron's grin wasn't humor induced. "You couldn't possibly imagine," he told Nevil and disconnected from the call.

~~~

"They went back for more?" Huron queried, when he saw that Cousteau was once again alone at the table.

"Ladies room and then we're out," Cousteau explained.

"Sounds good."

Cousteau inclined his head, noting the other man's preoccupation. "You gonna brood about it, or tell me what's up?"

Huron took a slow scan of the dim, swanky dining room before meeting Cousteau's expectant gaze. "That was Nevil on the phone."

"And since I'm guessing the man knows better than to intrude on your time with Kam, it must've been real important. One of the black hats?" he guessed.

Huron's expression seemed haunted. "One of the oldest in the closet- I've tried to burn it more times than I can count."

"Ah...the proverbial bad penny."

Huron's expression was confirmation enough.

Cousteau pushed his empty glass around in a small circle. "This black hat must've been a favorite one once, for it to keep rollin' up on you this way."

Genuine amusement flashed in the jade depths of Huron's gaze. "The guy never took hints all that well and um...his dad sort of gave me my start in the finance game."

"So it's safe to say that his son intends to milk that for all it's worth."

"Yeah..." Huron admitted with a slow nod. "But it wasn't hard for him to do. I loved the guy like a brother. Once."

"What changed?"

Huron seemed ready to offer a response. He expressed short, harsh laughter instead and changed his mind.

"There're things I need to come clean with Kam about- things she needs to know if she really wants to be with me," he said. "She's too special- too special not to be told and... besides..." he focused on his fist as though he'd just realized that he'd clenched it. "No woman should have

55

to be saddled with having a man in her bed that she doesn't know, especially when he's got things in his past that many would deem unforgivable."

"So? Did that call from Nevil give you the motivation to lay it all out for her?"

A harsh look slashed across Huron's gorgeous face then. "I wanted more time with her dammit," he all but growled, slamming a fist to the table before he stood.

"I wanted her the first time I met her," he admitted, observing the starlit view beyond the expansive bay windows in the alcove where the table was located.

"I did everything I could to get her and I succeeded. As much as she... devastated me... I wouldn't let myself believe there was anything more to it."

"And now?"

Huron's laughter rushed out on a gruff tone. "Now I don't want to let her go. Ever." He watched his fist clench again. "I don't want her going back to that job of hers-that's for damn sure."

"Ah man..." Cousteau reared back in his chair and folded his arms over the shirt that was the same brilliant blue as his eyes. "That business is her life."

"*I* want to be her life," Huron turned his head, but didn't look at his friend. "I could keep her very busy and she'd love every second of it." He gave an annoyed wince once silence had carried for a few seconds. He gave Cousteau the full benefit of his gaze then.

"Did that sound as oafish to you as it did to me?"

Cousteau cringed, spacing his thumb and index finger an inch apart. "It had slight caveman undertones."

"Shit," Huron groaned, leaning back hard against the wide window. "I'm not a possessive man, but she... she's found a way to draw out every possessive tendency I have. It's getting harder not to be ruled by them."

56

It was true, he thought to himself. Kamari drew out every possessive *caveman-ish* tendency he possessed. The way she melted for him, moved against him when he held her, sounded when he was inside her... She made him lose his mind with wanting her.

"I get it, B."

Cousteau's voice merged into his thoughts and Huron took note of the other man's strained expression.

"I want to enjoy Elly as often as I can before I tell her anything about my family. She thinks-assumes- I come from this protective Irish clan," he smiled. "It's true for the most part, so I've been content to leave it at that," his expression soured.

"Part of it is just being too cowardly to tell her all of it and have to sit there and wait to see if she'll hate me for it. The other part is feeling sick to my stomach over the thought of sharing that kind of ugliness with the most beautiful thing I know."

"She'd never walk away from you, Cous. Not over that," Huron resumed his place at the table. "That's all about your *family*- not you. You're one of the straightest arrows I know."

Cousteau's eyes crinkled just slightly at the corners when he burst into laughter. "Thanks for also making me sound like one of the most *boring* arrows you know!"

"Boring sounds pretty good to me right about now," Huron said once his own laughter had quieted. "Cous, the point is your folks shielded you from a lot of the negatives- whatever they were. You may have rebelled, but you never would've turned out like you did if they hadn't been there for you."

I wasn't so blessed in that area. I had to... do things to survive or at least I thought I did, but it was me, Cous. *I* had to do them," Huron clenched another fist and jerked his thumb into his chest for emphasis.

"Kam won't blame you for any of it, but you've got to tell her."

"You're right and that might be easier to do if I still wasn't so connected to it. You know all my income doesn't come from completely legit sources, Cous."

Cousteau's expression hardened. "I'm also aware that you don't need those *sources* anymore. You've found a reason to free yourself of them. You said it yourself, B. She's in a profession where the chances of her finding all your secrets is a high possibility."

"I could see to it that she couldn't."

Cousteau grinned. "I might buy that if you'd seen her coming with the Breck thing. Someone who can move that stealthily around you, has got talents you'd be wise not to underestimate."

Cousteau saw the women returning. He gave a pointed nod that drew Huron's uncommon gaze to the entryway where Kam and Eliza talked with one of the waitresses. Cousteau grinned, taking note of his friend's dazed expression. He stood, clapping a hand to Huron's shoulder when he drew near his chair.

"You also said she's too special not to know who she's sharing her bed with," Cousteau spoke close to Huron's ear. "Tell her the rest or walk away. I don't see things turning out well otherwise."

Cousteau walked on to meet the women, leaving Huron alone at the table to fixate on Kamari.

~5~

After leaving Teardrop Lounge, Huron, Kam, Cousteau and Eliza opted for a moonlit stroll along the shore while they enjoyed drinks from a small seaside bar. A short distance away, couples danced with drinks in hand and to music of a slower tempo courtesy of an island quartet that performed the most romantic tunes.

Kam swayed against Huron with one arm slung high over his shoulder where she held a fruity mixed drink. Her other hand rested palm down against Huron's chest and was sandwiched between it and her cheek where she swayed against him. Eyes closed, she felt utterly content.

"Kam?"

The soft smile curving her mouth gained definition when she felt his voice vibrating through his chest when he called her. "Hmm…?" Was all the response she could muster.

The lazy reply brought a smile to Huron's face. Gently, he eased a hand from her hip and used it to cup her chin urging her to look up at him.

"Sleepy?" he asked.

"Relaxed," she sighed, "we should just move here."

"Sounds good to me. But between the two of us, *you're* the workaholic."

"Hey," Kam slapped his chest in retaliation.

"You deny it?" Huron faked a show of surprise.

"I could," she sniffed indignantly.

"Would you really give up everything you've built to run away to Hawaii?" He kept his voice light, teasing, yet something serious had managed to settle in.

Kam reclaimed her spot on his chest. "Depends on who I'm running away with," she sighed.

Huron seemed to consider her words for a time, before he bent low to drop a kiss to the top of her head. For a time, his face lingered there in the curls that were being tossed about by the steady sea breeze.

"Would you run away with me?" He asked finally while caressing an invisible design on her back left bare by the cut of her satiny mocha halter dress.

She gave a lazy sigh. "Sure I would…"

Huron took her upper arms in a soft, sudden squeeze that drew Kamari's attention. She searched his outrageously gorgeous face with a look that hovered between desire and curiosity.

"We're speaking hypothetically, right? I mean… would *you* give up your job for me?"

Huron was seconds away from confessing that he'd do that and more. Instead, he opted for a teasing route. "You're right, we're speaking totally hypothetically, here."

"Mmm hmm..." Kam pursed her lips and returned to her relaxing spot against his chest.

"I'd have to keep my job anyway," Huron mused, "somebody's gotta pay for all this..."

"Exactly," Kam murmured and nuzzled into a more comfortable spot against his toned chest. "No way would I have work on my mind living here..."

"Good to know..."

The silence between them was colored then only by the quartet's melodies, the crash of the ocean waves and the breeze overhead.

"Kam?"

"Mmm...?"

Huron squeezed his eyes shut, hesitating for a second. "There are things I have to tell you. You know that, right?"

"I know," her response, merely solidified what had already been professed in her eyes when she looked up at him. "Are we going to have that conversation now?" she asked.

"No. But um...will the fact that I intend to have it be enough?"

Her expression shadowed. "That depends on when you intend to have it."

"Soon."

"Years?"

The fact that she imagined them together years later, made him want to kiss her. Somehow, he resisted the urge to lose his head over it. "It won't be that long," he promised.

"If that's the case," Kam resumed her relaxing spot on his chest, "guess that'll be enough."

"Enough to quiet your curiosity about me? About my past?"

That sent Kam's head lifting again. Her smoky gaze shimmered with expectancy... and suspicion.

"What are you asking me Huron?" *And why?* She had to ask that, even if she did so silently.

"I'm asking you not to look at me- at... my past. There are things you need to know about me. I want to tell you about them once they...are things I *used* to be part of and not *am* a part of." He rolled his eyes, clenching his jaw to send the muscles flexing wildly.

"It's stupid, but I need it. Will you do that for me, Kam?" He waited for the nod that came slowly.

Somehow she nodded. All the while, she prayed that he couldn't feel her heart thundering behind her ribs. That would be a dead giveaway to her uncertainty-to her... fear?

"Hey?" He bumped her chin gently against his fist. "Don't agree to this just because I ask you, Kam. I'll handle it if you find out things I'm not ready for you to know. I um...I'd just like the chance to do what I need to-first."

And what was it he needed to do? Her mind felt flooded by that singular question.

"Kam?"

She nodded decidedly then. "I mean it, Huron. I'll do what you asked me." Remembering her drink, she took a filling swallow.

Huron watched her closely and didn't know if her agreement satisfied or disturbed him. She hadn't raised one word in argument, but that was a good thing, wasn't it? Given his current predicament, her agreeing not to put to work her talent for peeling away a person's gloss to get to their core, was a good thing.

So why was he questioning; and with no small amount of aggravation, her decision to do it? He left the silent questions hanging when Cousteau and Eliza found

62

them through the maze of embracing bodies on the makeshift dancefloor.

Soon, the couples were returning to the Jeep Huron had driven into town. In minutes, they were leaving behind the dazzle of Lahaina.

~~~

The decision to call it a night in no way meant that the evening was over. Upon returning to the villa, the group exchanged chic eveningwear for sexy and less confining beach attire.

The couples converged on the stunning stone and marble patio. Cousteau played bartender and filled everyone's requests. There were Piña Coladas for the ladies and beer from the tap served in chilled mugs for the gentlemen.

Kam and Eliza reclined on the cushiony maplewood framed lounges while their guys reclined against them. Huron lay snug between the vee of Kam's bare thighs and took great enjoyment in the cradle her breasts provided for his head.

Cousteau mimicked the position as he rested against Eliza. The foursome savored the comfortable breeze and glorious evening view that was dotted by electric candlelight trailing a myriad of walkways leading down to the shore.

"This is the life," Cousteau groaned once the view had been relished in easy silence for over twenty minutes. "We should make this a yearly thing. Come down here to relax in the sun until we're in our eighties."

Eliza nudged Cousteau with her hip once the hearty laughter roused by his suggestion had settled a little. "Do you really want to see me in a bikini when I'm eighty?"

"Stop teasing me," he grumbled, "I'm getting hard just thinkin' about it."

More roaring laughter followed the comment. Cousteau turned on his stomach and nuzzled his darkly handsome face into Eliza's neck while she giggled.

"Stop laughing, I'm serious."

"Really?" Eliza practically gushed the word.

"Damn right, just *thinkin'* of us having sex in our eighties is enough to make me hard."

"You say the sweetest things!" Eliza laughed, until Cousteau was kissing her with unrestrained passion.

A second later, Cousteau shifted positions again and scooped Eliza up from the lounge. "See you guys later," he winked and rushed away with Eliza in tow.

"Much later!" Huron called after them.

"We won't see them 'til morning," Kam teasingly predicted once she and Huron were alone on the patio.

"Good, because I really don't want them back down here tonight."

Before Kam could scold Huron for being anti-social, he was turning to face her. He planted a bare foot on either side of the lounge and held his hands clasped between his thighs.

"Were you gonna tell me about that call from your office?"

Confusion stirred in the smoky depths of her stare and she propped up a bit on the lounge.

"At the club? You said you got a call and might have to head back early."

"Huron," Kam closed her eyes as memory struck, "baby there's always gonna be business to handle. If I tell you about every single thing that pops up, we'd never have time to talk about anything else."

"Kam-"

64

"Wait," she heard the warning chord in his voice and scooted closer. "That's the truth, I swear it. I love being here," she looked up and around in wonder of the environment. "For a person who never takes time off, it's gonna be *very* hard to tug myself away from it."

Huron dropped the argument, but wasn't done with his interrogation. "Why didn't you argue with me when I asked you to hold off on investigating anything to do with my past?" His voice was softer and uncharacteristically less confident.

"Why didn't you argue when I asked you to wait?" He rephrased when she offered no response to his prior question.

"Huron-"

"Answer me."

"This is crazy," she threw up her hands and let them fall with a muffled bump to the lounge cushions. "Did you *want* me to argue back there with you? Moonlight, music… I just didn't think an argument fit into that-"

"Are you afraid of me, Kamari?"

The question eased in so smoothly, so unexpectedly that she knew he'd glimpsed the flicker in her eyes that she hadn't had the chance to mask.

No, She wasn't afraid of him. Regardless of what she knew about him, what she may have… suspected about his past, she knew he'd never physically hurt her. What she hadn't been able to mask- what had caused the curious little flicker in her gaze- was the reaction to the small part of her that seized when she thought of the *things* he said he needed to do to distance himself from his less than legitimate affairs.

"I'm not afraid of you, Huron," she told him steadily while searching his captivating green stare. "I don't think you believe me, but I wish you would. I know you'd never hurt me physically."

"But I have, haven't I?"

"Huron-"

"I have and you haven't said a damn word to me about it."

"What-" Before she could finish, he had hooked a hand into the middle of her bikini and used his thumb to claim her in one swift, delicious motion.

She moaned. Sadly, the sound came after he saw her wince at the initial stab of discomfort caused by their numerous and enthusiastic romps.

"Right," he noted grimly and began to withdraw from her body.

"No!" she gasped, "please," she grabbed his wrist to stay him.

"Kam…" he shook his head, regret ruling his expression. "I haven't been careful with you."'

She wanted to laugh over his reasoning, but was too aroused then to do anything more than circle his finger. She bit her lip, feeling the slow ooze of her moisture. She knew he could feel it too.

"Does that feel like I want you to be careful with me?"

"Let go of me, Kam."

"No," she tightened her hold and circled her hips more intensely, hiccuping cries of pleasure the entire time.

It was too much stimuli for Huron to resist. He gave in happily and completely then. Tugging her close again, he crushed her mouth beneath his. His tongue silenced her ecstatic cries as the smothering kiss somehow deepened along with the intimate fondling his fingers provided.

Kamari linked her arms about his neck. By then, her bare feet had joined his on either side of the lounge chair.

66

Daintily, they rested atop his large ones which served as leverage while she took his finger with greater enthusiasm.

A low, intimidating sound rumbled in Huron's throat moments before he withdrew his thumb and replaced it with his index, middle and ring fingers. The thick digits plunged deep to rival his exploring tongue for depth of penetration.

Her shriek was a mixture of discomfort and delight. Huron only registered the tones of discomfort.

"Fuck," he growled and quickly left her.

"Huron no," Kam moaned, already squeezing his wrist to bring him back. "Huron, plea-"

"Stop."

Her tugs to his wrist were no match for his resistance. "Dammit, you haven't been hurting me," she snapped, losing patience with watching him work the bridge of his nose with the fingers that hadn't been pleasuring her into oblivion. The memory almost made her moan. "Huron, I'm just a little tender is all."

"Why haven't you told me that?"

"Dammit, do I need to tell you every time I have to go pee, too?"

Silence held as he took his time raking his eyes up and down the diminutive length of her. "I want you to enjoy everything we do together," his voice was soft- calm despite the erratic prance of his hormones.

"If you don't enjoy it because you're just not in the mood or because you're pissed at me or because you're *tender*," he spoke the last through clenched teeth. "I expect you to tell me all of that goddammit because when you don't, it makes me think you're afraid to upset me and I don't want that to ever be the issue," he expelled a breath following the presentation of his demands.

Kam swallowed when his uncommon eyes shifted her way.

"Do you understand that?" he asked.

"I do," she added a tiny nod and waited. Her luminous gaze narrowed when it scanned the broad, perfect plane of his chest. She studied the defined abs expanding and contracting enticingly as he worked to slow his breathing.

"Is that it, then?" Kam realized her mouth had gone bone dry as she lustfully observed him. "Are you um- done with me for the night?" She cleared her throat on the question and her eyes drifted and lingered on the crotch of his swim trunks.

The curse he muttered sounded like affirmation enough. Kam seemed to be wilting from disappointment when she flopped to her back against the lounge.

Huron looked ready to bolt from the chair, but he didn't. He couldn't. Instead, he hooked both hands behind Kam's knees and dragged her almost to the center of the lounge.

Kamari's lips parted, but she didn't dare make a sound. Huron was still facing her with his feet firmly planted on either side of the chair. The stunning green of his eyes appeared to have darkened from its vibrant jade to a shade closer to olive. He watched her as though she were an equation he was trying to solve. Deliberately, he trailed the lush line of her thigh as his thumb traced an invisible path along the inside.

Kam's heavy lashes brushed the tops of her cheeks as her hips arched in Huron's direction. "Huron," she whined.

"Quiet," his thumb skimmed higher, knuckles brushing her flesh, coasting her thigh until they met her clit beneath the sunflower yellow material of her bikini.

She pushed her head back into the lounge cushions and bit her bottom lip on the moan that wavered up past her throat.

The barest hint of a smile curved Huron's beautifully crafted mouth and he took pleasure from watching Kam in the throes of her own pleasure-spell. The pad of his thumb barely grazed her clit outlined against the flimsy garment.

Nevertheless, Kam couldn't have been more aware of his presence then. She wanted to feel his skin next to hers without barriers. Subconsciously, she moved to take possession of his wrist again and moaned her impatience when he turned the tables to imprison hers instead. He trapped them between her breasts that were on the verge of heaving past her bikini top.

He leaned in closer, never easing his hold on her wrists. His thumb was then applying more pressure to the bundle of nerves at the apex of her thighs. The sensitive patch of flesh vibrated choruses of radiant energy from his touch and Kam worked her hips in earnest to capture more of the dazzling sensations that branched off inside her body.

Huron never ceased his study of her, taking in every change of her lovely features as her expressions highlighted her approval. His gifted thumb made the slowest rotations while pressing down against her clit.

Arrogance mingled with the satisfaction evident in his smile. Her reaction to him was like an aphrodisiac all its own. He loved the way she melted for him. Simply put, he loved her.

He loved her?

The acknowledgement almost stilled his thumb's rotations, but only just. Kam's moans drew him back into the exploratory act.

69

He wanted to keep her. That was as definite as his love for her, he realized. He believed she would stay with him through it all if she had love for him, but would that be fair of him to ask, if he loved her?

An anguished sound wisped past his lips, the thought frustrating him. Kam didn't notice, still too enmeshed in the erotic assault on her clit. Her hips bucked with renewed fervor while she labored to find her release.

Huron was being too ruthless, too stingy with his touch she thought. She wanted him to do so much more. Since he wasn't letting her use her hands to direct his moves... "This is so good, mmm..." she tried using words to encourage him, "wouldn't you like to feel how much?"

"Shut up."

His manner brought a lazy smile to her face.

Huron leaned closer until they were nose to nose. He followed up his order by using the tip of his tongue to tease her lips.

Kam obliged the unspoken request to grant access to her mouth once he'd traced the seam of her lips a few more times. Instinctively, her tongue darted out to follow the action and Huron took swift possession. He laid claim to her tongue by swirling his around it and then suckling hard.

The effect on Kam was literally breathtaking given the fact that her hands were trapped inside his fist and between their bodies. His kiss was hungry and she met it with equal hunger. Driving her tongue against his, she moaned into his mouth and rocked her hips against the touch that didn't fully sate her hungry sex.

The moaning she put forth changed into a scream when Huron suddenly ceased the maddening rubs. She bucked her hips once firmly to relay her dismay.

70

Her disappointment lasted barely a second. That was about the time it took for Huron to exchange teasing the super sensitive nub of flesh for sliding his fingertips along the crotch of the bikini bottom.

Kam heard the distinct sound of ripping fabric moments later. She couldn't spend time regretting the loss of the piece when she was more focused on him fondling the folds of her sex as he tested the petal softness of the area. A growling moan left his mouth, causing his tongue to vibrate against hers when his fingertips breached the spot.

He didn't totally invade, only gave her a light fingering instead. Feverish, Kam contracted intimate muscles in a desperate move to keep his fingers inside. Huron wouldn't give her the benefit of *that* massage either.

She tried to tug her wrists free, but the move didn't budge him at all. "Huron..." she mewled during their kiss and yet again when he broke the kiss to skim his mouth across the soft curve of her jaw and neckline.

Again, she tried to free herself of his hold which; while not painful, was unbreakable.

"Stop," he whispered on his way down her body. Halting at her bosom, he worked his handsome face deep into the valley bared by the cut of her top. He helped himself to several deep inhalations, lightly tonguing the outline of one nipple beneath the top before he moved on.

Kam sobbed. With her wrists bound, she tried to relay her frustration by raising her bare feet to nudge his knees.

Huron let go of her hands then and took possession of her thighs. He spread them wider to accommodate his big frame. The bottom of her swimwear had already been ripped away. The garment lay in a tattered mound beside the lounge. She was bare and glistening wet for him.

At first, Huron simply used his nose to pleasure them both. Faintly, he thrust against her sex and she rode it without shame- seeking relief any way she could get it.

For Huron, her smell was a tantalizing drug that almost maddened him.

"Yes, please," she moaned when he at last gave her something more substantial. Elated, she bit her lip on a smile as pleasure hummed through her on a rich wave.

His tongue had plunged slow, deep, the organ penetrating in a lusty rotation that made Kam's hips surge wildly. His grip firmed on her thighs and Huron straightened, taking her up with him. Weakly, her calves dangled across his sinewy shoulders.

"Come for me?" he asked.

Kamari replied with something indecipherable and he smiled before his tongue invaded her body with another deep plunge. She shuddered out a moan, at once fisting her vaginal walls about his exploring tongue.

Huron kept one muscular forearm banded about her lower half as he dined. His free hand eased back up her body, making quick work of freeing a covered breast. He flicked the nipple with his thumb and then used the inside of an index and middle finger to squeeze.

Kam opened her mouth, but there was no sound forthcoming. She was mindless- a mass of sensation commanded by the relentless claiming she was being subjected to. She met those strong thrusts, clenching and releasing his tongue upon every stroke until a spasm wrenched her, encouraging a steady stream of liquid need.

Huron drank deeply of her, feeding from her long after her orgasmic shivers had ended. When he was done and she was draped over him depleted, he set his forehead to her inner thigh and took his own steadying breaths.

Kamari forced open her eyes when she felt him covering her with a towel before he took her from the lounge.

"What about you?" her voice was soft.

"That was for you." He left the patio with her snuggled tightly into his chest. "You should rest up. You'll need it."

She might have laughed, but exhaustion claimed her silently. She lost consciousness before he even entered the house.

Huron acknowledged his own exhaustion then. The feeling was heightened more by unsated need than physical depletion. He dismissed the fact, inhaling the fresh scent of her hair and anticipating the night he'd spend sleeping with the woman he loved.

~6~

In spite of her energetic activities the night before, Kam was first up the next morning. She'd already helped herself to some of the fruit and baked goods from the food cart placed on the patio by the discrete cook staff. She was enjoying her second helping of croissants and cantaloupe when Eliza joined her.

"Ah…" Kam gave her best friend a bright, welcoming smile that quickly transitioned into a teasing one. "I'm surprised Mr. Morgan let you out of bed."

Eliza beamed while shaking her head. "Mornings like this always make him sleep harder than usual," she helped herself to a mug of fragrant coffee. "Guess that still hasn't changed."

The morning in question was somewhat overcast, unusual given that every day thus far had been drenched in sun.

"I was able to sneak out while he slept."

"Sneaking out?" Kam made a face. "That bad?"

"That good." Eliza laughed and added some of the flavored cream to the brew. "He's definitely making up for lost time."

"It's good to see you so happy," Kam propped her chin to the back of her hand and smiled. "Things were kind of tense when he showed up again."

"Hmph, you can say that again. I felt so stupid wanting to trust him again the minute I saw him."

"You love him," Kam noted with a simple shrug, that nudged the strap of the white tee she wore.

"That didn't make me feel any less stupid," Eliza finished prepping her coffee and joined Kam at the polished, maple table between the lounges. "Guess I felt *more* stupid if anything," she took a sip of her coffee and nodded approvingly of the taste.

"There was all that crap with my family and the part he played in some of it."

"But none of that mattered?" Kam prompted, already knowing the answer.

"None of it mattered," Eliza confirmed, snuggling into the lounge cushions and smiling contentedly. She heard Kamari's sigh and observed her friend.

"What's that face for? And what the heck are you doing up so early?" A devious smile tugged Eliza's mouth then. "I know your night turned out same as mine."

"What?" Kam pretended to be confused. "You mean flat on my back with my legs over a pair of amazing shoulders?"

75

"Well..." Eliza seemed to consider the question. "I was on my back for *some* of it..." she dissolved into laughter and flopped to her side with her arms folded over her middle. "Ah Kam...I'm afraid we're at the mercy of two sex fiends."

"I know," Kamari wiped laugh tears from her expressive eyes. "Isn't it great?"

Another fit of giggles resumed among the friends. Kam was first to recover. Still curved on her side, Eliza's radiant stare had once again settled upon her friend's face.

"Kam? What? Is it Huron?"

Wincing, Kam turned her face into the fragrant breeze that stirred a bit stronger then. The day was overcast, but still beautiful. The dullness of the sky only seemed to accentuate the vibrant colors of the flora. The ocean crashed with heightened intensity and it was devastating to witness. The place was a smorgasbord for the senses and; for a while, Kam let herself be lulled.

Eliza didn't begrudge the silence, figuring her best friend must have needed it. She turned on her back, squirming a bit while straightening the mosaic print cover-up where it bunched at her hips. She drew up her knees, crossing one leg over the other and took in the surrounding loveliness.

"He asked me not to go looking into his business." Kam said after a while.

"Oh...but...you've already done that."

"Please."

The lone word was all Eliza needed to send her nodding in agreement. They both knew Kam hadn't uncovered half the mystery that was Huron Base.

"Did you promise not to look?"

Kam reached for the mug of tea she'd brought with her to the table and scooted back to recline on the lounge. "I don't know if I'd be here this morning, if I hadn't."

Eliza gave a startled sound. "You think he'd have asked you to leave?" She gaped.

"No," Kam rolled her eyes. "Leaving would've been all *my* decision...who I am, what I do...would've dictated that I leave, wouldn't it?"

"Why?" Eliza challenged, her blue stare then diamond hard. "Because you're so sure that what's in his past goes against what you stand for?"

Groaning, Kam set her mug back on the table and buried her face in her hands for a second. "People are very rarely what they show you on the surface. You know that, El. I've certainly seen it proven, more than *dis*proven often enough in my line of work," her coffee brown stare shifted out towards the environment again.

"I believe the man Huron wants to become is fighting to get free of the one he is."

"And you're sure he still *is* that man?"

Regret etched Kam's expression. "He's enough of that man to ask me not to investigate him until he's had the chance to...handle things related to it all."

"And you can't stop wondering what those 'things' are?"

Kam denied the guess. "What I can't stop wondering about is how he plans to handle them."

~~~

Huron woke to find himself somewhat relieved by the fact that Kam had already left the bed that morning. Not that he would've complained over finding her there. Still, he wanted to give her a little more time before he took her again sexually.

And just what the hell do you think you were doing last night?

Grimacing, he swiped fingers through his wet hair in an attempt to drive the reminder from his head. The heavy shower spray had provided a welcomed massage to the muscles that had been progressively bunching and tightening since early the evening before.

He'd felt like shit for asking her not to delve more deeply into his past than she already had. With age, had come a certain intolerance for things that were once a given.

Things like dishonesty...he'd begun to despise the trait the older he'd become. He'd begun to despise it, yet he'd asked the woman he loved to perpetrate that very thing.

She weakened him. Now; more than ever, when he needed to be firing on all cylinders for what he suspected may be down the pipeline.

Huron dipped his head and smiled as the hot spray of water pounded his nape. The woman he loved...that label didn't stun him as much then as it had the night before. The onset of the morning had brought with it a certainty of what he wanted-at the top of that list was Kamari Grade.

What he wanted from her though, was more than the fling they were then having such fun with. And it had damn well been fun, he thought and then grimaced. They'd probably been having *too much* fun if she was experiencing discomfort when he took her.

Discomfort indeed, Huron thought, unable to keep his mind off the erection below his waist. The pounding shower spray was doing nothing to soothe that particular ache. He'd called on every shred of his restraint to resist fucking her outright the night before and dealing with the consequences later. His mind had emerged victorious over his body, but his body had not ceased its raging.

He resented the idea that his body was then about to win out over the willpower it had taken to resist its clamoring. Slowly, he skimmed a hand down his broad chest, across the devastating array of abdominals to curve about his shaft. Fisting the lengthy muscle, sent a tremor of pleasure and regret coursing through him. A warped sound was forced from his throat when he palmed his cock and gave it one up and down stroke.

His thoughts were filled of Kamari from the night before. All he'd wanted then was to bury his dick deeper than his tongue could have ever hoped to reach. Squeezing his eyes shut, he pressed his forehead to the area of tiles directly beneath the wide shower head and conjured more images…

The way she surrendered herself, arched for him…yes, she weakened him and so often in the best way. His hand worked at a steadier pace as he tended the erection that was growing more rigid over memories of the way she sounded when she came- the hiccupping gasps and the uninhibited cries she released last night while his tongue penetrated, rotated and withdrew in relentless repetition…

~~~

San Francisco, California~

The offices of 'Grade' hummed along like a well-oiled machine. Employees moved around the floor, carrying files and holding conversations at every volume. Amidst it all, receptionist Mandy Keegan maintained a determined gait as she headed for her boss' assistant.

"Tenille?"

"Oh! Uh-just a minute Mr. Tate." Tenille smiled up at the woman who handed her a gold 11x13 padded envelope. Nodding, she held the phone receiver against her chest.

"Thank you," Tenille whispered in a tone of fierce gratitude, winking at Mandy before returning her attention to the man on the phone.

"It's just arrived Mr. Tate," Tenille told the caller once she'd checked the markings on the envelope's labeling.

"Thank you for checking," Daniel Tate's voice held a wealth of appreciation and relief. "It occurred to me that it might help for Kam to have a little insight into what I'll want to discuss with her when we meet," soft chuckling came through the phone line. "That way our dinner discussion won't be so awkward."

Tenille laughed. "I doubt Kamari would ever feel awkward talking to you, Mr. Tate."

"You're sweet to say so, Tenille but I'm sure your boss won't be all that jazzed about meeting once she hears it's me requesting the meet."

Tenille laughed again. "I think you're being very unfair to yourself."

"I'm the guy who asked her to marry him, Tenille. The guy she turned down, remember?"

"You're also the guy she still considers a friend."

Daniel chuckled. "Has anyone ever told you that you really know how to keep the customers happy?"

"Thank you, Mr. Tate. It keeps the boss happy too."

"And we all appreciate it. Thanks for your time Tenille and tell Kam I'm looking forward to hearing from her."

"Will do," Tenille promised, setting the receiver to its cradle once the connection broke. Curiously, she eyed

80

the padded envelope Daniel Tate had messengered to the office.

~~~

Kamari took her time returning to the suite she shared with Huron. She'd left him sleeping and thought it'd do him well to get as much as possible.

Clearly, he was on edge. While she was all too aware how business matters could wreak havoc on one's calm, Kam sensed there was more to what had him so agitated. His past? But that topic had always existed between them. It was after all, what brought them together in the first place. Yet, he'd pursued her anyway.

Why would he do that if he wanted to keep her from wanting to know more about him? Because he wanted her in bed? That too was a credible reason, but surely he'd had his...fill of her by then? She knew enough about him to know he didn't keep the same woman on his arm for any extended period of time. She wouldn't be naive enough to try convincing herself that he thought she was different.

Even so- he wanted her to wait for him. He'd hoped to ensure that by asking her not to do what came so naturally to her and go looking for answers on her own.

Kam eased open one of the double doors and tipped inside the bedroom in case he was still asleep. The bed was empty and she was contemplating snuggling back beneath the soothing coverings when she heard the shower running.

A coy smile teased her mouth as she sauntered toward the bathroom door that was half open. Her thoughts were set on invading his privacy. She was eager to enjoy the pleasure that six and a half feet of insanely sexy caramel-toned male was capable of providing. She'd planned to spy on him bathing. Instead, her legs went rubbery when she found something more entertaining going on.

Huron had barely left the shower before realizing he'd need to return to it. That time, it would have to be for an icy cold spray to rid himself of the maddening arousal that struck him again shortly after he'd left the spacious stall. He'd restarted the water, but gave into the demands of his body before returning to the shower. He cursed his weakness, even as he braced one hand to the countertop and cradled his swollen cock inside the other. He was grunting from faintly satisfied need after only a few powerful strokes.

"Fuck," he growled, bowing his head and squeezing his eyes shut as a second climax hit him mercifully fast.

"Shit," he hissed when his need marked the counter before he could catch it in his palm. Partly sated, he gulped in air and tried to summon the ability to move away from the counter.

"So does that do it for you?"

He tensed, but didn't look back. Her question drew his mouth into a tight line. "I was just getting in the shower."

"Oh...is that what they're calling it these days?"

"Give me a minute," he asked, making an effort to clean up the mess he'd made on the counter.

Kam moved further into the bathroom. "I was hoping for more than a minute."

"Kam," her name was wrapped up in a growl. "You don't need that right now."

"From where I'm standing I'd have to disagree."

"Kam- enough, alright?" He pleaded in earnest then. She needed him to be slow and gentle with her. Every part of him roared with the lust he had to cool. He was liable to break her in half as badly as he wanted her. Being

82

under the same roof with her had an abundance of advantages and its fair share of drawbacks. He wanted her *all* the time.

"Out Kam," the words were a whisper then.

She moved closer though, until her breasts nudged his back. The wispy barrier of the white, strappy tee she wore over bikini bottoms was the only barrier between her nipples and his skin.

"I'm happy to go as long as you come back to bed with me."

"No," he fisted both hands to the counter when her fingers skirted around to his abs where she toyed with his naval and then lower until she'd taken him into her hand. Lightly, she tongued his spine.

"Appears you're out-voted," her smile was devilish when she gave his once again rigid dick a slow pump for emphasis. Triumph blasted when she felt his back tense under her tongue.

"Don't," the word seeped raggedly past his mouth.

Kam's next slow stroke of his heavy endowment, sent the muscle flexing noticeably on her palm. "Are you sure?" She asked.

When he finally turned, Kam knew she'd taken her teasing a little too far. His big hands squeezed her upper arms, but the hold wasn't painful.

"I won't do this with you now," he spoke through clenched teeth.

"Why?" Emboldened, she moved closer until her breasts crushed into his chest. "You think you'll hurt me? Or," she searched the remarkable green of his gaze, "is that really even it at all?"

"Kam," something pierced the hardness of his stare.

She cupped his cheek before he could lower his head. Moving to her toes, she sealed her mouth to his and eagerly thrust her tongue inside.

She moaned when his hold firmed as though he were using it to steady himself. Kam continued to taunt his tongue with hers, bathing it, enticing it into play with the gentlest swirling moves. It didn't take much teasing to persuade him to give in. She felt her toes leaving the floor when his grip flexed on her arms as he lifted her.

The kiss became deeper, wetter. Huron held Kam flush against his big body. He needed only an arm about her waist to keep her where he wanted her. Kam draped her arms about his neck and released small cries whenever her tongue tangled with his.

One of those cries held on an erotic shriek when she discovered he'd removed her bikini bottom. His fingers skirted the cleft of her ass and then delved in for more intimate contact.

Her gasp was more of a shudder and Kam locked her legs around Huron's back to grant him better access. He skimmed the sensitive circle of anal nerves, just barely dipping inside before easing on to take possession of her sex. Her shuddering, transitioned to a moan at the onset of a three-finger caress. Shamelessly, she bucked and swayed to the sensual beat they stirred.

Sadly, Huron wasn't in the mood for much foreplay then. He'd warned her to leave- she hadn't listened.

Disappointment fueled her sob when he withdrew his skilled fingers. Before she could complain or even thump a fist to his chest in frustration, Huron was yanking her away from him.

He set her to her feet and crowded in behind her half a second later. Kam winced when the edge of the porcelain counter pressed rather uncomfortably into her

84

belly. She didn't dwell on it once Huron had snaked a hand around her waist to cup a breast while insinuating a beefy thigh between her legs.

The move opened her up to a more thorough exploration. She wilted when his fingers next made contact with her core. His thumb and forefinger ruthlessly assaulted one nipple while the corresponding digits on the opposing hand treated her clit to the same molestation. Kam was rendered virtually motionless given the way he held her. She'd have preferred being able to move and enjoy every thrust and rotation of the thick middle finger. It had invaded to assist in the erotic performance which had already commenced. Still, she had to admit there was a definite delight in being handled as she was just then.

Huron's breathing was labored, ragged against her ear where he panted in sync to the long slow drives of his finger. Kam tried to clench and keep the digit where she wanted it, feeling her climax at hand. He, of course, denied her the pleasure. Conditioned then by the torture of being led to ecstasy only to have it withheld, aided Kam in resisting the urge to complain over his selfishness. She was learning that his denials were usually topped by the sweetest acts.

He gave her a little shove, indicating that he wanted her to bend over the counter. Spreading her ass cheeks, the wide head of his dick breached her from behind. Kam eagerly moved to her toes as Huron proceeded to ease the stiffness home. She clutched the rim of the rose blush porcelain sink and used the improved purchase to meet his robust thrusts with her own fire.

The telltale sounds of flesh meeting flesh surged faintly amidst the water spraying from the shower head. Huron slid a hand beneath Kam's thigh and angled it outward just a bit. The penetration deepened

85

instantaneously. His hand at her breast firmed as well when he directed her to straighten before him.

Kam hooked her arms around his neck and moaned his name while she bucked and arched. The triple sensations stemming from having her nipples teased, her clit stirred while her vaginal muscles were repeatedly stretched and filled ushered in a powerful climax. The effect was made more delicious when strong waves of semen erupted deep inside to coat her inner walls with a rich dousing that made her convulse from the rapture of it.

Huron came hard, given the way her pussy fisted his ejaculating cock. "Kam," he shuddered once his forehead rested on her shoulder while his body was wracked by potent spasms of release.

Kamari was a mindless mass of sensation. There was no way she could resist responding especially when both his hands lowered to her clit and his thumbs launched a dual caress to the tight nerve center. Spasms rocked her as well, jolting through her body and shooting sparks of renewed arousal.

With nothing left to give, they slumped against the counter at an awkward angle. Huron's demanding erection had abated, yet he remained snug inside Kam. She had no complaints, knowing it was by his contact alone that she was even able to stand up against the orgasmic aftershocks that rippled in her belly and down to her core.

Huron was first to recover; his grunt following Kam's sob when he withdrew his sex. She smiled when he lifted her and she anticipated being carried to bed where the plan would be to doze and sex the day away.

Huron had another item on the agenda first though. "I should have run this for you instead," he told her.

Kam's sated mind received an undeniable shock when frigid water hit her body. She shrieked, fighting to get

86

free of Huron who laughed and held her relentlessly beneath the cold spray. She fought as best she could, until the need to laugh got the better of her as well.

~7~

The couples spent four more days in paradise before deciding that the real world was calling and wouldn't take kindly to being shut out for much longer.

At least that was the way Huron and Kamari saw it. Business was calling for them both and they acknowledged having ignored their entrepreneurial responsibilities for way too long.

It was a different story for the other half of the foursome. Cousteau and Eliza were off for more fun and relaxation. Cousteau had decided he and Eliza would head back to Malibu to plot their next move.

Still, the group set out late on the day of their scheduled departure. Everyone agreed how difficult it was to leave behind the beauty of Hawaii. Once Huron's jet had delivered them safely back to the private San Francisco airstrip, the couples said their goodbyes and settled into the chauffeured cars that waited to carry them to their next destination.

Cousteau and Eliza were first to set off. Huron and Kam's departure from the strip wasn't quite so expedient.

Kam took a spot on the car designated to transport them from the remote airstrip. The evening promised to be a chilly one and the slight warmth radiating from the car's polished hood, beckoned her. Her vantage point gave her the opportunity to observe the goings on of the jetport which kept her from just blatantly staring at the only thing that truly held her interest.

Huron Base. Although, she had to admit that her interest at that point was more on what he was discussing with the two dangerous-looking men standing next to him.

She recognized them from one of her earlier visits to Huron's office. She'd been surprised to find them at the airstrip once she and Huron had deplaned with Eliza and Cousteau. She hadn't gotten their names when she'd seen them at Huron's office before. He introduced her then to Rave Grant and Nevil Willis before dropping a quick kiss to her mouth and promising they'd leave once he had a quick talk with the men.

Kam hissed a criticism to herself to stop trying to guess at the details of the intense conversation taking place across the tarmac. After all, how would she abide by Huron's request that she not go snooping any deeper into his background when she couldn't even keep her mind off a simple chat he was having with friends?

Friends? Ha! She'd sooner believe that those two were hired muscle. *Kam...* Silently, she chastised herself and reached over the car hood to dig out her mobile from

89

the depths of her tote bag. Maybe the device would keep her mind to safer things.

Yeah Kam...keep telling yourself that.

Rave Grant and Nevil Willis had in fact made names for themselves as hired muscle. They were also however, two of Huron's oldest friends- ones who had known him long before he'd ever thought of changing his name- ones that had taken and would take a bullet for him without hesitation.

"Have there been any waves, besides Theo?"

Nevil shook his head over Huron's question. "Quiet since that initial call," he said.

"Guess Sturg'll wait 'til you get back to share the rest," Rave added, referring to Theodore Sturgess.

"Great," Huron sarcastically celebrated his rotten luck, but remembered to keep his expression schooled. Chances were high that Kamari was covertly observing his chat just then.

"Has somebody checked out her place?" Huron switched topics, not worrying about being misunderstood.

"Nobody's gonna touch her, man. But yes- everything's good over there." Nevil added when Huron shot him a look.

"You really think somebody would come after her, B?" Rave's slanting dark gaze seemed narrower in light of his interest.

"Folks will do anything when they think their money's being threatened," Huron muttered.

"But nobody's money is bein' threatened," Nevil's broad shoulders rose quickly beneath the fine material of his suitcoat. "You bought your way out from Breslin for three times what you put in."

"Yeah," Huron shifted a grim stare across the tarmac, "and that's all the money they'll ever make off my name. Dutch and his wife are angrier over losing their connection to my name than my money."

"Stupid reasoning," Rave's voice was hushed. "Just because you aren't partners on paper-"

"Means folks might start wondering what they did to piss B off and make 'em think twice about doin' business with 'em," Nevil interjected, his ruggedly handsome features adopting a colder quality on his milk chocolate face. "Any off-the-cuff deals they work, might bite 'em badder in the ass without B havin' any interest in protecting them from the fallout."

Huron and Rave studied Nevil with looks of playful amazement.

"Wasn't it *you* who said he had no idea what a brain was for?" Huron posed the teasing query to Rave.

Laughter broke out among the men.

"All I'm sayin' is they'd be even bigger fools to come after you and especially Kamari." Nevil clarified once the mood had somewhat sobered.

"I still want her watched," Huron insisted, risking a glance at Kam across Rave's shoulder. "Keep it light at first, just check in on her subtly. She'll sense a tail in a heartbeat."

"Have you told her who we are?" Rave gave a faint half shrug. "Who we really are and what we really do for you?"

Huron gave his friend an 'are you kiddin' look, "I haven't even told her what it is I'm trying to distance myself from so I definitely haven't told her that those things often require me to have two or more people watching my back because there's usually a target on it."

"Got it, man," Nevil clapped Huron's back and smiled encouragingly. "But you need to tell her anyway."

"Thanks Cous," Huron snapped.

91

Undaunted, the men shrugged.

"Cousteau's right, B," Rave said. "She's the one who's got to decide if she's ready to ride or die with you."

Huron risked another look at Kamari then. She'd struck up a conversation with the driver of their car. Slowly, he followed the petite length of her, adoring the way her bowed legs looked beneath the short hem of the cream denim skirt. "I'm afraid to give her that choice," he admitted. "Just found her- not ready to lose her."

Rave set a hand to Huron's shoulder. "In our world, that could happen whether you tell her or not. She deserves to know what she's letting herself in for."

Huron didn't respond, but he knew his friends were right.

"Catch you later, man," Nevil traded a nod with Rave and left Huron alone.

Huron barely registered the men's departures. His focus had returned to Kam.

***

Malibu, California~

"I'll take all the 'hellos' to mean that you spend a lot of time here," Eliza told Cousteau once a couple had moved on from their table after inviting them to a beach barbeque later that week.

Cousteau gave a noncommittal shrug and scanned the spacious seaside bar and grill. He'd suggested the place once the chauffeured car had dropped them off at his home.

"The owner may've asked me to come on board as a partner a time or three."

Eliza laughed. "Well, I'm both impressed and proud to know such a renaissance man."

"Hey, I haven't bought in yet!" Cousteau joined in on the laughter.

"Will you?" Eliza reached for her beer and sipped from the frosted mug.

Cousteau shrugged again. "Depends."

"On?"

"Whether I plan to stay here. Put down roots."

Eliza blinked, obviously intrigued by the response. "Is that something you've thought about?"

"What? Buying into a bar or settling down?"

She frowned. "Buying into a bar, of course."

Cousteau decided to play along. The left dimple spliced his cheek when he grinned.

"I've thought about it for years," he admitted.

Eliza set her mug to the distressed beechwood table. "But you haven't done anything to make it happen."

"I have...but my ways were kind of unorthodox."

"You mean, slow."

"I mean, cautious."

She studied her mug. "What's been the reason for that?"

"Misunderstandings... outside complications."

"Do you think all that could be fixed?"

"I pray for that every day."

"Cous-"

A shatter silenced whatever else Eliza meant to say. Cousteau had already turned, his startling sea blue gaze immediately fixing on the source of the noise.

A crowd had already gathered outside on the deck- an understandably popular spot among the patrons. Unfortunately, it was hell on the bouncers when it came to breaking up fights. There was often standing room only once all the overstuffed sofas and chairs had been claimed.

Despite the fact that the shore was at their disposal, patrons of Malibu Jacks held a special love for its deck.

Such was evidently the case that night, Cousteau and Eliza discovered. The barkeep had rushed out to see to the commotion the two on-duty bouncers were attempting to quell. Cousteau and Eliza left their table to get a closer look at the ruckus, as had many of the other indoor patrons.

"Never bodes well for a woman's husband and boyfriend to turn up in the same establishment," barkeep Chad Wadson told Cousteau and Eliza when they sidled up next to him. "'Specially with women *other* than the one they're 'sposed to be sharin'."

Cousteau whistled. Eliza could only shake her head, her eyes wide over the scene she observed. Having never witnessed a real-live bar fight, she was undoubtedly fascinated.

Fascination though, took a quick detour to horror when an unsuspecting woman got caught up in the brawl. Obviously, the woman believed she was far enough from the melee to make her way off the deck unscathed. Sadly for her, one of the brawlers on scene didn't agree. Eliza watched horrified as a man- who must've outweighed the woman by at least one hundred pounds, yanked her collar and gave her a backhanded fist without an ounce of regret.

Eliza cried out when she saw the woman fall. Cousteau roared- at least, that was the best descriptor Eliza could think to use for the sound.

"Cousteau!" She cried, watching him bolt off into the clog of bodies.

"What's he doing?!" She called, the volume of commotion in the establishment had to have gone up another two or three decibels since Cousteau had literally thrown himself into the ring.

"Dammit to hell!" Chad Wadson slammed a fist to his palm. "Ol' Jack ain't never gonna get that man to buy into the bar if he's gotta moonlight as one of the bouncers every time he shows up for a drink!"

Eliza dragged her incredulous gaze from the rowdy deck display to the bartender. "Are you saying he does this all the time?"

Chad shrugged. "Often enough. The place is popular- pretty good rep among the tourists. It's the locals who always show their asses."

"Well can't you do something to get him out of there?"

"You serious?" Chad gaped; appearing to blanch beneath the haphazard smattering of freckles across his nose and cheeks. "That guy's a better bouncer than the *actual* bouncers!"

Speechless then, Eliza looked back toward the sea of brawlers. She squinted, searching for Cousteau amidst the wild dance. She found him and was at once captivated. Before that moment, she'd have never imagined him capable of the violent display he performed. His fists delivered precise, lethal blows that downed virtually every man he touched.

He took a few hits himself and Eliza forced herself not to look away. She couldn't- not when he recovered so gracefully from the abuse and punished his attacker beneath an onslaught of fists.

The bouncers...and their scrappy assistant managed to bring the brawl under control a little over seven minutes later. It was just as well, for Cousteau appeared to be gearing up for another battle.

Eliza watched in relief when reinforcements finally got there. Additional bouncers arrived on the scene and set about clearing the deck of troublemakers. The bouncers who had been first to enter the fight, then retreated. They kept hold of Cousteau, supporting him between them.

"Where are they taking him?" Eliza wrung her hands while angling her neck to keep sight of the men until they disappeared up a back stairway.

"They're heading up to the owner's office," Chad squeezed her elbow. "Follow me."

~~~

"Chad."

Men greeted the bartender as they left the upstairs office. Many did doubletakes when they noticed Eliza.

"Careful, Miss, he's still in a helluva mood," one man cautioned on his way past.

Eliza hurried to Cousteau the moment she spotted him in the back of the sparsely furnished paneled room. He was having his hand tended by whom she assumed was a medical professional.

"Eliza Breck, meet Dr. Paul Emery, one of our local vets."

Eliza gave the veterinarian a wan smile and then dropped to the sofa Cousteau occupied. She hid her face in his neck while Cousteau spoke briefly with Chad Wadson. She took no interest in the men's conversation; preferring to inhale the subtly spicy cologne that was enhanced by Cousteau's naturally intoxicating scent. Taking deep inhalations, she was able to prove to herself that he was alright.

"It's okay, Elly...it's okay..." Cousteau soothed, using his less injured hand to pat her back and squeeze her nape.

Eliza sniffled and pulled her face from the base of his throat. "Did he break his hand?" she asked the doctor.

"Isn't even sprained," Dr. Emery seemed to be in awe of the fact, "where do you get your vitamins, man?"

"Does he need X-rays or to have it wrapped or something?" Eliza queried amidst the men's laughter.

"No, ma'am," Paul Emery answered dutifully, "best thing for him is to ice it and keep those fingers in motion. You might want to grab some OTC pain meds," he said to Cousteau. "They'll ease any stiffness that sets in overnight," he stood. "Sorry I can't be more help. You get that looked at if need be."

"You did good, doc." Cousteau moved his arm from Eliza's back to use his uninjured one to shake with the doctor.

"Goodnight," the veterinarian left Eliza with a polite smile and motioned toward the office door as he headed in that direction. "You want this door locked, Morgan?"

"Yeah, thanks!" Cousteau called.

"What the hell did you think you were doing?!" Eliza waited until they were alone to shove her hands into Cousteau's chest. "Jumping into that crazy mess," she clutched the collar of the denim shirt he wore unbuttoned over a faded Nirvana T-shirt. "Somebody could've had a knife, gun-"

"Elly, Elly, shh...come on now. I've been through worse," Cousteau brushed a lazy kiss across her temple. "Besides, the locals who start this mess are idiots. They'd be quicker to shoot or stab themselves before anybody else."

Eliza wasn't convinced and took the injured hand to perform her own layman's exam upon. Gently, she pressed her fingertips against the scrapes and cuts across Cousteau's knuckles.

"Please don't scare me like that again," she was running her fingers across the injuries and intermittently kissing them. "Ever, Cousteau," she warned.

He dropped another kiss to her temple, and then his expression chilled. "That guy shouldn't have hit her-"

"Stop. You were amazing for coming to her rescue. I was so proud," Eliza slid her fingers through his hair and then gave a tug. "Just try not to throw yourself into the line of fire on a date night, okay?" She smiled, letting him see the teasing element in her gaze.

Eliza resumed her study of his hand, but Cousteau kept his eyes fixed on her. "I told you I've been through worse. Made my living as a bouncer before. In Brooklyn-at a club that belonged to my uncles…"

Eliza felt her breath catch. She was looking down at Cousteau's hand without really seeing it. Much of what she'd suspected about his family, she'd pretty much assumed. Never, in all the time she'd known him had he spoken a word about his family- not one iota. He'd never mentioned a mother or father, let alone uncles. He squeezed her hand then, until she met his gaze.

"The place they owned was like a private club for their friends, but *their* friends were a rowdy bunch and there was always someone who came to fight and needed to have their ass kicked out the door," he grinned faintly on a few passing memories. The amusement didn't last long.

"And then there were the nights those *friends* brought their girlfriends and…those were the nights my job was really fun. My uncles gave the bouncers free reign over *any* man who'd put his hands on a woman to hurt her."

"Sounds like an exciting place to be," Eliza's smile wavered, her voice was soft.

"Had its moments."

"Did the fight out there bring it to mind?"

98

"Sort of," Cousteau reached out to toy with a lock of her hair. "I should've told you a long time ago."

Eliza smiled a little brighter. "Is this your way of telling me you want me to meet your family?"

"Baby, I never want you to meet them," he responded without hesitation. "You're not the only one who comes from a well-known family," he gave her a grim smile. "It's just more beneficial for mine to stay out of the public eye."

"Well at least you have the luxury of not having to be around them," Eliza sighed as her own family came to mind. "At least you never got yourself involved-"

"You're wrong there, beauty. I was involved a whole helluva lot."

"Was." She pointed out.

He smiled a haunted smile that sparked the lone dimple in his cheek. "You know how you walk away from things but they still follow you?"

"Have they threatened you?" her delicate brows drew close as a frown emerged. "Are they coming after you or something?"

Cousteau was already shaking his head. "It's not like that."

"Then why are we talking about it?"

"Elly…"

"Unless you're about to tell me there's a contract on your life, then I don't want to know." She had a feeling their perfect peace would shatter once he shared what was on his mind. Whatever he had to tell her, it was the last thing she wanted to know.

"It's important that you do," he seemed to challenge her silent decision.

Eliza shook her head, resembling every bit the stubborn child who was moments away from covering her ears to prevent hearing something she didn't want to.

Cousteau was pressing a kiss into her palm.

"Can't it wait just one more day?" She pleaded. "Just one more day before the world comes rushing back in?"

"Come 'ere," Cousteau took pity, understanding her need for just a bit more of the normalcy they'd enjoyed over the past few weeks. He brushed kisses to her forehead, cheeks and temples when she complied.

Moments later, Eliza found herself straddling his lap. "Cousteau? Stop," she gasped, tugging at the hem of the purple tennis skirt riding up her thighs. "Your hand-"

"Doc said I needed to keep my fingers in motion. I know the perfect type of exercise for that."

Her cheeks burned and she tried to leave his lap, but he held her fast. One steely arm at her back, kept her virtually immobile.

"Anybody could walk in-"

"Door's locked."

"It's not your office."

"Actually, it is," he stroked a thumb across her knuckles where her hand clutched her skirt. "I finally decided to tell 'ol Jack that I'd come on board as his partner- get something for all this pain and suffering."

The apprehension that had been squeezing Eliza's heart, lifted when he shared that news. That; along with the kiss he pulled her into, seemed to set her to rights again.

***

San Francisco, California~

"Just a nap, huh?"

Huron murmured the question when he walked into his bedroom to find Kam asleep on top of the covers. He was glad he'd talked her into an early dinner at his place-the closest stop when they left the jetport following their return from Hawaii.

Kam had opted for a quick nap while he took a business call that had come through. The plan was that he'd go along when the car took her home. Of course, *that* part of the plan was one he'd agreed to but had no intention of following through with.

He'd known she was exhausted. Finding her asleep did him a world of good as well. He enjoyed his penthouse, same as he did his home in Marin County. Like the place in Marin, he hadn't truly considered his penthouse a home until he found her there on his bed.

Kamari Grade had smoothly and irrevocably become home to him and he wanted to keep it that way. By any means necessary? No...he wasn't that kind of man anymore, remember? Correction he was *trying* not to be that kind of man anymore. He was still a long way from accomplishing that, however.

Kam shifted her position on the bed and he went to her. She had kicked off her sandals shortly after walking inside the condo. Huron decided she'd sleep better once she lost a few more articles of her clothing. He figured he could benefit by losing the rest of his clothes too and doffed his shirt, jeans and socks before he joined her.

She fidgeted when he coaxed her to her back and proceeded to unbutton the fastening along her skirt. Gently, he eased the denim down her hips, over her bottom and grunted a low curse when he saw the scrap of peach-colored lace panties beneath. He quickly made the decision that she'd be better off if she kept those on.

Leaving her clothed in that garment however, did nothing to discourage him from exploring all the other areas the removal of her skirt had bared.

He ran his knuckles along the lush line of her outer thigh, smiling when she moved her legs, shifting one higher than its mate. The position parted her legs and his knuckles journeyed toward the middle of her underwear. There, he grazed the outline of her sex against the fabric.

She had shifted so that the hem of her shirt rode up above her navel. The circular dip beckoned his attention and then he was tracing it with the edge of his thumb. He celebrated the easy access of the shirt's zip front and swallowed noticeably while debating on whether to remove the bra that matched her panties. He knew enough about women to know she'd be more comfortable without it. He realized that he'd have probably removed it regardless.

The more vibrant color of his striking stare pooled with a darker olive tone when he fixated on her breasts. Supple, they heaved with every breath she took. He was so in tune to her, he noticed when her nipples reacted to the air skimming them once he'd tugged her out of her bra.

Huron watched, his mouth literally watering as he observed the peaks firming and beginning to pout in anticipation of the kiss he was eager to give.

What was intended to be a peck of his lips to the bud, easily morphed into something wickedly sensual. His tongue circled the nub and then bathed it a few times in rapid succession until he was suckling the morsel outright.

Driven by the taste, smell and feel of her then, he cupped her other breast, plumping and squeezing the mound while his mouth worked on its twin. Faintly, he acknowledged the sound of her moaning. Utilizing admirable willpower and a great deal of restraint he withdrew.

102

"Huron…" she moaned sleepily.

"Shh…I'm sorry…shh…back to sleep," he urged, feeling like an ass for waking her.

Quickly, he tugged down the covers and got them both settled beneath. It didn't take much for Kam to drift back into sleep. He tugged her back against his chest, enveloping her in a spooning embrace that radiated relaxation and sensuality in the same vein.

He listened to her breathing, recognizing when she fell into deep slumber. For him, sleep would be a long time coming when thoughts of the past renewed their haunting chorus in the recesses of his memory.

He hid his face in her hair and inhaled. Part of him pitied the tiny woman who lay so trustingly in his arms. She had tempted a dark soul- one that would do anything, use any means to keep her. He wanted her so in love with him that she wouldn't- couldn't walk away once he'd shared it all.

And do you really believe she won't bolt when she discovers that on multiple occasions…you've killed?

Huron closed his eyes tightly. The question continued to loop like some grotesque chant in his mind.

~8~

"She'll probably be at her office most of the day- I'll have a car take her home," Huron spoke to Rave Grant by phone the next morning. "I want two of your best guys outside her place when she leaves to head in."

"I'll take care of it, but I want it on record that I'm about to be paying my men to virtually kick back and do nothing," Rave said. "I really don't believe she's in any danger, B. Nobody would dare touch her and not because folks are learning that she's yours.

Everybody knows how she makes her living. Nobody's gonna do anything stupid enough to get themselves a front row seat on her radar."

Huron laughed. "Except me, right?"

Rave chuckled, thoroughly amused then. "Well you weren't always the brightest bulb in the lamp."

"Thanks for havin' my back on this, man," Huron spoke through the laughter still claiming him.

Rave sobered. "It's about time for some dime piece to cross your path and make you take note. She's one of a kind and you're not the only one who sees that."

"Have your guys stay out of sight, alright?" Huron softly urged. "It's my ass if she spots them keeping tabs on her."

"Understood."

The connection broke then and Huron studied the phone without really seeing it. His mind settled on the decision he'd just made. He would gladly bow down to a little paranoia if it meant keeping Kam safe. His instincts were telling him that was very necessary.

A dull thud and a hissed curse caught his ear. He looked up to find Kam making her way into the den that connected to his master bedroom suite. Huron smiled, taking in her agitated state while he enjoyed the sight of her battling with her top to tug the zipper over the gorgeous breasts that had filled his hands the night before.

"There's breakfast," he called, catching the look of exasperation she threw his way.

"I was supposed to be home after dinner."

"Well *you* were the one who opted for a nap," he cleared his throat when her eyes narrowed threateningly. "This is some thanks I get for tucking you in and making you comfortable for the night."

"Mmm…" Kam strolled into the den at a slower pace then. "And was taking me out of my clothes part of the comfort process?"

"Of course," one massive shoulder lifted in a shrug.

Kam slowed the zipping of her top. "Why'd you let me keep my panties on then?"

Huron broke eye contact, appearing interested in something in a folder on the table. "You wouldn't have gotten any sleep otherwise-neither would I. Sit and eat," he said before she could say another word.

"I really need to go. There's a bucket load of work waiting on me."

"Having breakfast won't get rid of it any sooner," he spoke while reading the contents of the folder.

"But I've let it wait too long already-" Kam cut off her argument when he suddenly stood and headed toward her.

Taking her by the elbow, Huron simply escorted her into an empty chair at the intimate round table where he worked. "Car doesn't move 'til you eat," he said.

Smiling curiously, Kam tilted her head and looked up at him. "So you'll keep me here against my will?"

Huron's stunning gaze swept her from head to chest and he slid a hand inside her half zipped top until it was inside her bra and cupping a bare breast. He swept the nipple beneath his thumb, arrogance curving his mouth when her lashes fluttered and she swayed in the chair.

"I won't really have to do that, will I?" He pinched the puckering nipple between his thumb and forefinger.

Instantly affected, Kam leaned into the throb-inducing caress.

"Will I, Kam?"

"No," she breathed.

"Good," he took his hand out of her top.

The feeling of abandonment was sobering. Kam forbid herself to reach for his hand. Huron provided her with a plate of turkey sausage medallions, buttered English muffins and fruit before he returned to his seat. She quickly
106

fixed her clothes, then helped herself to some of the coffee from the carafe in the middle of the table. Silence hovered for a while then. Kam discovered she was starving and ate heartily of the light breakfast while Huron made notes in the folder he'd been mulling over.

Taking advantage of his preoccupation, Kam observed Huron across the table. She loved the sight of him in the silver gray three piece suit that molded to his superb physique. As finely crafted as the suit was, it did nothing to mask the potency of the body it adorned.

"How long have you been up?" She asked when he caught her staring.

"'Bout an hour and a half," he returned to studying the folder.

Kam gasped. "You didn't wake me."

"You needed your sleep."

"Hmph, you're right."

"I know," he closed the folder then. "I had your stuff brought in in case you want to shower and change before you head out," he made the offer, not surprised by the unease he sensed from her. "Did I say something?" he asked.

Kam shook her head, biting her lip and then squarely meeting his gaze. "It's probably not a good idea. I can just go home and do all that from there."

Her reasoning didn't satisfy him and he knew there was no reason she could have given that would have. The admission made him angry with himself over how badly he wanted her to stay. God, how had she gotten so far under his skin?

"What's the rush?" he couldn't resist the question.

Surprise registered in Kam's rich cocoa gaze and her mouth twitched on the verge of laughter. "I really don't have anything in that case that would be suitable for a day

107

at the office." She leaned over the table and leered at him. "We were trying to forget all about business, remember?"

Huron couldn't resist smiling then and shook his head. "You're right, I'm sorry."

"An apology?" Impressed, Kam arched her brows.

"Don't get used to it," he said.

Smug, she settled in to finish her breakfast. "Are you riding back with me?" She asked, when she was done eating.

"Hmm...what was that you just said..." he pretended to try remembering. "Ah! 'It's probably not a good idea'."

"Why?" She smiled.

Huron looked serious. "Chances are high that you won't get to use your shower let alone get to your office if I go back with you."

"Does that mean we won't see each other anymore today?"

"I'll see you for dinner. We'll go out."

"So, will it be the deli or the sandwich shop?" she teased, remarking on the family owned deli they both enjoyed and the sandwich shop just around the block from where Kam lived.

Settling back in his chair, Huron watched her coolly. "I think I can do better than that. We'll discuss it later."

Kam nodded and caught sight of the clock. "Good idea," she noticed the time. "I need to get going," she dabbed a napkin to her mouth and then leered at him again. "Is the driver allowed to leave with me now?"

"You're good."

Smiling, Kam stood and rounded the table to kiss him goodbye. The simple peck however, turned into a throaty act within a split second. Moans intermingled the longer their tongues engaged. It was Huron who broke the kiss, easing her back gently as he averted his head while steadying his breath. "Get your ass out of here before I change my mind."

Kam dropped a quick kiss to his temple and left the room.

***

"Is it as clandestine as he made it out to be?"

"'Clandestine'? Nice," Kam smiled but didn't look up from the papers she reviewed.

Tenille gave a pride-filled shrug. "I'm working on expanding my vocabulary."

Kam shook her head amusedly. "It *does* look pretty involved," she agreed.

She had arrived in the office around lunchtime and spent the remainder of the afternoon reviewing the thick envelope that Daniel Tate had delivered by courier. Much of the documentation appeared to be bank statements with rows highlighted to show withdrawals. Not every withdrawal was highlighted which told Kam that Dan Tate's main concern had to do with those transactions.

"Someone's done a lot of my work for me," she quietly noted.

"How?" Tenille took a few steps closer to the desk in order to peer over her boss' shoulder.

Kam dragged an index nail across the sheet. "These highlighted withdrawals are recorded on the following sheets along with the recipients of those funds. In addition to the printed documentation," she set aside the paperwork, "are several photographs but none feature anyone I recognize," she shook her head.

"What does he expect you to do with all this stuff?" Tenille asked.

109

Kam continued to shake her head, feeling as bewildered as her assistant. "Hopefully, Danny'll tell me that when we meet."

"So you'll take the meeting?"

"Not much I can do to refuse," Kam dropped the photos and reared back in her desk chair. "Danny knew he'd get me curious by sending me this stuff," she fixed Tenille with a pointed look. "Did you think I wouldn't take the meeting?"

"I thought you would," Tenille put distance between herself and the desk. "But you guys almost got married, so…"

Kam grimaced. "We were never anywhere near marriage, as far as I was concerned. We were still at the 'just friends' stage when all of a sudden, he was proposing."

"And now there's this 'problem' of his that he just has to have your help on," Tenille propped her hands to her hips and walked the room like she was debating. "I smell another proposal coming on."

"I hope not. He'll find himself disappointed again."

"Because of your sexy travel partner."

"We're definitely *not* going to talk about him," Kam thinned her lips to stifle a smile.

"You're in love with him."

"He's dangerous."

"You knew that already."

"This is a whole other kind, Tenille."

"How?"

"Because I don't mind forgetting who I am when I'm with him."

Tenille perched on the side of the desk. "I hear that's one of the side effects."

110

Kam rolled her eyes. "I can't afford to let that happen."

"Why not?" Tenille's dark, pretty face tensed with curiosity. "You deserve to be happy, don't you?"

"Not if it means shirking my responsibilities."

"Dictated by who? You've never been a woman who cared about what people thought."

Kam rested her head back on the chair. "Probably because I didn't have anything really worth protecting. But my business has been good to me for a long time. I have a responsibility to it regardless."

"And you think that responsibility would dictate you walk away from the man you love?"

"It could."

"*Would* you?" Tenille sighed when Kamari didn't answer. "You know, I admire the self-righteous act but I don't buy it for a minute." She reached for the folder she'd tucked beneath a paperweight when she'd arrived for the meeting.

"I mean, I might be willing to back it a *little* if not for the fact that you both hinted at wanting a go-to person, *and* had me work up a packet of candidates."

Tenille dropped the folder right in front of Kam. "Nighty, night," she said on her way out the door.

~~~

"I was wondering when you'd get around to calling me."

Huron grinned at the sound of the husky voice that always held a hint of laughter. "Word has travelled, huh?"

"Travelled like a muthafucka. What the hell you been up to, man?"

"Not a clue. I only know it feels good."

"But?" Sheldon Gerringer probed on the other line.

111

"When you were trying to clean up your business for Lyd, did you ever think it'd be easier to just let it stay the way it was?"

"Easier?"

"Safer." Huron clarified after some hesitation. He heard the man sigh over the other end of the phone line and figured his old friend was thinking of his wife Lydia.

"Safer-yes," Sheldon finally answered. "Easier-*hell* yes."

Huron joined in on the laughter the other man sent through the line.

"Now if you'd like to know whether it would've been *better* for me *not* to clean up my act," Sheldon stated after the majority of their laughter had cleared, "if it would've been better in the long run for her- or for us as a couple- no. No man, not one damn bit."

"Shit," Huron grunted and grimaced, "that's what I thought."

"Well wait a minute, now. You do realize our situations are different here. Lyd wasn't a... troubleshooter."

"Kam's job isn't really factoring into this, Shel. She's the woman I love. She-" Huron massaged the tension from the bridge of his nose and forced out the rest of his sentence, "she deserves a man she can be proud of."

"So I'll take that to mean you haven't told her everything? If you had, then you'd know she'd definitely be proud of you."

"Shel..." Huron swiveled his desk chair to and fro. "One thing doesn't cancel out the other."

"Maybe you should let *her* be the judge of that."

Huron replied with a snort.

"Listen, B. All I'm trying to say is that maybe this isn't the right move for you and Kam. It's kind of moot for you to try shaping up now anyway, isn't it? She already knows you play the bad guy every now and then."

"What are you really tryin' to say, Shel?" Huron had gone still while listening to his old friend ramble and rationalize- two things he rarely did.

"You've got a lot of folks upset with these moves you're makin', B. Worse than that, you've got 'em scared."

"You're sayin' they won't be scared if I stay in business with them?"

"They might feel better about it, considering who your significant other is. The fact that you're trying to distance yourself might give some of them the idea that it's because Ms. Grade's lookin' to take down some folks while sparing her sweetheart."

Huron erupted into laughter. "If they knew her, they'd know she'd have no qualms about taking me down with the rest if I deserved it," concern warred within him however. "What have you heard, Shel?"

"Just rumblings...the little fish aren't happy. They've got the most to lose in all this, so don't underestimate 'em, okay?"

"The most to lose," Huron spoke the words like they were obscenities. "They're makin' dollars hand over fist. I'm buying' 'em out so they can have total control- a thing they constantly griped about *not* having when we first became partners."

Sheldon chuckled over the other man's exasperation. He had been friends with Huron Base for years with such displays of emotion becoming things he'd grown accustomed to witnessing.

"All better?" Sheldon asked when it appeared that Huron was done with his tirade.

Silence held for a time and then both men gave into unrestrained laughter.

113

"Sometimes respect is more powerful than money, B." Sheldon philosophized afterwards, "folks get used to being treated well when others find out who's got their backs. Especially when they're backed by a legend."

"Shel," Huron groaned. "Don't start with that shit."

"It's your story. You should be proud."

"It's the past- no sense going back to it."

"It made you who you are."

"Why does that have to fascinate people so much?"

"That kind of story always has. David taking down Goliath? It's classic!"

"Right," Huron's sour expression came through in his voice. "And David went on to become a king, not a convict. This story you think I should tell...it doesn't have a happy ending."

"Is that right?" Sheldon sounded playfully bewildered. "'Cause I could swear you called me to discuss the woman you're ready to spend the rest of your life with."

A low, amused sound swelled inside Huron's throat and grew when Sheldon chuckled.

***

"So he's serious about her?"

"It would appear so," Dutch Breslin studied the couple at the cozy table across the room.

The man having drinks with Dutch didn't seem convinced. "This is Huron Base we're discussing, remember? He's been rumored to take two or three women to bed with him at the same time- lucky bastard."

"That's why she's got everybody nervous," Dutch fidgeted with the end of his red silk tie. "The woman doesn't just oversee some little P.D. firm. She's not some half-assed investigator snapping pics of cheatin' husbands.

114

She's got the ear of some key players in business *and* law enforcement."

"Huron's no snitch," the other man argued.

"Fuck that," Dutch eyed Kamari with a covetous look. "A man would drop a dime on his mama while he was balls deep in that."

The other man considered Dutch more astutely. "Is this you regretting that you never drew Huron more into your shady dealings? There *are* things the man could claim no knowledge of, aren't there?

Given that fact, his lovely trophy over there could forge ahead full steam were she to uncover illegal deeds calling for justice," the man continued. "She wouldn't even have to feel edgy about protecting a guilty lover," he grinned, "pity you didn't see this coming sooner, Dutch." He grinned devilishly while Dutch Breslin cringed.

~~~

"Thank you," Kam smiled up at the waiter before he left with the orders. She looked over at her dinner partner. "Why'd you bring me here?"

Huron shrugged, focused on the ice he twirled in his drink glass. "I said I wanted to take you out for dinner."

"Here?"

"You don't like the place?"

Her eyes narrowed into a look of playful disgust. "Stop the innocent act, it's not convincing on you."

"So I've been told," he nodded as though the observation were nothing new.

"So?" Kam leaned into the table. "Why *did* you bring me here?"

"There are people I know here," he scanned the casual elegance of La Kruze- "people *you* know here...right now, we're just two associates out for a business dinner.

We could eat and leave and no one from my circle or yours would be the wiser."

"But people are already talking," She pointed out.

"And they've got no real proof," he countered, "we haven't confirmed anything in public, have we?"

"How would we confirm it?" Kam studied the cut crystal base of her wine glass.

Huron observed the table. "I'm envisioning you on your back."

She laughed. "Is there a less X-rated way?"

"Lots. But you have to be sure, Kam."

"Are *you* sure?"

He shrugged. "I brought you here, didn't I?"

"So the ball's in my court?"

"The balls are all yours."

Her laughter turned several male heads in appreciation. She didn't notice or care about the attention she drew when she left the chair. The sexy swish of her body inside the black cocktail dress was an equal attention grabber. Kam deposited herself on Huron's lap and claimed his mouth in a lusty kiss. The gesture drew not only appreciation, but a fair amount of envy from both sexes.

~~~

The two men who had been watching Huron and Kamari with such interest, traded looks.

"Sandra's right, Dutch. You'll want to wait on this. I think you'd be wise to let this play out another way but if this is the route you want to take, you'll want to give him a few more people to point fingers at when you do." The man sighed, stretched his lanky frame in the chair he occupied.

"All that'll do though is give him more people to go after should anything happen to her." The man looked to Dutch. "Is this just about you being pissed for not realizing

116

how in debt you were to a guy like Base and wanting payback or do you *really* think laying a finger on that woman will get him to play along like a good soldier?"

Dutch squirmed a bit in his chair. "This is just a precaution if Sandra's plan doesn't produce the necessary results."

The other man grinned and reached for his glass. "You're a brave man to tangle with Huron. Not many have done that and lived to tell the tale."

~9~

"It's good to know some deals are easier to close than others," Huron was chuckling into the headset he used.

"You serious?" The man on the other end of the line tried to sound stunned and failed. "Do you know how long I've wanted my business back under my whole thumb? She must be somethin' else, B. Somethin' else to make you give up all your money."

"Jorge, man. I'm not giving up *all* my money."

"I see," Jorge Raez, was the one chuckling then. "Just the money you have to look over your shoulder to collect, right?"

"I've been steppin' back from the game a long time. I don't get why everybody's waited 'til now to have cows about it."

"'Cause you've never met a woman who many in our circle have cause to be wary of."

"She's got no interest in your business."

"Her interests go hand in hand with those of her clients, B."

"So stay out of her way, then."

"The suddenness of this, along with the lady on your arm, is making people jumpy is all."

"So can I count on you to keep your ear to the ground for me?"

"You know that you can, my man," Jorge's accent grew thicker then. "But no one wants to move against you, B. We take our cues from you which forces me to ask if there's anything the rest of us need to know? Any moves *we* should be making to clean house?"

Perched on his desk, Huron studied the view beyond his office, tossing a baseball back and forth. "For some of you, cleaning house is never a bad idea. But none of this is about taking anybody down."

"All for love, huh?"

"Stupid- you can say it," Huron groaned.

"Fuck that, man. Love is the best reason I know." Jorge cleared his throat. "So can I also count on you to keep your ear to the ground and share info on anything that might be coming down?"

"You know you can."

"Mmm...won't that put you at odds with your lady?" Jorge didn't bother to hide the slyness in his voice.

"It won't- because she doesn't and won't have anything going on that would involve you."

119

"Her job involved you at some point. It's how you met, after all.

Just promise to keep me posted," Jorge urged again when Huron remained quiet. "Give me time to cover my ass, alright?"

"You got it, man."

"Alright, B."

"Later," Huron waited until Jorge dropped the connection before he dragged off the headset and tossed it to the desk.

He thought of the night before, the statement both he and Kam made during their rather demonstrative date. Anyone who'd been speculating about how serious they were would have pretty concrete evidence after last night.

He wasn't a man prone to public displays of affection. A woman or three at his side was nothing surprising, but rarely was there ever the same one on his arm or even called for a follow up date for that matter. Last night had changed things in a big way as he'd intended.

Huron realized he hadn't bothered to ask what *she* thought of them 'coming out' so to speak. She hadn't seemed to mind, he recalled, smiling over the memory of her on his lap in the middle of a crowded dining room.

The contentment coasting through him didn't last however. Would her feelings change if certain aspects of her business once again bumped up against his? He knew the chances of that were heavy in spite of his casual manner with Jorge Raez.

Distancing himself from those he thought Kamari would deem less than desirable, wasn't about making himself respectable in her eyes at all. She was just the excuse that would mark his true motivation. Not that she wasn't a valid excuse, she was the best reason he could think of to turn away from old habits and interests. But his

120

true motivation for it had been festering for years. Distancing himself was an effort to bury who he'd had to become to survive. Until Kamari, there had been no incentive for him to remain faithful to the endeavor. Even branching off into more legitimate business arenas hadn't panned out. He'd been fine with straddling the line between legal and...barely.

Now there was another chance and, while Kamari Grade wasn't the actual motivation, she was a damned good catalyst for it. She was the best he'd ever had.

You're making folks jumpy, Huron. He was aware of that and would be jumpy too if the situation were reversed. He had no doubts that he'd be able to protect her. There were few with nerve enough to cross him- another thing he'd had his past to thank for. That part wasn't so bad, though.

Yes, there were lots of folks loyal to him. That left a lot of room for the not so loyal ones to hide among.

***

Malibu, California~

Cousteau abided by Eliza's request to keep the real world at bay for two days. He'd enjoyed showing her why he loved Malibu and loved changing her thoughts that it wasn't the snobbish place she'd always found it to be when she'd visited in the past.

Cousteau told her she hadn't been visiting the best parts. But he'd gone as far as he could in holding the lid down over the can of worms he'd finally pried open. There was more he needed to tell her. The fact that she didn't want to know any more soothed his fears and fed the cowardice that was fine with keeping her ignorant of facts she didn't know she needed. Nevertheless, love and loyalty wielded their hands.

A genuine smile tugged at his mouth. He leaned against the doorjamb to observe Eliza across the bright, spacious kitchen.

He'd come full circle in understanding what nagged at Huron about coming completely clean with Kam. Eliza deserved to know who she was sharing her bed with. She deserved to hear every grimy detail about him. That included details about the family he came from. Unlike Huron's situation with Kamari, his past aligned with Eliza's in ways she'd never suspect.

His single knock to the kitchen's open doorway, got Eliza's attention the instant it echoed through the room. She looked up from where she sat out a platter of bacon on the round oak table in the alcove.

"You're up early," she smiled, "I wanted to surprise you. All the pampering *you've* been doing deserves some payback."

Cousteau had crossed the kitchen and was behind Eliza, preventing her from turning in his arms, when he eased them around her waist. He rested his handsome face in her neck and inhaled the fresh scent clinging to her hair and skin.

"Trust me when I say you've paid me back more than I deserve," he told her.

Laughing, Eliza patted one of the muscle packed forearms bound about her waist. "Sit down and let me get you a plate."

"We need to talk now, babe," Cousteau felt her stiffen against him. "We've waited long enough."

Eliza grimaced, wiggling in his arms to make it known that she wanted out of his hold. "Is this important?" She asked when he let her go. "I don't care who your family is-"

122

Cousteau stopped her before she got too far. "You should care, Elly."

She stilled, her blue eyes narrowing in surprise and mild curiosity. "So say it, then." Quietly, she convinced herself that there was a reason he was being so insistent.

"Sit."

She shook her head. "Let's just get it over with. You're not about to tell me anything good."

Cousteau mopped his face in his hands and began a slow stroll around the big kitchen. "You remember what I told you about my family- my uncles and their club? You remember what I said about their friends?" He asked when she nodded. "If I tossed out some names, you'd be sure to recognize them if you follow politics, sports, music or movies."

Eliza gave a weak smile. "Sounds like your bouncer job was pretty entertaining."

Whatever easiness held in Cousteau's mellow expression, faded. "It was...except on the nights when there were lovers' spats like the one we were fortunate enough to catch the other night."

"Were those common?" She felt some of her apprehension ease at the idea of his needing to confide being due to the bar fight earlier that week.

Cousteau stepped to the cozily set table. He studied it and then his ocean view in the distance.

"They were common enough," he spoke after a few silent moments, "but the game changed when the upsets involved the famous."

Eliza took her place at the table then. "In what way?" she asked.

"My uncles gave me free reign to intervene when I saw a woman being abused regardless of who she was

123

with," sighing, he pulled a hand through the brown waves of silk that fell across his forehead.

"I won't deny that it greatly satisfied my ego to put a few quarterbacks and so-called action movie heroes on their backs," his grin was short-lived.

"But my heroic endeavors were only as good as my reaction time," Cousteau leaned back in his chair to study a spot on the hem of a wrinkled white T-shirt. "And that wasn't worth a shit if I got there after the bastard hit his date with a bottle or put his fist to her temple- instantly killing her."

Eliza clamped a hand over her mouth to mask some of her horror. "Did that happen often?" She asked.

"Wish I could tell you it didn't," he couldn't look at her. "My um...my bouncing skills also involved maintenance duties from time to time, but my uncles kept that to a minimum," he joined Eliza at the table then.

"I never had anything to do with the actual um...disposal of the bodies."

"Cousteau I don't understand. Why do I need to know-"

"My dad was never alright with me working there, so of course I wanted to be around it more than anything," he gave the bacon on the table a disinterested look. "When he died, I couldn't get away from it fast enough- felt like I was betraying him by being around it.

My uncles still looked out for me though- put me through school and everything. They didn't seem at all on edge by the fact that I wanted to be a reporter. They even gave me the lead on some of my biggest stories- including the one I did on the Brecks."

Eliza blinked several times and straightened in her chair. "Cousteau?"

124

"I had no plans to air it once I met you," he wouldn't look at her. "I would've rather died Elly than give you a second of pain, but then I found out what the real reason for the story was and it wasn't to help solidify my name in the news business." He looked at her then, his turquoise stare hauntingly serious.

"They wanted your mother to know they knew where she was. If that didn't occur to her, they at least wanted her to know she was in the public eye and it'd be easy for her past to come knocking."

Cousteau shook his head, propped his elbow to the table and braced his forehead against his palm. "I realized that last part too late."

"How did your uncles know her?" Eliza barely felt the words vibrate in her throat as they left her tongue.

"Mutual friends- the guy's a senator now."

"Senator-" Eliza lost her voice, feeling like she was trying to climb a progressively steep hill.

"In the early days of his career, the man had certain...addictions-porn was one. Only thing better than seeing a flick was having one of the starlets in his bed. Your mom happened to be the lucky lady on the scene the night he raped a waitress at my uncles' establishment. Afterward... he left her there for the rest of his campaign staff to um...enjoy." Cousteau rubbed at his chest as though he were discomforted. "The senator was an alderman then, I think."

Eliza pressed her hand to her mouth again as nausea set in.

"Stick with me, babe," Cousteau leaned closer then.

Eliza failed, an anguished cry left her throat as she rushed from the table with both hands over her mouth. She went to the sink for water, gulped down half a cup and then braced against the counter.

"What does any of this have- have to do with my-my mother? Did the senator and his men try to-"

"No baby, no…" Cousteau soothed from his seat at the table, he didn't dare to go to her. "Honey before I get into that, you need to understand that even though these celebrities and politicians were friends of my uncles, my uncles saw them as…benefits first and foremost. They weren't friends with people who couldn't benefit them in the long run." Sighing, Cousteau risked a glance toward Eliza.

"The club was private because it was a place that accommodated men who had interests that might be frowned upon by their wives, constituents, bosses…interests like that, along with the power some of those guys wielded that made them great friends for my uncles to have. They um…" he reached for a strip of bacon and debated on whether to bite in. "They solidified the beneficial aspects, by keeping records of every visit those guys made to the club."

"Records?" Eliza barely turned her head from the sink.

"Logbooks, recordings- audio and video."

Blinking then, Eliza finally turned from the sink. Memory stirred of what her mother had said about 'taking things'- information.

"My uncles say they didn't know exactly how, but your mom got her hands on the proof of what happened that night and left before anyone knew she was gone. It was longer still before they pieced it all together and figured she'd even taken anything like that."

"How do they know she took-"

"They know."

Defeated, Eliza went back to the table. Dropping into a chair, she rested her forehead in her palm. "This all

126

happened a long time ago. It's monstrous but who would care about it now?"

"Honey, the alderman is a senator now, remember? All his campaign staff have gone on to make names for themselves high up in various areas of law enforcement."

Eliza paled.

Cousteau nodded, realizing she'd understood the full weight of what he was trying to tell her.

"So my mother's screwed whether she keeps her mouth shut or not?"

"Elly-"

"Why'd you tell me this?"

"You needed to know, babe. I already waited too long to tell you."

"And why is that?" Eliza straightened at the table. "Why didn't you reveal all this when that story broke?"

"Your mother didn't deserve that."

Eliza coughed out a laugh. "But the rest of my family deserved to be dragged under the bus?"

"Honey-"

"Or maybe you just wanted your big story, but not at the expense of casting any unwanted attention your family's way."

A storm began to brew in his eyes. "Did you just hear what I said? Throwing my family under a bus wouldn't have been an issue. If they were willing to go up against Huron, they could've had the story pulled before that ever happened."

"And so you went with what you had," accusation simmered then in her stare. "It busted up whatever we had going and made me an outcast among my family for a long time." Angrily, she swiped at the hot tears flooding her eyes. "I told you what I went through when that story broke."

"Babe-" a chill scourged his spine when he reached for Eliza's hands only to have her draw back, hiding them under the table. He forced himself to calm.

"Elly...the story airing was all on me. When your mother found out I was a reporter and started causing you to doubt how you felt about me," he shrugged. "I let that rule my temper and I put that story out to show the Brecks were no better than everyone else they tried to look down on. I had the info about her involvement with Fine Lines, but I wouldn't use it."

Eliza rolled her eyes. "Gee thanks."

"Elly," Cousteau bowed his head, working his jaw muscle frantically when he squeezed his eyes shut. "I don't want to lose you over this but being with you and having this," he clenched a fist for emphasis, "you deserve to know what I came from."

"I need to see my mother," Eliza nervously fingered a lock of her hair.

"There are good people out there, Elly. Ones who could help her out of this. They'd be very interested in what she knows and what she can prove."

"Right. And *all* she has to do is share it and then walk around with a target on her back for the rest of her life." Eliza stood. Cousteau followed, blocking her way before she could leave the dining alcove.

"I need to get back."

"Let me take you."

"Cousteau...no I-"

"When can I see you?"

"Soon."

He knew she was lying when her gaze faltered. His insides felt hollow while a dull ache began to throb at the base of his skull.

"Cousteau please," she skirted the edge of the table in an attempt to pass.

He listened to the voice that told him to ease off. He could give her time- *some* but he would not lose her- not ever again. He gave her barely enough space to inch past and Eliza left the kitchen at a quick walk.

Cousteau reclaimed his place at the table. He sat there calmly for a few moments until, he brought his hands down on the surface causing everything there to jump in response.

***

Kamari flashed a bright smile for the man who stood and held his arms open wide to envelope her in a hug. She joined him in laughter when the embrace tightened and he gave her a quick rocking before setting her back to take a slow scan of her body.

Daniel Tate shook his close-shaved head, his hazel eyes pooling with playful disbelief. "I may not have been able to convince you to be my wife, but at least I had the good sense to ask."

Kam squeezed his hand. "I'm glad we can be friends, Danny in spite of our past drama."

"The drama was all on *your* part," Dan playfully insisted. "*You're* the one with the commitment issues."

Kamari laughed, though something cooled in her warm gave.

Recognition flickered on Dan's attractive dark face, hinting that he'd witnessed her reaction. "I was all planned to ask again and accept the punishment of being turned down a second time."

"All *planned*?" Kam smiled curiously. "So you decided against asking me again? Why?" Her head tilted. "Could there be a special woman in your life?"

129

"Nah," Dan's eyes twinkled. "No courage to risk the waters of denial again," he waved toward their table.

Kamari laughed and allowed Dan to escort her to their table. "Still a drama king," she raved.

"True, but that's not why I changed my mind about asking again."

"Alright," Kam's tone, prompted explanation.

Dan grinned and took his place at the table. "I don't know how many men are brave enough to risk the wrath of Huron Base by making a play for his woman."

Kam's peaking interest was evident in her expression. "I didn't know you knew him."

"Only by reputation."

Kam smiled. "You were quick to make *that* distinction."

"Hmph, it'd be wise to, *considering* his reputation."

"Well respected?"

"On one side."

"Ahh…"

"And you're his main squeeze- talk about opposites attracting."

Kam shrugged, making the sequins sparkle along the oversized collar of her shirt. "Never know who you'll meet in a business like mine."

"Clearly," Dan nodded, "I remember the wild stories you used to tell me about your cases. I miss hearing them. Guess you're still coming up against all sorts."

"And I was starting to think that I was almost done with being surprised, but it looks like I've got *you* to thank for my latest stunner."

Dan raised a brow. "So there was something of use in that package I sent."

"Very much so."

Daniel looked pleased. "I told my boss you were our best choice if he wanted to get to the bottom of this."

"Mmm…" Kam accepted the compliment coolly. "I'm surprised you haven't solved most of the mystery yourselves."

Dan shrugged, but intrigue shone on his long face. "We can't all be investigative geniuses, like you."

"It wouldn't have taken a genius to discover that half the people on that list don't exist." Kam dropped whatever effort she'd made at appearing polite. She leaned closer to the table. "If this little fishing expedition was supposed to get my attention, you have it. Now what's the job you really want me for?"

~10~

"So they already knew some of the names were phony?"

Kam smiled over the exasperation she heard in Tenille's voice when it rushed through the phone line. "Dan and his people thought they may've overlooked some stuff which is why they called me in. They think it could be an inside job. To look any deeper...from the home front could spook someone and adios to their chances of finding how the money is leaking."

Kam leaned over to set her tea glass to the living room coffee table. "They think there could be a connection between the names on the list and whoever the weak link is within their ranks. They want me to find those connections."

"Sounds like a pretty hefty request," Tenille's voice held a rushed tone.

Kam smiled, propping her small bare feet to the coffee table. "I already know where you're headed and I already made a lunch appointment with Roya and the others."

"Well, well...I'm impressed."

"Yes, yes sure you are," Kam accepted the compliment with mock hastiness while she grinned. "What you should be doing instead of giving me a rough time, is taking care of your husband. Aren't you guys supposed to be on vacation?" She knew that Tenille and Blake had set out for parts unknown three days earlier.

"Alright, alright, I just want to be kept in the loop."

"You'll hear everything else when you get back. Say hi to Blake for me."

Tenille promised to do so and the call ended some time later. Kam set aside her mobile and got back to work on the packet of info Daniel Tate had shared. The mysterious transactions that had been draining dollars from Laramie Brothers Consulting had been administered among twelve accounts.

So far, Kam had exposed seven of the so called account holders as non-existent. The other five *appeared* to have strings to tug. Whether or not they would lead anywhere, remained to be seen.

Kam was about to write down the names on a separate pad, when her phone chimed. At first, she barely glanced at the faceplate, but did a double take when she noticed the name there. Forgetting the pad, she answered.

"You busy?" Huron asked.

"That depends," she gave into the customary lash fluttering that was usually stoked by the rich sound of his voice.

"That depends on what?"

"On what I get for *not* being busy."

"Damn...I didn't think to bring anything but myself."

She warmed in the most incredible way. "That'll do."

Half a second later, there was a singular knock to her front door. Scooting off the sofa, she padded barefoot to the door but hesitated to check her clothes. The ratty, off shoulder T-shirt and cut off sweats weren't prime entertaining attire, but with any luck, she wouldn't be in them for long.

Wearing an inviting smile, Kam pulled open the door. Her breath stopped dead center of her throat when she saw that Huron had brought along two men who were almost as imposing as he was.

"Huron?" She whispered.

He moved just inside the door and dropped a quick, thorough kiss to her mouth. Kam blinked when he added a firm pat and squeeze to her bottom.

"Kamari Grade, this is Jonathan Aidan and Mike Edmond," he gestured to the men in the hallway. "They're your security. They've been following you for about a week now."

Huron evidently took Kam's silence for understanding and not that she was absolutely stunned stupid. A guileless smile curved his mouth when he studied her at length before turning to the men at his back.

"Thanks guys, that'll be it for the night."

The men nodded, tipping invisible caps in Kam's direction before taking their leave. Kam inched back when Huron crossed her threshold and closed her front door.

"Huron what the-bodyguards?" She gaped.

He seemed to shudder. "Don't call them that. They prefer being called security."

"And what about what *I* prefer? Which is not to have them at all."

"I prefer that you do," Huron eased past Kam and entered the living room at an easy stroll. Coolly, he observed the stacks of papers on the chairs and coffee table.

"I don't need anyone following me," Kam continued to fume. "*I* have people followed- not the other way around."

Huron, having enough of observing the chairs in the living room, took a seat on the back of the sofa. "I need you to go along with this, Kami," he said.

"Why?" Suspicion plumped the word.

"You know what I'm trying to do with closing out some of these partnerships."

Kam's mouth thinned. She didn't need to be spoon fed the rest. "People aren't happy with your decision. Which means, they're probably pissed with me."

"I should've emphasized that part a little more before we put on that show in the restaurant the other night."

"Then let me take this moment to emphasize what I do for a living," Kam threw a hand behind her in the general direction of the door. "It's way too sensitive to have a security detail following me around- calling attention."

Huron tented his fingers, studying them. "The guys have been on you for a week and you haven't noticed," he risked a peek at her reaction when she didn't respond right away.

Kam accepted what she'd perceived as a dig at her skills of perception and then she bristled. "There's gotta be another way."

135

"It's either them or me, sweet thing," he gave her a take it or leave it shrug and then slowly tracked his jade eyes over every inch of her bare skin from his spot on the sofa. "I can promise you'll know I'm there."

Excitement crackled beneath her agitation. "When can you start?" she asked.

He didn't seem to find humor in the question even when he cupped her hips as she draped herself against him.

"I wouldn't keep my distance," he warned her.

"I'm good with that," she murmured in a wholly contented manner. Leaning in, she began a hungry suckle of an earlobe.

Huron fought against allowing himself to be swayed. "Your ex might not appreciate it so much."

Cooling the attention she paid to his earlobe, Kam eased back a fraction. She studied his insanely gorgeous face which was, of course, unreadable.

"My security detail *is* good," she commended.

Huron gave a shrug in confirmation.

"Is that why you stopped by tonight?"

"I'm not a jealous man, Kamari but I'm protective of what's mine," he stroked a patch of her skin visible through the torn T-shirt. "I needed you to know the guys are around, because they're also protective of what's mine," he released her T-shirt as if he weren't sure of himself in that moment.

"It might be a good idea for you to tell that to your ex in case he's got plans to toss his hat back in the ring."

Kam felt her jaw drop.

"He should know that by putting his hands on you, it could get him hurt."

Kam resisted the urge to smile when Huron looked so menacingly serious. She inched a smidge closer and cupped his cheeks in the gentlest hold.

136

"Sweetie, you know most of my clients are male."

"I'm aware of that," his admission charged in without hesitation.

Kam bowed her head briefly in order to give into a smile. "Maybe if you'd dug a little deeper, you'd have known that he wants to hire me for a job."

"That's what I told the guys when they came to me with this."

"And yet you're here giving me this warning?" Curious amusement flooded her warm stare.

"It's not a warning. Not for you."

His meaning was clear and she let him see her smile. "What were you saying about not being a jealous man?"

Huron bowed his head then, smiling at the way his hands were almost smothering her hips where he held her.

"I own a lot of stuff, Kam. *A lot* of stuff," he sighed the words as though the fact made no sense to him. "But until just recently, I didn't know how little it all meant to me. You're the only thing I give a damn about keeping.

I knew all this would make you mad," he shifted a look towards the condo's foyer. "I know what it's like to have people tailin' you. I was trying to make the experience as painless as possible, but I can't take 'em off you, babe. Not yet."

Kam nodded, not having the heart then to argue the subject further. Her finger slid across the silky whiskers shading his cheek and unforgiving jaw. She searched the jade filtering the bold green of his eyes and she knew arguing would be a futile exercise.

"How far do you think these crazy partners of yours will go?" she asked.

137

"For some of them, it's very advantageous to have my name tied to their businesses. Losing that worries them."

"Well, do you really have to do that, then?" Kam chewed her thumbnail and debated. "I mean, if you're not hands on with any of it, why go to all the trouble of buying them out? No one would know-"

"You'd know."

Kam's eyes drew to the spot where a muscle flexed in his jaw.

"You'd know I still have these attachments and-"

"But I don't care."

"*I* do."

"Huron," Kam rolled her eyes, "I know the man you are now. You're the man I-" she caught herself before she said she loved him. "You're the man I want."

He pulled her hand from his jaw, kissed the back of it. "How long before who I am, the connections I have, start to impact what you do for a living?"

"Can't we worry about that when the time comes?" She stood on her toes and tipped closer to him.

Huron was nodding his agreement. "If I have my way we won't *ever* have to worry about it."

"And you really believe tossing all that money to your questionable contacts will work?" She focused on her thumb encircling a button along the front of the walnut colored shirt he wore outside midnight blue trousers. "That's what all this... security is for, right? You think more than a few of them will fight you for wanting to back out."

Very long lashes settled slowly over his stunning gaze and Kam saw him considering her words. She didn't require an answer to the question- she already had it. He was too smart for the thought not to have occurred to him at

138

the very onset of this plan to walk away from the darker aspects of his lifestyle.

"Huron?" She squeezed his face a little. He'd gone so still that it roused her concern.

He blinked and then fixed steadily on her face. Suddenly, he was jerking her into a crushing kiss. Huron exchanged his hold on Kam's hips to clasp her upper arms. The grip wasn't painful, but Kam didn't need to test it to know there was no way she was getting free of it until he meant for her to.

A chill skimmed her spine when she heard the unmistakable tear of material. Her hands curved into loose fists near the open collar of his shirt.

"Let me undress," she proposed, attempting to ease back out of the embrace. It was also an attempt to salvage what remained of her clothes.

Huron wasn't interested in the proposition. One hand released the hem of her shirt to slip up to her nape. Securing his hold, he kept her in place to accept the stifling yet all too sensual kiss he plied her with.

The act was intensely drugging. Kam wasn't so passion drunk however, that she didn't sense the urgency beneath the heat of the ragged thrusts of his tongue against hers. Still, she gave up on any notions of talking him into letting her save her shirt. She looped her arms about his neck and he released her nape. Shredded, the shirt fell past her waist and hit the carpet without a sound.

Kamari wore nothing beneath the garment. Her heartbeat skipped when she picked up the lethal sound that surged deep in Huron's chest upon his discovery of that fact. He moved on to remove her shorts, emitting a sound that hinted of frustration when he discovered the panties beneath them.

Kam stepped from the pool of gray cotton and attempted an awkward straddle of Huron's lap where he perched along the back of her sofa. He assumed control of directing her moves, hands cupping her hips again in order to steady her on his lap. She began a slow wind in his arms, a move that flattened her breasts into his shirt. She moaned, drawing delightful sensations from the friction of the fabric on her bare nipples. The peaks stiffened in sync with the building moisture she felt pressuring her vaginal walls to produce an arousing ache.

Her slow grinding on his lap took on a new urgency especially once his erection was thick and pronounced against the fly of his trousers. Kam shivered over the mere promise of the climactic pleasure the organ was capable of rendering. Her tongue battled with his in a play of frenzied desire and he mimicked the increasingly unrestrained movements of her hips.

Huron rumbled out a fierce curse then. He'd come there planning on a battle once he'd informed her of the security detail he'd assigned. From there, he'd assumed the conversation would steadily decline until he was certain he'd have nothing more to lose by telling her the whole sordid story of himself.

He'd known it wouldn't be that easy. Just then, he was happy to hide beneath the cloak of cowardice until she demanded more. While he expected those demands were still to come, he'd hoped to at least get out in front of it all. He'd come there to at least open the door to the conversation, not to get caught up in a love scene.

Who the hell was he kidding? She filled his hands in the most sensational way. Her lace clad sex teased his cock relentlessly, the longer she moved against it. Maintaining a firm hold on her hip, he insinuated a hand between their bodies to cradle her breast. He brushed a

140

nipple back and forth beneath his thumb until she cried out into his mouth. Her reaction stroked his tongue and massive ego at once.

"Please," she curved her fingers into the waistband of his trousers and gave an insistent tug.

Huron decided a heavy conversation was the last thing he was interested in.

Kam felt him undoing his belt and trouser fastening and elation swept through her on a more heightened level. Feverishly, she raked her nails through the close cut blue black curls atop his head while arching closer when she heard the distinctive release of a zipper.

She remembered her panties too late. They met the same fate as her tattered T-shirt. Huron applied a few yanks to the middle and ripped them off her hips.

"I'm gonna make you take me lingerie shopping."

"Promises, promises," he murmured, positioning her over his lap and easing her down.

A gaspy, hiccup crowded Kamari's throat when the wide crown of his dick pressured her entrance. Slick as she was, it took no time for his engorged sex to penetrate deep. She gave him total control over her body then. Not that she'd had much choice. She'd gone entirely boneless from the pleasure of him stretching and probing her sex with his.

Huron rested his forehead on Kam's shoulder and willed himself not to submit to the weakness that was laying claim to his strength. Thankfully, his hands maintained their ability to direct her to his satisfaction. Once he'd fully seated himself snug inside her, he let her take control. Kam needed no persuasion and immediately began to ride and rotate as she greedily took her pleasure. That combined with the clench and release of her exquisitely tight channel was excruciating in the most amazing way. So much so, she threatened to make him come much sooner than he wanted.

Huron resumed control somehow. Squeezing Kam's hips in warning, he slowed her heated moves to set a pleasurable tempo. It was one that would stave off the onset of orgasm and grant him the joy of her body a little longer before he was emptying his seed inside her.

Unfortunately, Kam wasn't terribly pleased at being made to wait. She put her hands to his, squeezing to try preventing him from maintaining full control. Huron lowered her and she held his gaze. She bucked and rotated in an almost seamless move that sent his lashes fluttering and a curse to his lips.

Kam smiled her triumph when he shuddered her name and groaned out another lurid curse. Satisfied that he'd not put off imminent pleasure, she repeated the shattering buck and rotation, topping off the move with a deep clench of her already tight inner muscles. Again, Huron gasped a curse following a guttural groan of her name.

"It's alright..." she teased, "just give me what I want and I'll stop."

"Fuck that..."

"I'm trying to."

"Kam..."

"Shh...mmm...shh..." she felt him grow even more rigid inside her. "That's it..." she encouraged, then cried out when he seemed to stretch her more as his dick swelled on the brink of release.

"Don't stop," he begged.

"Don't worry," she gasped.

Cursing again, Huron cupped her breasts. He took one mound into his mouth, smothering the pouting nipple while fingering the other. The delicious double torture

142

made Kam come powerfully. She sobbed, feeling the flow of moisture oozing and coating the long muscle relentlessly tapping the most sensitive spot she possessed.

Huron felt some last portion of his control snap and he all but devoured the nipple he suckled. Both hands were then cradling her ass, spreading the full cheeks while claiming her with more vigor. Deep, repetitive thrusts quickly brought him to a peak that spewed jets of liquid warmth.

The feel of being saturated by the merciless dousing of the thick release had Kam's arousal back-building. She got off on the sensation of being filled by his sex and the proof of his satisfaction. Depleted, she somehow managed to milk him until she could no longer feel him ejaculating. His cock was still marvelously stiff and she actually resented the exhaustion that crept in. It warred with her desire to have him again. She moaned her disapproval when he withdrew and tucked his sex inside his trousers which he then half zipped to keep around his lean hips. All this, he did while keeping Kam secured against him in a one-arm hold about her waist. He left the sofa to seek her bedroom.

~~~

Huron and Kamari collapsed into the welcomed abyss of sleep shortly after their arrival in her lamp-lit room. Kam was first to recover and decided to wake Huron with an oral treat that quickly had him moaning himself awake. The resulting orgasm almost rendered him unconscious again, but he resisted and repaid Kam's kindness in a similar fashion.

The lovers collapsed once more, but didn't slumber. Instead, they settled beneath the covers to embrace.

Kam smiled, contented by the strong steady thud of his heart beneath her cheek where it rested against his chest. The vibration had a lullaby effect. She was succumbing once more to the sweet enticement of drowsiness, when she heard his voice.

"How serious was it between you and Tate?"

Her content smile merged into one of playful suspicion. With effort, she raised her head to look down into his steady gaze.

"Are you serious?" She almost laughed.

He wasn't so amused. "I asked, didn't I?"

"But you're not a jealous man, remember?"

"No. Just a curious one."

"Huron-"

"Humor me," his expression softened and he gave a lazy shrug against the pillows behind his back. "I'd like to know a little about a man I'm so thankful to."

Still smiling, Kam cocked her head. "Thankful."

"Mmm hmm," he eased a hand beneath his head, cradling it on his palm. "I'm thankful to him for being such an idiot to let you go- a move that's since gone on to benefit me greatly."

Kam gave into her laughter then. She rested her forehead against his sternum while the gesture had its way.

Huron waited for her humor to spend itself. Losing his fingers in her auburn curls, he let his thoughts rewind to waking up to the sensation of her mouth riding his dick. He remembered tunneling his fingers into her thick, glossy curls and groaning without shame every time her head lifted to nudge his palms.

"Actually," she cleared her throat as her laughter eased. "Danny was pretty smart to let me go."

"Oh, *Danny* was, huh?"

"Stop," she snorted a laugh and slapped his shoulder. "He asked me to marry him. I turned him down," she shrugged. "I'd say walking away after that, was a smart move on his part."

"Well, he had the good sense to ask you to marry him, so I guess the man isn't a complete fool," Huron noted, sounding playful. Still, it gnawed at him knowing she'd once been close enough to another man that talk of marriage had come into the picture.

"Why'd you turn him down?"

Amusement continued to lurk in Kam's smoky browns and again she raised a slender shoulder in a lazy shrug. "Guess I was saving myself for a bad boy."

"Uh huh," he appeared to ponder her response, "and how many bad boys have you known?"

"You're my first. *Only*," she rephrased when he gave her a playful jerk.

"So why'd you turn Tate down?"

"Huron...why do you need to know? It was a long time ago."

"Was there something about him you didn't feel right about? Was that why you told him no?" Huron softly persisted. He didn't much care for the sound of her extolling another man's virtues, but he'd asked, hadn't he?

"It was me. I just wasn't ready for marriage," she said.

"Because of your business? Trying to get it off the ground?"

"Some of it was that," her gaze; less amused then, faltered and she eased off Huron to roll onto her back.

"I knew my business would require lots of time and marriage is about commitment- obligations to things I didn't want to think about."

145

Huron couldn't tell whether she still held those beliefs and he had to know. "It's about a lot of other things too- good things," he said.

"Yeah," she kept her eyes on the vaulted ceiling of her bedroom, "but some of those good things require agreement from both sides. I don't think I'm a woman who's cut out for the bulk of it."

"Sounds morbid, Kam."

"Yes it does…"

Huron lay on his side, his fist braced against his chin while he looked down at her. He didn't care for the faint lines that marred her brow then. "Wanna talk?" He brushed the lines with his thumb.

Sighing, Kam appeared to be forcing a smile. "Talking's not high on my list right now…"

"You can talk to me, Kam," he said while she pushed him to his back.

"I know," her smile was easier then. "Now shut up."

Huron watched her drag kisses across his chest and abs. "Kam," he called upon guessing at her intention.

Her lips skimmed the dark, glossy curls above his sex and then she was taking him in her mouth, teasing the slit at the head of his caramel-toned shaft, motivated by the taste she found there. Kam sheathed him deep, holding his hips when he jerked at feeling the crown of his sex nudging the back of her throat.

"Okay…" he groaned…submitting… For the second time that night, he'd lost whatever motivation he'd had for an involved discussion.

~11~

Kam woke without the aid of an alarm clock that morning and felt a rush of accomplishment over the feat. She couldn't recall the last time she'd done that, her recent vacation notwithstanding. She knew she couldn't take *all* the credit, though.

Huron had left her tucked in bed. She wouldn't find him anywhere in the condo. She knew he was gone. In spite of the great time they'd had, it was just as well that he'd left. She had a feeling that their conversation about marriage would be one he'd want to continue.

Her easy breathing, became strained as his observations filled her memory. He'd called some of her ideas morbid and she had agreed. They *were* morbid and in ways she'd never want him to imagine.

Her phone rang then and she celebrated the interruption. The celebration went into overdrive when she noticed the name on the faceplate.

"Well good morning! I take it your better half is taking time off from shoveling more sunrays into your system?"

"I wish to hell that was true, Kam." Cousteau's voice grated through the line like sandpaper.

A frown wrinkled Kam's brow and slowly she pushed herself up in bed. "What happened?"

"We um," Cousteau cleared his throat apparently not liking the emotion-induced thickness that made his voice sound rather distorted.

"We had a-um-difficult conversation," he laughed shortly but there was no humor. "She wanted to go home afterwards- wouldn't let me take her back."

"What'd you talk about?" Stunned by the turn of events, Kam sat unmoving in the middle of her bed.

"I um…" Cousteau breathed out a curse. "I'm sorry, Kam but it's up to Elly to say… I-she mentioned going to see her mom. Have you heard anything from Jessica yet?"

"No I-" Kam fell back into bed and lay there with a hand pushed into her hair. "We were going to see her together after all the travelling, but we haven't yet. El hasn't called to set a date for us to go. Cousteau? Are you guys on the outs again?"

"I hope not," Cousteau shared once silence had carried for a while. "This- our talk- didn't have to do with us specifically but it...it wasn't easy for me to tell her. It was harder for her to hear."

"Dammit Cousteau! What the hell?"

"Kam I'm sorry I- I called because I- Jesus…"
Cousteau took a moment, his breathing labored as it rushed
through the receiver. "I just need you to call her. She's not
taking my calls and I- after everything she found out about
her mother, I don't know how she'll handle this latest."

"So this is about Jessica," Kam calmed a bit over
the prediction.

"Yeah," Cousteau grated. "Hell yeah and I
should've told her all of it back when I was unloading the
rest. I've got my own pettiness to blame for this shit- trying
to get back at Jessica for the way she got between me and
Elly before-"

"Cousteau, stop." Kam pushed herself up and out of
bed then. "None of that's important now. I'll get in touch
with El and have her call you."

"Thanks Kam," the man's relief was evident.
"Thanks," he said and then disconnected the call.

Kam gave into a sigh of her own and tossed the
phone back to the covers. "What now?" she groaned.

***

"Dammit, nobody's *that* squeaky clean." Sandra
Breslin slammed a fist to the white lacquered desk and
threw a stony blue glare towards the speaker box on the far
corner.

"I'm afraid such people *do* exist," a male voice
transmitted through the speaker.

Sandra snorted. "Such people are boring. No one
goes into a business like the one she's in, just *because*.
Experiences drive passions to do work like that."

"Not necessarily. She could just be a nosy twat," the
man pointed out. "Do you want me to stick with this?"

Sandra leaned over her desk and browsed the print
out of the report her contact had emailed to her. "Where the

149

hell was she before Aspen?" She queried, sounding as if she were posing the question to herself.

"Come again?" The man asked.

"There're years missing," Sandra thumbed through the stapled pages. "She didn't start school in Aspen 'til the fourth grade."

The man's laughter suddenly came through the line. "Hell Sandra, do you think Kamari Grade came out of the womb with a scandalous past?"

"Maybe the scandal isn't hers...but someone she knows?" Sandra rolled her eyes, frustrated that she couldn't admit there was nothing to be found.

"I'm not ready to buy that the little bitch doesn't have something she wants to keep quiet. Find it."

"What if-"

"Jesus Monroe, are you trying to tell me that Kam Grade is better at hiding things than you are at finding them?!"

"You'll hear from me soon," Monroe disconnected from the line.

Settling back in a leather armchair that was the same pristine white as the desk, Sandra observed the report. She tapped a French tipped nail to the top of the page. "What's your story, Ms. Grade?"

***

The disbelief on Jessica Breck's face had merely intensified. She'd been told who her visitor was, but believed she'd misheard the name. That was until she got to the visitation cell.

The woman on the other side of the dreary space could have been her sister. They'd met because of men who liked the same type of woman- tall, blonde, busty. Physical

150

similarities however weren't what could have made them sisters, Jessica thought.

Sisters shared secrets and kept them from others. She and this woman hadn't developed what most would call a friendship. It had been almost three decades since they'd even spoken by phone, let alone seen one another. Yet, *for* one another, they had harbored secrets that were monstrous.

Synthia Errol's collagen-enhanced mouth crept back into a curious, happy smile. "Jessie?" She called.

In spite of the years (and the work) Jessica recognized the woman. She wondered though, if it was the circumstances of their association that had so indelibly stamped the image of the woman *she'd* known as Synthia Reed on her brain.

"Syn?" Jessica replied in a softer tone than the other woman had used in her greeting.

It was enough for Synthia Errol who rushed over to envelope Jessica in a crushing hug. "Oh, you're still so beautiful! I can't believe-"

"No contact!"

Synthia gave a start and turned to glare at the guard who had spoken from the corridor. Synthia discovered her glare was wasted on the man who had called out from a small desk further down the hall. Jessica tapped her shoulder and pointed to a corner of the cell's low ceiling. Synthia grimaced, noticing the security camera perched there.

"Christ, this place is as depressing as the people," Synthia snapped.

Jessica shrugged. "It's why they call it prison, I guess."

Synthia's pale blue gaze narrowed when she re-focused on the woman she'd come to visit. "It's not prison yet, Jessie. You haven't even had a trial."

"Well Syn, I *did* confess," Jessica rolled her eyes and trudged further into the cell. "I *am* refusing to defend myself, so the lawyer my daughter shoved on me is trying to make a play for an insanity defense. I'm only letting him try for Eliza's sake."

"Jessie...Honey why would you give up that way?" Synthia slapped her hands to the tight black linen pants she wore. "I remember the fight you've got inside you. You can't fake that Jess. Why aren't you fighting now?"

"Because I did everything I've been accused of," Jessica leveled a gaze at the woman.

"I don't care what you're accused of," Synthia's gaze was just as level. "You've got a 'get out of jail free' card that'll absolve you of all this mess. You *do* still have it, don't you?"

Jessica blinked rapidly, stunned. "I can't!" she gasped.

"You can. You should. You will."

"They'll kill me faster than prison will."

"They won't."

"Syn-"

"Haven't you ever wondered how I knew there would be a recording and where to find it?"

Jessica stilled, listening intently while Synthia Errol revived her memories of an old haunt they used to frequent back in their wild old days. Club Indulge was a place where all indulgences were tolerated.

"I was there, Syn." Jessica interrupted, to quiet the woman's unwanted recap. "I knew it well."

"But what you *didn't* know was that Laird Riley and his brothers were in the habit of recording their very

152

influential and up and coming friends for insurance and security. By the time anyone realized this was all going on, it was too late. Tons of recordings had already been made and copied." Synthia waltzed to the battered chrome table and settled gracefully to one of the metal chairs there.

"All those *friends* were trapped, but it was still a symbiotic relationship." She made a pretense of studying an expensive manicure and a far more expensive diamond. "The Rileys were beneficial friends to have especially when it came to election time and, of course, *indulging* in those vices that would've been scorned by so many.

I didn't begrudge them the idea," Synthia's sigh carried a playful element. "Even though my ass graced so many reels of recordings...but it got me to thinking of my own security and so I took to recording my own choice tidbits." She gave a serene smile. "If I do say so myself, they're ones that have served me well up until this very day."

"Synthia..." Jessica's lovely face registered bewilderment. "What the hell are you doing here?"

"I'm here to tell you, you're free to use that recording." Synthia placed her elbows to the table and held her hands clasped. "Pull the blanket off all the dirt that's laid the foundation for the corruption that's made the careers of those sons of bitches."

Jessica sat then as well. "Syn, how in the world can you believe I'm free to do that?"

Synthia smiled as though the other woman's confusion hadn't surprised her in the least. "I have enough material on my husband and his friends to make that recording look like a cartoon, but what you've got tucked away will be damning enough to cause them all a lot of frustration."

"Husband?" Was all Jessica could draw out of everything Synthia had said.

The woman laughed merrily. "Sweetie, I told you that recording idea paid off for me in the best way. How do you think I was able to convince your jailers to let us speak uninterrupted until we're done? No touching, of course," she slid a look toward the security camera.

"Use that reel, Jessica. It's old, but-"

"I had it transferred to videotape a long time ago."

Synthia's merry laughter returned. "There's that fightin' spirit!" More animated then, she leaned in and tapped the surface of the table.

"Look Jessie, unless you're happy as a clam, window dressing this drab slice of hell, you better find that tape and scream for a deal to anybody who'll listen."

Satisfied that she'd said enough, Synthia stood and walked around the table to pull Jessica up into a hug. She made it a lengthy embrace and turned to salute the camera when she heard the guard call out his warning.

"Someone's always watching," she made a show of straightening the collar of Jessica's county issued attire. "Use that tape. Chances are high that someone already knows I'm here talking to you. It won't take long to figure out about what."

The jingle of keys alerted the women of the guard's return. Synthia had been fluffing Jessica's hair about the jumpsuit collar while she talked and totally tuned out the man's persistent warnings.

"Don't bother. We're done," Synthia issued a flip wave to the heated guard. "Call me when you're out. I'm sure it won't be long," she left Jessica with a wink and then strolled past the guard when the cell door opened.

***

Huron admitted he'd procrastinated in getting around to seeing Theo Sturgess. The man hadn't made a point of contacting him since the message Nevil and Rave had relayed shortly after his return from Hawaii.

Huron thought of his recent string of activity, trying to distance himself from questionable associates. He shoved the keys to his truck into a side trouser pocket and headed toward the beige stone scraper across the street where he'd parked.

Silently, he mourned the fact that it wouldn't be so easy to distance himself from the likes of Theodore Sturgess. His other friendships had been forged out of necessity, violence or common interests. The friendship with rich kid-wannabe bad boy- Theo Sturgess, had been forged through a mutual acquaintance.

Theo's father, Franklin Sturgess had taken an instant liking to Huron, who had been assigned to an afterschool entrepreneurial program. Frank Sturgess' accounting firm had put the program in place to benefit at-risk kids.

At thirteen, Huron was far beyond the 'at-risk-stage. The actions that had put him there however, had earned him many influential friends. They were friends who had pulled strings to get him the most advantageous community service assignments. Such opportunities came in handy when life happened and Huron found himself in danger of adding another line to a growing criminal record.

As much as Frank Sturgess tried to hone the potential he saw in Huron, his son strived to hone the thuggish element that he imagined could serve him well. Theo Sturgess saw Huron as the kind of friend that; through the violent intimidation of others, could send him through the corporate ranks higher and faster than his father may have approved of.

155

While Huron was no one's fool, he was a young fatherless male with a lot of anger. The… favors he did for Theo Sturgess, among others, fed that anger and he welcomed it. He welcomed it in much the same way that he welcomed and needed Frank Sturgess' involvement in the shaping of his future.

Frank Sturgess had proven to be a good connection to have when the 'less than legitimate' lifestyle lost much of its deceptive sheen. Unfortunately, Huron doubted he could keep a 'stress free' friendship with the elder Sturgess and turn his back on the one with his son.

Huron puffed out his cheeks, hesitating briefly before pressing against the tall, turnstile doors that brought him into Sturgess Finance. He'd called Theo earlier that day to let the man know he'd be around. There was no need to make an appointment. Theo knew him well enough to know Huron would come see him following his message to Base Holdings.

Theo Sturgess knew the debt Huron felt he owed to his father. Frank Sturgess believed he had received all the 'payback' he wanted when Huron had become the businessman he knew he could be.

Despite all Huron had done for him, Theo shamelessly and consistently played on the fact that Huron's debt to his father went far beyond satisfying the man's peace of mind. Huron allowed Theo to drive that line of reasoning, because he'd believed it himself.

~~~

Theo Sturgess had never been a man who instilled a sense of intimidation when he entered a room. He was however, a big, barrel-chested man with a big personality. The combination had served him well and had made him an undeniable success in the finance world that had changed

156

considerably during the time the reins of Sturgess Finance had passed from his father's hands into his own.

To the uninformed, one might believe Theo Sturgess to be a man in a constant state of elation. Those who knew him better could recognize the frame of paranoia that often encased the delight.

"B!" Theo crossed the big corner office to shake hands with Huron when he arrived. The handshake rounded out with a hug and hearty clap to the back. "You're a hard man to get a sit down with!" Theo gave Huron another shoulder-clap and grinned. "Guess I'd be hard to find too if I had a sweet thing like Kamari Grade to keep me occupied."

Huron's easy smile remained, though a hint of menace flared amidst the extraordinary green of his stare. "You know her?" he asked.

Theo's laughter blustered out. "Anybody with a problem in business knows Kam Grade," he perched on the corner of the L-shaped desk that filled almost the entire rear corner of the office. "As you know," he sighed, "in business problems are always dreaded but can always be expected."

Nodding, Huron went to the wall that accommodated a fully-stocked bar.

"You guys made quite a show at La Kruze the other night."

Huron grinned. "You were there?" He didn't look up from preparing a glass of bourbon from Theo's impressive stash.

"Didn't have to be," Theo folded his arms over his round chest. "Almost everybody in business goes there. Every man in Cali probably knows to cease fantasizing about Kam because she's yours."

"Giving me too much credit, Thee," Huron chuckled.

Theo shrugged. "That was still quite a statement you made. What was the point? You just want it known how you feel about her?"

Huron downed some of the bourbon and kept his eyes fixed on Theo. "This what you called me for?" he asked.

"Alright, alright," Theo raised his hands as if to acknowledge that he'd gotten too nosy. "Just want you to know I'm happy for you, is all. It's about time you got somebody real on your arm. Kam Grade is about as real as they come," he gave a clap and stood.

"We got a snitch in the ranks, B," he said on his way to the big chair behind the desk.

"Snitch," Huron finished off his bourbon. "You've got your dad's seat now, Thee. There's no need to make moves anybody would have to snitch about."

"This is business, B."

"Yeah- a legal one. You've always been blessed in that." *Pity you could never see it.* Huron kept the last inside his head.

Theo pulled a glass and bottle of Scotch from a drawer at the bottom of the large desk. "Finance isn't the respectable game that it once was, you know? Certain plays have to be made that others might frown upon."

"Others? As in the law."

Theo sighed. "It's complicated, B."

"Is that why you called me?"

Theo poured the scotch. "I need you to find out who's leaking info to the board."

Chuckling renewed, Huron returned his glass to the bar. "You're getting me confused with Kam."

"I doubt it. She doesn't offer the services I need for this particular job," the man toasted Huron with his glass. "I need you to locate the leak and shut it off." He added, taking Huron's silence as encouragement to continue.

"I'm not the one for this job either, Thee."

Theo laughed. "Are you serious?!" His laughter intensified causing his expansive torso to roll. "Is this because of the lovely Ms. Grade?"

"Theo, do you have any idea what I'm doing?" Huron's voice held on a tone of frustrated disbelief. "You know where I had dinner the other night, but do you know I'm closing out interests that connect to things 'others' might frown upon?"

"That don't apply to me, B." Theo still appeared jovial. "You and me go back-"

"And it's got nothing to do with this."

Theo's joviality showed hints of stress. "The hell it doesn't. You owe me, B."

Huron called on restraint before he spoke again. "It's Mr. Frank I owe. Not you. As far as he's concerned, the debt's paid."

The wildness in Theo's hazel gaze glinted with a harsh light. "That's bullshit. If it wasn't for my pop, you'd still be some fool on the corner breakin' bones for money."

"You would know, wouldn't you, Thee? Seeing as how you benefited from that service more than once. But I'm done."

"Where's all this comin' from, B?" Theo smirked, the scotch glass forgotten in his hand. "You never had an issue with helping me before-" Realization beamed in his eyes then. "So you think she's the one, huh?" He laughed and finally sipped of his drink.

"Jesus, B, do you really think she'd ever tie herself to you legally? You're trying to clean yourself up to make

159

her your wife, aren't you? Ha!" Theo's rotund chest shook while he laughed heartily and finally drained the rest of the liquor from his glass.

"B..." He snickered, shaking his head while heading back to the desk for a refill of the drink. "I guess it's true that love can make the strongest man pool like water. Hmph..." Theo's humor faded into something stern, cautionary.

"Word to the wise, B, women like Kamari Grade don't marry often. When they do, they sure as shit don't marry men like you- no matter how many millions you got in the bank or how good you are in the sack."

Huron stepped toward the desk. Theo swallowed noticeably- nervously- but stayed rooted to his spot.

"Remember what you said about if it wasn't for your dad, I'd still be breaking bones for money?" Huron smiled, detecting fear in the other man's eyes. "Thanks to Mr. Frank I'm not that man anymore, but I'm still a long way off from the man he thought I could be. Don't call me for this shit anymore, Thee."

"You're leaving?" Theo looked incredulous when Huron headed for the door. "What the fuck, B?"

Huron didn't acknowledge his old friend. He kept walking until he was slamming the office door behind him.

Alone, Theo Sturgess raised the glass of scotch he'd poured. He paused, taking notice of his shaking hand. With an enraged cry, he threw the half-filled glass across the room.

~12~

"Yuck," Kam gave a miserable smile when Eliza opened her door that evening.

Eliza rolled her eyes. "Don't expect improvements anytime soon," she walked away leaving the door open.

Kam slowly entered the condo, freezing in place when Eliza's voice suddenly thundered out.

"Bolt it." She ordered.

Kam hesitated, sweeping her eyes along Eliza's rigid frame. "I talked to Cousteau," she shared while easing the deadbolt into place. Kam turned in time to notice Eliza's steps slow before she continued her trek toward the living room.

"What happened, honey?" Kam rushed into the room behind her friend. "You guys looked happier than I'd ever seen you."

"Cousteau didn't tell you?" Eliza faced the fireplace where she studied artwork above the mantle.

"He said it was for you to share."

Eliza threw her head back and gave into a long, but shaky laugh. "Can you believe I finally found someone with a more screwed up family than mine?"

"Cousteau's family?" Kam found that hard to believe.

"They're mafia," Eliza finally turned from the fireplace. Curiosity beamed past her strained expression. "Or should I be referring to it as organized crime? They're Irish so...not sure what's politically correct..."

"Honey what did he tell you exactly?"

Eliza wearily made her way to the sofa while recapping what Cousteau had revealed about his uncle's club, it's clientele and the sort of work they did outside of being nightclub owners. Kam was sitting on the loveseat by the time Eliza finished. Her mouth was hanging open from what she'd learned.

"I can't believe he could make a living as a reporter with family ties like that- not without looking over his shoulder, anyway," Kam noted dazedly.

"Well his dad was real concerned about having his only son hanging around his brothers- in-law," Eliza crossed her legs beneath her on the sofa. "After his dad died, Cousteau couldn't make peace with being a part of it. So...sounds like they loved him a lot- did whatever they could to make sure he was a success."

Kam frowned. "Why are you here, El? Is it Jessica? I mean, you're not turning your back on Cous because of his family, are you?"

162

Eliza gave an abrupt laugh and dragged a few fingers through her unkempt locks. "I love Cousteau, Kam. That hasn't changed but knowing my mom's sitting in a jail cell because she's afraid to rat out the sons of bitches who know his family, is making it kind of hard to be around him right now."

"Huh?" Kam leaned forward on the loveseat, her eyes stretched until they were almost the same circumference as her open mouth.

Eliza raised her knees, propping her chin against them. "Cousteau told me about a man my mom was seeing-she met him through Fine Lines. He was some kind of city councilman or alderman or something," she trailed trembling fingers across her brow and seemed to fight against closing her eyes.

"One night, the alderman and some of his campaign staff, raped a waitress at the club owned by Cousteau's uncles. All this happened while my mom sat unsuspecting at the bar."

Kam finally blinked and tried to shake her head. "El, what the- did she see? Did she- do they think her being in jail would make her tell that? Surely they know they won't be prosecuted after all these years and I'm guessing it's safe to say the victim didn't report the crime."

"You're right," Eliza tired of sitting and moved off the sofa to walk the living room. "Guess they'd feel pretty confident if there wasn't a recording of it."

Kam didn't think she could take any more shocks and sat silently for a moment. She made a couple of attempts to form questions, but failed. "How'd Jessica get her hands on something like that?" She finally managed.

"Cousteau doesn't know all the details," Eliza tugged on the hem of the blue cotton sleep shirt she wore. "He's gotten this info second hand from his family, but he

163

says they're pretty sure mom- with the help of another woman who was there- got their hands on the recording of the attack."

Eliza sat on the sofa arm and mopped her face with her hands before sighing heavily. "She said she...took things when she left working for Fine Lines. I thought it was about the studio, but it was altogether different."

"Honey," Kam left the loveseat and crossed to Eliza. "Have you seen your mom?" She cradled Eliza's face in her palms.

Eliza's eyes watered. "I don't know what to say to her," she sobbed. "How do I get her to come clean and save herself if she's got that recording and it's why she felt she had to protect us for all these years?"

"Listen El, we need to see her. We've put it off long enough. Now do you want to set it up or do you want me to do it?"

Eliza sighed again as though she were resigning herself that time. "I'll handle it."

Kam nodded slowly, straightening. "What about Cousteau?"

"Ah Kam," Eliza buried her face in her hands again. "I can't think or talk about him right now, okay?"

"Alright, it's alright," Kam rubbed the woman's arms briskly. "How about some hot tea? Does that sound good?" Kam smiled when her friend visibly relaxed.

"Sounds better than you know," Eliza's sigh was a more relieved one then.

"Relax, I'll take care of it." Kam slipped off her sandals and headed for the kitchen.

"Kam?" Eliza waited for Kamari to turn. "Thanks."

Kam threw her a kiss. "You'd do it for me," she pointed to the sofa. "Relax."

***

164

"Sounds like a big waste of time."

"There's something there. I know it." Sandra Breslin countered her husband's opinion while considering her selection of earrings. Trying to decide which pair was more appealing, she held various pieces to her earlobes. She'd observed her reflection through the lit vanity near where Dutch Breslin relaxed on an armchair in the bedroom alcove.

"And if you find somethin'?" Dutch queried, his face twisted in doubt. "Exactly how do you think it'll benefit us?"

"That depends on what it is," Sandra sang, merrily evaluating her earring stash.

"Let's say it's somethin' good."

Sandra finally turned to observe her husband. "Then, we take it to Mr. Base who I'm sure will agree that it's something his sweetheart wouldn't want made public. We assure him that won't happen as long as he continues with business as usual."

Dutch squirmed in the big chair. "There's a lot of unknowns there, Sand. One final act could save us a lot of trouble, you know? Give us a stronger name in the process."

"And Huron Base has a lot of friends we'd need to keep happy when he's gone. Subtlety, not flashiness will suit us much better here, sweetheart."

"And what if you find somethin' Ms. Grade doesn't mind makin' public?"

Sandra turned back to her earrings. "Again...that depends on what it is. We latch onto something really damaging...she won't want it out and he'll do whatever it takes to save her that pain." Sandra paused to study her mirrored image. "That man would move mountains for her. I could see that when they were here."

"There's a chance the bastard would flat out kill us anyway just for threatening to expose his woman," Dutch theorized.

Sandra stiffened on the cushioned bench she occupied before the vanity dresser. "You're right," she gave a resolved sigh. "Well, my love, if that becomes the case I'm afraid a little flashiness might be appropriate after all."

Dutch gave a lengthy stretch in the chair. "I appreciate your cunning, darlin'. Despite my playin' devil's advocate, I really do think subtle's the only way we can come out on top in this. Unfortunately…" he let the word hang while he pushed out of the chair.

"We've already overstepped too many times because we had Huron's backing and therefore no fear of reprisals. We move forward the way you suggest, we not only have *his* wrath to suffer, but that of everyone we've crossed, unless we kill him and give folks pause before they think about fuckin' with us."

Sandra smiled to concede her husband's point. "If that becomes necessary, then I suggest we do it right, my love."

***

"We thought Tenille was fuckin' with us when she told us why you wanted to meet."

Kamari laughed as she often did when initially confronted by Roya Sams' gregarious personality. She and the woman shared a warm hug and then Kam greeted the other members of Roya's usual team.

"You guys know this is long overdue," Kam took a place at the big round table she'd reserved at the cozy soup and sandwich bar near the harbor. "I've been running my business like a lone wolf for way too long."

"Alright," Roya offered up a slow nod. "Tenille said you wanted to talk about easing up on the work load. What's that mean for us?" She glanced around the table at her small, yet effective team.

As Kamari's presence in the field of troubleshooting started to garner praise, respect and a fair amount of fear, she'd been approached to take on cases that often went hand in hand with law enforcement agencies that handled the bulk of their investigations below the grid of adherence to law and ethics. Nevertheless, they got results. Kam was honored to play a role in bringing some very loathsome characters to justice.

A waiter stopped to take orders which were then confined to drinks. It was usually the case when Kam met with various members of her teams.

The drink orders took a little longer to collect what with the waiter's stupefied expression as he oogled the women at the table. The women didn't mind, especially not Roya and her crew who had been shamelessly complimenting the attractive waiter before their boss' arrival. The young man's wavy, black braid, that hung almost to his well-shaped ass, had garnered quite a few flattering yet outlandish comments.

Kamari was happy to settle in and enjoy the episode. If Roya Sams and her team were men they would've been labeled as sexist pigs. The fact that they were an ethnically diverse group of women- tall, beautiful ones at that- first stunned and then intrigued nearly everyone they met.

"You guys know I usually bring in teams for the footwork the investigations require once I'm done following all the paper trails that make our cases," Kam said once the blushing waiter had taken his leave.

Roya nodded, dark thick curls sliding across her head as she did so. "We all know that, Kam."

"The system's served me well," Kam felt as though she needed to defend her decisions at least a little. "I've enjoyed being hands on, but the popularity of our services has made doing business that way a bit much for one person."

"Oh, I get it," Tearza Reynolds grinned. "Tenille's finally getting the promotion we all know she deserves."

"Tenille's earned a promotion and more. I couldn't run 'Grade' without her," Kam scooted closer to the table. "But even Tenille agrees that what we need is someone with working knowledge of the office *and* the field. That's you." She looked to Roya.

Grins broadened on every face. Every face, except Roya's.

"Beggin' your pardon, Kam," Roya raised a hand to silence the other women's congratulations. "I'm no executive type," she said.

"I'm not asking you to be. The last thing I expect is for you to spend your days inside an office," Kam explained, "I'm not attempting to dump everything in your lap either, but I need someone like you to have my back."

"You know you've always got that in me, girl." Roya's husky tone, deepened with meaning.

Kam nodded once, decisively, understanding the look. She and Roya went back a long way and the way had not been an easy one. She reached for a black two-pocket folder that had been sitting next to her on the table. "This outlines everything I expect of the person I'm asking to take on this responsibility." She pushed the folder in front of Roya.

"I don't want you to look at that until you've wrapped up whatever you're currently working on." Kam clasped her hands atop the table and scanned the faces looking back at her. "How's that shaping up? Has our information generated any leads?"

Everyone looked to Roya who wore a satisfied grin.

"Our reputations as...couriers are serving us well," Roya stretched her long, curvaceous frame in the chair she occupied. "It's a comfort to know we've got another career path should this one not pan out."

"Is the cover getting you any closer to finding out what our client's heir is really involved in?" Kam asked once laughter had settled.

Olymph Harris cleared her throat and smiled when Kam looked her way. "Looks like our client's suspicions that his son has involved himself with a criminal element, are correct. We knew he'd been responsible for the theft- which required him to reach out to various sources to fence it, but we weren't expecting that those sources would become more involved business associates."

Conversation paused when drinks arrived at the table.

"The mere fact that he reached out to them to sell his stolen property makes them business associates," Kam sipped her Rum and Coke.

"That makes them business associates by default, Kam." Mist Blackmon chimed in to support her teammate's information. "We think the guy reached out for other reasons."

"Thankfully, we weren't hired to discover those other reasons," Kam enjoyed another sip of her drink. "Our job is to find him, confirm he's tried to move the merchandise and let the client know so that he can move forward. Once that's done, we can talk about a shift in your job duties." She gave Roya Sams a pointed smile.

The woman grinned and reached out to shake Kam's extended hand. "You're an insistent bitch," she said.

Laughter roared at the table. Kam's laughter roared the loudest.

***

Marin County, CA~

"He hasn't been in the best mood lately, Miss," Lukas Moyers stepped back from the door.

"I figured that," Kam sighed, following the man's wave directing her to enter.

It had been a few days since she'd spoken to Huron. She'd been so busy that she'd assumed he was as on the go with work as she was.

"He's in his study, Miss Grade."

Kam gave a watery smile. "Thanks Lukas," she watched as the man left her alone in the foyer. Letting out a slow breath, she headed for the study.

Of course, there were reasons beyond business hassles that had played into her maintaining distance from Huron as well. Their last discussion had unsettled her more than she wanted to acknowledge but that never failed to happen when talk involved marriage and family.

Those were things she could never consider. Not with anyone-most especially not with Huron. He was the only man she'd ever truly loved or been *in love* with. He deserved much more than what she could give him.

She dropped a light knock to the study door and then pushed open the heavy oak when there was no response.

170

"Huron?" There was no answer. She'd gotten halfway to the massive desk in the corner of the dim room when she heard him.

"Want a drink?"

Kam commended herself for not shrieking in response to the sudden booming of his voice. "Sure," she slowly walked toward an L-shaped bar that spanned two walls of the study.

"Lukas says you're not in the best mood."

Huron smirked while preparing a Rum and Coke, Kam's favorite. "The man thinks I'm at the edge of rage if I don't eat all my dinner."

She leaned against the bar, curving her fingers over the beveled edge. "Haven't heard from you in a few days."

"Didn't think that'd be a problem."

The pointed reply sent Kam's heart thudding strangely beneath the scooped, ruffled neckline of her dress. "Why would you think that?" she forced out the question.

"You didn't much care for our last conversation."

"It wasn't that."

"Care to elaborate on what it was- exactly," he passed her the drink.

Kam studied the fizz and bubbles clinging to the carved glass. "Why are we having this conversation?" she kept her eyes on the glass.

"We aren't having *this* conversation. We're discussing why we *can't* have it."

She raised the drink to her lips and savored the crisp flavor. "And why are we doing that?" She asked once the bubbles had dissolved on her tongue.

"Because it's the only conversation I want to have with you."

Kam had taken another sip of the drink and remembered to swallow before she choked on it. "Tell me this isn't why you're in such a bad mood."

Huron rolled his eyes and took a drag from the long neck of the beer bottle he'd opened. He set the bottle down with more force than needed and abruptly rounded the bar to dwarf Kam where she stood.

"I'm in such a bad mood because I love you and don't much care for forcing you to have a conversation we're definitely going to have."

Kam had to remind herself not only to breathe, but to speak. After all, the man just said he loved her. A response was not only polite, it was expected. She opened her mouth, but there was no sound.

"Don't bother," Huron didn't seem at all surprised by her inability to respond.

"Huron-"

"I said 'don't bother'. I get it Kam." he went back behind the bar.

"Get what?" Baffled, she spread her hands.

His smile was coolly knowing, yet it hinted of sadness. "You said you were holdin' out for a bad boy, but loving him was never part of the plan, was it?"

For a moment, her eyes were fixed on the logo centered on the T-shirt stretched across his chest. She discovered the amazing torso hadn't stunned her nearly as much as his words did. "You're putting words in my mouth," she said.

"Is that a problem?" he added a dry laugh. "Doesn't look like you've got any of your own in there."

She rounded the bar. "Huron-"

"I got some calls to make," he moved to leave the bar, halting when Kam stood in his way. The move caused him to utter a genuinely amused chuckle as his green eyes scanned the diminutive frame she thought to trap him with.

"This is fun, babe, but I'm busy."

"Will you shut up for just a second and let me talk?" She nodded when his fake, easy expression hardened. "I love you too," she said.

Huron blinked, at first appearing stunned and then satisfied until shadows of his recent agitation returned. He moved, seamlessly turning the tables on Kam until she was the one being trapped inside the bar. He smiled down at her then, a hint of knowing darkening his vibrant stare.

"Marry me," he said.

Her gasp seemed to echo in the soft lit, panelled room. Kam knew that, had she been sipping her drink then, she would have surely choked on it. He waited patiently and she was thankful, for words were taking their own sweet time to form on her tongue.

"Huron," she finally felt able to verbalize her shock. "Where is all this coming from?"

He invaded more of her personal space. "*This* is where it's been going for me from almost since the day I met you." He laughed then, rolling his eyes at her bewilderment. "Did you think I was just having fun with you in my bed for a while?" He turned his head and muttered a curse. "Course you did."

"Huron!" She was beyond exasperated.

"You love me enough to let me have you anyway I want you but not *quite* enough to marry me."

"Dammit, what the hell is going on with you?!" She snapped, not sure how much longer she could stand there being stunned witless. "Where is all this coming from, Huron? We haven't even known each other long enough for you to be talking-"

He moved away from her so abruptly, Kam actually felt a sense of loss.

"Lukas is right, I *am* in a bad mood. Stay here. He'll be through to show you out."

Kam slammed a hand down to the bar. "So you're just walking away?"

"Trust me, Kam. It's best for both of us if I do just that."

Mouth agape, Kam stood behind the bar and watched him leave the study through an inconspicuous panel at the back of the room. She was still rooted to her spot when Lukas arrived as if cued some ten seconds after the panel thudded shut behind Huron.

Kam looked to the dapper man who spread his hands in a silent 'told you so' gesture. Motivated then by temper and recklessness, Kam stormed from behind the bar. Her steps gained speed as she left the study through the exit Huron had taken.

~13~

"You son of a bitch."

Huron paused halfway down the stairwell when he heard her. "Go home, Kam," he bowed his head while issuing the quiet warning.

Kamari bristled, going cold beneath the mauve curve-adoring frock she'd chosen for the night. That was when she'd hoped to spend a romantic evening with the man she- loved. Now she had to settle for the fact that she'd be speaking to his back for a while.

"I'll be happy to go home once I have my say or are you the only one with permission to run your mouth like a goddamn idiot?" Her chin lifted when she noticed his already broad shoulders stiffen and appear impossibly broader in the process. She glared down at him when he finally turned to look up at her.

"Go home, Kam. I meant what I said about not being in the mood to continue this."

"You don't have to continue a thing. I'll do all the talking."

But for the long, sweeping glance he gave her and the tensing of a jaw muscle, there were no other clues to his mood. Huron knew his temper was creeping into scary territory. His warnings to her were not hollow ones. He'd die before he ever harmed her physically, but he knew there were all sorts of ways to exercise his temper. While those ways were ones he believed he could make her enjoy, he was sure she'd want to kick his ass for subjecting her to them later.

As she'd reminded him a few minutes ago, they hadn't known each other long. That didn't matter. He knew her well enough to read the look on her face. She wouldn't leave until she had her say- to hell with his temper.

Huron gave her small, curvy frame a few more sweeps, lingering on her provocative bowed legs a little longer each time. Then, he turned and continued the trek into the lowest level of his home.

Kam gave into a quiet sigh and revealed an expression of intense relief when she realized she'd won their battle. She wouldn't acknowledge what was probably more accurate- that he'd just *let* her win.

On determined steps, she followed him down the stairway. Mild concern began to filter its way into her eyes as she took note of the increasing dimness that shadowed the area. She ignored the cautionary voice that asked if she knew what the hell she was doing.

The L-shaped staircase reminded her of the construction of the bar in the study. Some of her concern

176

eased when she saw a more inviting golden light spilling from the area the stairs led into. The golden lighting however was about as 'inviting' as the area got.

"Jesus," Kam breathed when she discovered where they were.

It was a weapons room of sorts- a well-stocked weapons room at that. For what had to be the fifth time that evening, Kam could feel her mouth hanging open.

Who could blame her? Astonishment was a fair reaction to a room such as the one before her eyes. An entire wall was dedicated to a vast assortment of cutlery- from the 'tamest' looking pocket knives to ones that would've looked like broadswords next to her scant frame.

Kamari passed a row of rectangular boxes that reached her waist. The tops were covered with a heavy looking glass to protect an array of handguns. She saw no semi or automatic artillery, but guessed that the painting depicting the guns in question was adorning the wall behind which those items were kept.

Kam concluded her survey of the room to find Huron leaning against a wall decorated with what looked to be various plaques. She made out the writing on a few of the largest and realized they were awards for marksmanship.

She swallowed and forced herself to look at him then. "Thought you had calls to make?"

He smiled and strolled but a few feet away to the wall behind one of several sectional sofas in the room. An expansive tapestry covered most of it. Not surprising, its artwork was dedicated to yet another gun- this one a medieval-looking cannon. He rested back against it.

"Felt like I needed to come down here first," he spread his hands. "You had something to say to me."

She reciprocated his smile then, refusing to be intimidated by his sudden desire to be in such grotesque surroundings.

"Why is it alright for you to ask me not to go digging around in your background, that we not even discuss it until *you're* ready, but I can't have the same courtesy when it comes to something *I* don't want to discuss?" She'd approached him on bold steps, propping fists to hips while she confronted him.

His handsome features contorted to display an incredulous look. "It's not alright because this conversation has to do with our future." His voice was dangerously soft and reflected the same incredulity as his expression.

In a weak attempt to keep her composure, Kam curled her fingers into her hair and tugged out of sheer frustration before making another attempt to reason with him.

"Please tell me why we have to discuss something *that* massive at *this* point in our relationship?" She spread her arms wide. "We just made our relationship public after only knowing each other for a hot second."

"Have you been listening at all when I say I'm distancing myself from certain things for you?"

Kam sent one hand slicing through the air. "I never asked you to do that-" she jumped at the thud his boot made when he slammed his heel into the wall.

"Maybe I wanted to do it, Kam. Maybe I'm trying to be the kind of man you'd want to change your last name for."

"Don't put that on me," she shook her head while stepping closer to him. "I love who you are. I never even hinted that I wanted you to change."

Unmoved, he smirked, resting his head against the tapestry covered wall. "You're right," he studied her beneath a hooded stare, "you turned your back on good guys because you prefer the bad ones."

"You're right," she returned his smirk then sent a scathing look around the room before setting it upon him. "Call me if that bad guy shows up anytime soon." She turned on him, but not before spotting the stricken look that sparkled in his unforgettable eyes.

Huron watched her walking away and bowed his head. Squeezing his eyes shut, he willed his temper to retreat as it encroached upon the hurt her words had inflicted.

His temper didn't listen. He shoved off the wall to catch Kamari before she'd taken five steps.

Kam resisted the hold on her arm, but it was useless. He was jerking her back against him and there would be no escape.

"You want him, you got him." His voice sounded harsh in her ear as Kam braced against his hold. She refused to beg, but fought in earnest as he tugged her to the midnight blue sectional before the tapestry-adorned wall.

"Stop."

"I will."

The guttural timbre of the promise sent her heart to her throat. She struggled a little more insistently then. Huron didn't seem to take much notice as he led her behind the sofa.

Kam bristled when he set her to the back of the long chair. He released her arm and she immediately sought her escape. His hand smothered her nape, applying the slightest pressure to encourage her compliance.

"Stop," her command sounded like a gasp, given her choppy breathing.

"Stop fighting me," he countered moments before crushing her mouth beneath his.

179

She melted. Of course, she melted. All she wanted was to feel his tongue invading her mouth which it did and deeply. Repeatedly, the strokes penetrated. Kam accepted what was meant to punish, but the act drenched her in far too much pleasure for that.

She struggled on principle then, determined not to just eagerly dissolve into a puddle of need. She slammed her fists into the impenetrable wall of his chest and followed up with another, weaker blow when he didn't bother to stop her.

He knew there'd be no need, she discovered, for she stopped fighting him on her own seconds later. His hand eased beneath the snug hemline of her dress and curved into her panties. Her blows to his chest halted at once when two fingers filled her.

Huron broke the crushing kiss and set his forehead to Kam's shoulder. "Stop fighting me," he set a rhythm to the intimate massage. "Stop fighting me, stop fighting…" the phrase continued like a litany that kept time to her moans and gasps. His voice distorted into an unintelligible groan when he felt her moisture bathing his skin.

He wanted to make love to her, but his bruised ego demanded humiliation over tenderness. That was what bad boys craved, right?

He waited until she was in the throes of the climax his fingers stirred inside her body. He raised his head from her delicate shoulder, watching her very lovely face made more enchanting in the grips of sexual enjoyment.

His thumb joined the caress to graze her clit, causing her to bite her lip and wince before she whimpered his name. He withdrew from her then without a hint of remorse. Jerking her from the sofa, he made her face the wall.

180

Kam blinked, trying to make sense of the unexpected change in her position. She heard the familiar sound of material ripping. She felt the scrap of fabric that had once been her panties, slide down her thighs to pool about the heels of her cream ballet pumps.

"Huron-"

"Don't."

Kam heard the unmistakable grating of his jeans' zipper. She wanted to face him, but he took her wrists and held them above her head against the plush tapestry. Unease battled with anticipation inside her when she felt the lower half of her dress being shoved above her waist. He held her hip captive and settled her beautifully.

Kam sobbed out a moan when the wide crown of his dick nudged the folds of her sex. He didn't need to guide himself inside her, his shaft was rigid enough to locate the spot he wanted to claim. He'd released her wrists to recapture her hips, but Kam hadn't moved them from their place upon the tapestry. Too in awe of desire rippling throughout her body, she wiggled her ass, hungry for what was breaching her core.

Huron groaned loudly, shuddering as his cock was coated by her thick need. Enjoyable as it was, he wouldn't torment himself by taking her slow. This wasn't about tenderness.

She cried out when he began to thrust relentlessly. His hips slammed hers in a display of dominance.

Huron wouldn't allow himself to care whether her cries were ones of pleasure or pain. Directing her moves, he guided her up and down the extensive length of his erection. Selfishly, he reached for his own pleasure plateau and commanded himself not to care about hers.

He did give free reign to her supernatural effect on his hormones however. His satisfaction came quickly and strongly.

Kam blinked as though emerging from a daze when she felt the heavy eruption of his seed drenching her intimate walls. She was more disappointed than delighted by the sensation since she was far from reaching her peak.

The disappointment merely heightened when she felt him withdraw, fix himself inside his jeans and tug the zipper back into place. An internal cold rushed her spine and seemed more tangible when he used her tattered underwear to wipe his release from her thighs. She turned her head and saw him toss the garment to the sofa.

"Find your way out," his voice sounded hollow and unmistakably chilling.

Hands shaking, Kam smoothed down her dress, turned on unsteady legs and made her way out of the room. Vaguely, she acknowledged the stairway banister, grateful for the support it provided back up to the main floor.

Huron kept his back toward the staircase while he paced the room for what seemed like hours. The area had never struck him as depraved until that moment. A wounded sound escaped him and in the next instant, he was beating a path to the stairs. He scrambled up the first flight and was roaring her name by the time he'd reached the landing.

She was gone, which he found surprising given her slow departure from the room. Still, the reality of her leaving and the true weight; the true horror, of how he had treated her, hit home.

Drained, he settled to the landing and remained there until he'd lost track of time.

***

"He's a Riley."

"On his mother's side."

Jessica Breck blinked out of clear devastation and confusion. "But how could he be a reporter if-"

"Thieves and murderers love their nephews too, mom," Eliza stared past the morose steel-mesh security screens that covered the windows. She shared her insight and barely registered anything she saw beyond the myriad of criss-crossing bars. Not that that was a bad thing considering the depressing view of the morning outside.

"Cousteau's dad didn't like him being involved with his uncles." Eliza went on, "He rebelled, but cleaned up his act when his father passed. Did you know, mom?" She asked in the same monotone she'd been using for the past week. The haze claiming her since Cousteau's confession wasn't going to lift anytime soon.

Eliza blinked, realizing Jessica hadn't answered her question. "Mom? Did you know about Cousteau- who he was?"

"No," Jessica breathed the word. "No, Liza. I swear it." She saw the disbelief shadowing her daughter's face.

"What about the recording?"

Jessica looked away, shaking her head. "I don't want to talk about it."

Eliza responded with abrupt laughter. "Well, that's just great Mommy, but unless you want to become a permanent resident in digs far less plush than these," she gazed around the visitation cell in phony wonderment. "You'd better find it and use it to save your ass."

"Hmph, isn't *that* the advice of the week?" Jessica muttered, rolling her eyes sullenly.

Eliza's frown sharpened and she moved closer to the chrome-topped table. "Cousteau's uncles believe you had help. Is that why you're dragging your feet here, mom? Trying to protect someone else?"

The misery on Jessica's face transitioned into something harder. "The only people I *ever* tried to protect were you...and your father. Everything I've done has been for you."

"Mom..." Eliza's chilly demeanor melted and she sat across from Jessica, pulling the woman's hands into hers across the table. "Then do that now, tell these people what they need to know so you can get the hell out of here." She sighed and released her mother's hands.

"You say you didn't know who Cousteau was- who his family was, that it's got nothing to do with why you tried to ruin things for us."

"No Liza, it never had anything to do with that," Jessica sounded panicked.

"It was only because he was a reporter."

"That's right, that's all it was. We both know having reporters nosing around a family like ours brings nothing but trouble."

"So who's to blame for our current state of troubles now, mom?" Eliza's blue eyes darkened and she gave another tense laugh. "This may all be a pipe dream anyway. I mean, who knows? What went down forty some odd years ago might not even raise an eyebrow and then you'd get your wish to stay here."

"So naive..."

Eliza stilled. Jessica's words had trailed away, but they had been spoken with a steely conviction that Eliza hadn't heard from the woman in months.

"Mom-"

"Guess I could consider that a plus for my parenting skills," Jessica's smile held a wistful appeal as she studied her daughter. "You have no idea how much ugliness I'd

184

seen by the time I was your age. I admit I put myself in the position to view a lot of it, but I saw it just the same."

She leaned across the table, the chains hanging from the cuffs at her wrists clanged against the chrome. "The thing about ugliness, baby is that it doesn't make class distinctions. It rears its head in every walk of life. Money, family, occupation- doesn't matter," she tapped a brittle index nail to the table.

"The men I knew, the men on that tape were on their way to power even back then. Now, they're obscenely connected. Connections like that mean there're a lot of people with a lot to lose if any of those bastards are exposed."

"And you're okay with that?" Eliza gawked at her mother in disbelief.

Jessica shrugged, resolve casting an attractive light to her already stunning features. "If it means you're safe then you're damn straight I am."

"Mommy-"

"Enough, Liza." Jessica's tone allowed for no argument. She smiled, reaching out to smooth her fingers across her daughter's cheek. Her thumb brushed the faint darkness beneath one of Eliza's eyes.

"My little beauty," she caressed Eliza's face for a second longer. In a motherly fashion, she fussed with Eliza's bright hair, pulling trapped tresses from the collar of her denim shirt. Silently, she gave thanks for the fact that the guards relaxed their 'no contact' rule when it came to her child. Smiling tightly then, she eased back from Eliza and settled against the uncomfortable metal chair.

"I want you to go be with Cousteau," she said. "Despite my earlier concerns, I know he loves you to obsession. It'll do me good to know you've got that kind of love and strength in your life."

185

Eliza was stunned yet again. Her mouth opened so wide, her jaws ached. "You can say that, when it's his family who-" She silenced, watching her mother stand.

Jessica rounded the rectangular table and leaned close to drop a kiss to Eliza's forehead. Her mouth lingered there as she spoke. "Cousteau's *family*- not Cousteau. Don't let him go, baby." She straightened. "Guard!"

Eliza blinked rapidly, feeling her eyes water as she tried to hold her mother's gaze. She nodded obediently, returning Jessica's smile until the guard came to escort her from the room.

***

"Sorry," Kamari fixed Daniel Tate with a harried look.

"Kam it's-"

"I've been caught up in so much at the office."

Dan smiled encouragingly. "It's not a problem, we-"

"Have you guys been waiting long?" Kam smoothed a hand across the silver buttons adorning the navy blazer she wore with matching slacks. "It seemed that everybody in the world needed me today-"

"Mar? Shh…" Dan urged, stopping in front of Kamari to ply her arms with brisk strokes tailored to soothed.

"It's alright," he bent a little to smile into her face, "you're right on time. My boss had a phone call that ran late. Thanks for sending me the text to let us know you were on your way inside. Gave me the chance to come meet you before we got started. We've only been here about ten minutes, which is good because my boss likes to arrive earlier than the people he's meeting."

Somewhat calmed by the explanation, Kam accepted the arm Dan offered. Together, they followed the maitre'd into the casual elegance of the restaurant's dining room.

"It's okay," Dan leaned over to encourage Kam when he heard her sigh, "my boss is like puddy in the hands of women- *silly* puddy in the hands of the ones who are as fine as you."

Kam laughed, thankful for the joke. It helped to ease a little more of the apprehension that had nagged her over the last two days. She began to feel a little more upbeat about the meeting with Dan and his boss. That was until she scanned the lightly crowded room and saw Huron seated at a table several feet away. She clutched her escort's arm in reflex.

Dan noticed her hold tighten through his suit coat. "Mar?" he dropped his free hand over hers. "You okay?"

"I um," Kam tugged at the shoulder strap of her leather briefcase. "Starting to feel a little overworked lately is all," she looked to Dan and dissolved into laughter at his look of disbelief.

He cupped a hand behind his ear. "What was that? I don't think I heard you right." He chuckled, then tugged the arm she held to draw her closer. "Finally getting sick of the grind, huh?"

"Finally getting old."

"Ha!" Dan threw her another disbelieving look. "Sure as hell can't tell by looking at you."

~~~

"I'm sure it's just business, B." Nevil Willis clapped Huron's shoulder. He'd seen his friend's gaze trained across the room on Kamari laughing and walking arm in arm with another man.

Believing that what he witnessed then was innocent or, at the very least, business related would've been easier for Huron to swallow had it not been for his massive screw-up a few nights ago. He had allowed Theo Sturgess' ranting to get in his head and cause him to second guess the only thing that really mattered in the current mess that was his life. What was worse, he'd taken out his frustration; and a fair amount of anger at his own self, on the woman he loved. The woman he was starting to love more than his own life.

~14~

"Look B, Nev's right. They're meeting somebody." Rave Grant gestured toward the table Kam approached with the man escorting her.

Nevil, Rave and Huron watched as a tall, well-dressed man got to his feet with the help of a cane and shook hands with Kam.

Huron both welcomed and despised the relief that coursed through him at the knowledge that the gathering did, in fact, appear to be business related.

"So can we eat now?" Nevil was already settling back to review the steakhouse menu.

Huron attempted to follow suit. No matter how diligently he tried to focus on making a dinner selection, his thoughts were distracted. Eventually, the whole of his attention was once more fixed on Kamari.

Nevil and Rave traded looks.

"Guess we'll just have to order for him," Nevil muttered.

~~~

"Give us about ten minutes to chat before you come back for the dinner orders." William Cormack instructed the waiter and then looked to Kamari. "Is that alright? You aren't starving too much, are you?"

Kam smiled and waved off the man's concern. "I don't have much of an appetite anyway."

Will Cormack's then unreadable face, suddenly revealed a surprisingly inviting smile. "I hope you won't make us eat alone?"

"Don't worry, I never pass on a free meal."

Kam's admission released a round of laughter that effectively shattered any remaining ice.

"Dan tells me you solved our little mystery in record time," Cormack was saying when the conversation veered towards business after several moments of light chatter.

"I'd say I solved half of it," Kam guarded her expression then so that it was as unreadable as Cormack's. "And since your people solved it too, I'd probably not be sitting here if I hadn't."

"It would've been overlooked if you hadn't," approval dwelled in Cormack's light brown eyes. "You're well preceded by your reputation Ms. Grade and then, of course, there was Dan's glowing recommendation."

Kam gave both men appreciative nods and then reached for her briefcase. "The second half of your list is shaping up to be as useless as the first," she retrieved a pad and two folders from the case.

"The way it stands now- only one name has any validity- James Bolton. I suspect those seemingly useless names will eventually link back to him."

"In what way?" Cormack asked.

Kam moved her wineglass and opened a folder. "Money is draining. The likely explanation is that Mr. Bolton is using these phony identities to shelter funds."

Cormack reclined in the wide arm chair he occupied at the square table. Stroking his jaw, he nodded as though Kam's theory held merit. "Can you prove this?" he asked.

"With a little more time," Kam relaxed in the chair that all but engulfed her petite frame. "That'll help me get a stronger sense of James Bolton. I'll start there before making any other attempts at linking those names."

"How hard do you think that'll be?" Dan asked.

"Well, I expected to hit a bunch of brick walls, but I'm no where near ready to accept that I've reached a dead end."

Cormack's glee was increasing by the moment. Grinning, he looked to Dan and then back to Kam. "I can see nothing this man told me was an exaggeration." He reached for her hand and held it when she obliged the unspoken request.

"I look forward to hearing your findings," Cormack gave Kam's hand a squeeze and smiled when he noticed the waiter approaching. "I hope your appetite has improved?"

Kam reached for her menu. "Let's find out."

~~~

Kamari's appetite made a presentable showing at dinner that night which surprised Kam most of all. She hadn't felt much like eating for the last several days- ever since the blowout with Huron and he was there that night…

She was sure his being there wasn't on purpose given the way things had ended between them the last time they were in the same room. Regardless, she was of a mind to finish her meeting with Will Cormack and Daniel and then make her exit before coming face to face with Huron.

Kam studied her reflection in the lit mirror above the pink-tinged marble sinks in the ladies washroom. She wondered if she could leave undetected by way of the kitchens she knew were on the other end of the hallway. The idea made her laugh, which added a little pep to her step when she left the ladies room.

The smile still tugged her lips when a man that matched her height, but vastly outweighed her, appeared in the corridor leading to the patron's washrooms. Paul Simmons, Esquire, spread his arms wide when he spotted Kam heading towards him in the hall.

Kam's laughter returned. Paul's trademark toothy grin and deceptively guileless brown gaze never failed to rouse her amusement.

"Good to see you," she embraced the man as best as she could, given the fact that her arms barely encircled him. "How's the most well-known lawyer on the West Coast?"

Paul chuckled over the playful dig that referenced the media's coverage of his client Jessica Breck.

"I'm very good, but my 'well-known' status may soon be a thing of the past if I don't get a new media darling for a client."

Mild concern pooled Kam's eyes. "Are you dropping Jessica as a client?"

"Oh no, no," Paul shook his head, "nothing like that but if all goes well, she may soon be seeing the last of a jail cell."

192

"That's great news," Kam itched to prod Paul for more details- ones he'd be unable to give as Jessica's council. The realization of that reminded Kam of how much time had passed since she'd spoken to Eliza.

"I hope to see you on the news soon announcing that very thing," Kam squeezed the lawyer's arm.

"I'll get you a front row seat to the press conference," Paul tugged Kam into another hug before they parted ways.

Kam remembered Eliza and dug out her phone from the pocket of her short waist blazer. She drew her thumb across the faceplate, activating the phone's touchscreen. She got sidetracked then by a few notifications she'd received. She was so absorbed; it scarcely registered when her path was blocked. Without looking up, she tried to sidestep the person she'd almost run into.

Sidestepping didn't work. When Kam moved one way, the other person moved the same way. They performed the dance twice before Kam stiffened, clutching her phone in a death grip while she trained her eyes upon it. Swallowing with effort, she inched back in an attempt to ease around the taller, well-dressed body.

Once again, her moves were thwarted. She saw a wide hand brace the wall nearest her head. The move effectively barred any escape. Kam finally looked up.

"Are you going to pretend I'm not here the whole night?" Huron asked.

"Are you serious?" Kam was surprised by her need to laugh. "I think that's the proper response when someone pretty much kicks you out of their house." She averted her eyes when she saw his mouth thin into a harsh line.

Her jab stung, but the anger it instilled quickly gave way to Huron's guilt. "Would it matter if I said I was sorry?"

193

"It would," the soft lost tone of his voice made her want to melt. She resisted. "It wouldn't change the way I feel about marriage, though."

"And you won't even tell me why?"

Her eyes flew back to his. "You of all people should understand being reluctant to share what shapes a person."

Understanding filtered the bewilderment in his stare and Huron hesitated only a second longer before he straightened and took his hand from the wall.

Kam wasted no time accepting her freedom.

Alone, Huron put his hand back to the wall. He drew a fist, hoping it would help him resist the urge to go after her.

~~~

"Uh-oh," Will Cormack's eyes were fixed on Kamari. He'd witnessed her heated departure from Huron's side. "Still interested in the lovely Ms. Grade?" he asked the man seated to his right. "Looks like there's trouble in paradise."

Dan had witnessed the scene as well. He had thoroughly enjoyed having Kamari dine with he and his boss that night. When she'd gone to visit the ladies' room, his eyes had followed her until she was gone from his line of sight. Smirking solemnly, he shook his head and considered his boss' query.

"It's too late for us," Dan said.

Cormack chuckled, the action bringing much needed emotion to his light, honey-toned face. "And I thought *I* was the cynical one," he mused.

"Trust me, boss, I'd happily risk having my heart stomped again if I thought there was a chance I could really make her mine," Dan scanned the room for Kamari and smiled when he saw that she'd stopped at a table to chat

194

with some people she knew. His smile waned. "Anyone with eyes can see she's thoroughly involved with Base."

"I haven't seen a ring on her finger," Cormack sighed.

"But she loves him." There was a finality to Dan's tone. "That's for sure, no matter what kind of lover's spat they're having."

"I'm sorry you two couldn't have a happier ending," Cormack patted Dan's shoulder and added a reassuring squeeze. "You're a wise man, though," he settled back in his chair. "In light of what's coming, you're very smart to let her go."

***

Sleep had been a laughable endeavor for Kam the night before. Seeing Huron at the restaurant hadn't shown her at one of her finer moments. She could tell that her words had cut him deeply. In spite of the way he'd treated her that night in his home, hurting *him* hadn't been her intention last night. Why couldn't he let this go? *Because he loves you, dammit!*

Kam dropped to the chair she was about to pass and just rocked herself. She knew she was acting crazy and knew she was driving *him* crazy with it, but this had never been an *easy* topic for her. Hell, she didn't even want to think about it much less discuss it.

She loved him and; despite his certainty that he was too much of a bad guy, she trusted him with her life.

She could trust him with her life, but not this?

Kam doubled over, clutching at her hair until she groaned. Somewhere in her warped sense of thinking she had convinced herself that as long as they were just...seeing each other, just enjoying one another as lovers, there would be no need to delve into such serious issues.

195

She hadn't expected them to go from seeing each other to M-word discussions in 0.2 seconds. A man with marriage on his mind deserved to know that the woman he loved couldn't (wouldn't) give him kids, didn't he?

She thought on that for a moment. She could at least tell him that. Her freaking out over that was understandable after all. She could tell him that part and they'd be done with the conversation. They'd be done with the conversation and she'd never have to tell him the rest.

The sharp rap of her doorknocker caused Kam to jump. The sound of it had come within a second of those last words stirring inside her mind- *the rest...*

Her steps to the door were slow, but didn't falter as she prepared to greet him. Kam realized she didn't know how he even felt about kids. She'd only assumed he wanted them. Perhaps he didn't- perhaps what she'd tell him would have no negative effects on his feelings for her.

The knocking resumed and she quickened her pace to the door. "Coming!" She whipped open the door, not remembering the last time she'd felt more relieved.

"El?"

"You did say nine a.m., right?" Eliza barely glanced in the vicinity of her watch, too busy glaring at her friend.

Eyes closing, Kam rested her head against the side of the door and nodded. She had finally gotten around to calling Eliza after arriving home from the dinner meeting with Dan Tate and Will Cormack. The ladies had decided to meet that morning for breakfast at Kam's place.

"I'm sure I don't have to tell you how bad you look," Eliza brushed by her friend.

Kam shut the door. "Well good morning to you too."

"I didn't mean it as an insult," Eliza tossed a sour look over her shoulder. "I look like shit myself. The last

196

thing I need is to walk in here to find you looking gorgeous as usual."

Kam rolled her eyes, evidently not putting much stock in that outlook. She shuffled towards the kitchen behind Eliza who was then lifting her hands and letting them fall back to the wrinkled denim cladding her thighs.

"Where the hell's breakfast?" She threw Kam an accusing look.

Kam tossed up her hands as well. "You said it yourself, I look like shit. Making breakfast is the last thing on my mind. I saw Paul Simmons last night," she said before Eliza could inquire about *why* she looked like shit. "Sounds like he's hopeful your mom will be home soon. Does that mean she's made a deal to use that tape as her bargaining chip?"

Eliza rolled her eyes and went to slump against the counter closest to the refrigerator. "Paul's very accurate to say he *hopes* she'll be home soon. Maybe he's got some trick up his sleeve to encourage her to use that tape."

"Why wouldn't she-"

"Because she's still hung up on this thing about protecting me!" Eliza pushed off the counter and stalked across the sun-doused kitchen.

Kam retrieved an iron skillet from a lower cabinet and set it to heat on a stove burner. "Does she think Cousteau's family will come after her?"

"Hmph, she's not half as concerned about them as she is over the men on that tape." Eliza fingered a wayward strand of hair that had fallen from her messy ponytail. "Sounds like they're all big shot senators or movers and shakers in federal law enforcement."

Kam separated strips of turkey bacon from the pack she'd taken out of the refrigerator. "Sounds like they should be more afraid of her. They may be a bunch of fat cats, but

197

if that tape comes out, they'll be too busy scrambling to save their own asses."

Eliza gave a quick, solitary clap. "That's what I've been trying to tell the woman…"

"Don't be so flip," Kam used a long fork to spread the bacon across the skillet. "People with a lot to lose don't often hesitate to do anything to keep it."

Eliza settled to the small round kitchen table and braced her forehead to her palm. "Kam I know that… this is such a mess."

"Have you talked to Cousteau?" Kam lowered the heat under the bacon and turned.

"Not since I got back from Malibu." Unable to sit still, Eliza left the table and made a beeline for the coffee maker on the kitchen island across from where Kam worked at the sofa.

The women worked in silence for a while. Gradually, the air filled with mouthwatering aromas that signaled the morning. Cinnamon rolls plumped in the oven, flavoring the kitchen with deliciousness. The smell of fresh roast coffee mingled in with the eggs, bacon and rolls soon after.

~~~

"She told me to go after him. Cousteau." Eliza clarified while taking two mixed-matched mugs from the cabinet above the coffeepot. "I never heard her sound so defeated as when she told me that."

"I'm sure she meant it," Kam said while searching for her favorite cream inside the refrigerator.

"Oh I know she did. I could tell." Eliza set the mugs to the table and returned to lean against the island. "What I mean is, it sounded like she'd already given up, like she's not looking for anything to save her." Sighing Eliza

198

reached for the coffeepot and returned to the table to fill the mugs.

"Even if she *could* use that old recording to bargain her way out of this mess, she'd probably feel like she was still a prisoner."

Kam walked over to hold a plate of the tempting breakfast beneath Eliza's nose which effectively silenced her. Like a starving woman, Eliza focused unblinking on the platter of food.

"I think Jessica has the right idea if you ask me. Your thoughts are all over the place right now. Fixing them on Cousteau Morgan isn't a bad idea at all."

Eliza obediently followed Kam to the table and sat before the breakfast and a piping hot mug of French Roast.

Kam patted the top of her girlfriend's head and then returned to the wooden countertop for her own plate. She was pleased to see Eliza eating upon her return to the table, but Kam was still concerned by her faraway expression.

"Hey?" Kam squeezed Eliza's arm, giving her a shake until their eyes met. "Eat up and then go call Cousteau and tell him to get his cute butt back here. He's the only one who has a chance in hell of getting you through all this with your sanity intact."

"Hmph," Eliza gave a wry smile and propped her fist to her cheek. "That's definitely true."

The women dived into the fabulous breakfast and ate in comfy silence for over ten minutes.

"So when are you gonna clue me in about your drama?" Eliza asked between sips of her second mug of coffee.

Kam didn't play at confusion. "Huron wants to marry me."

There was a clatter when Eliza's mug hit her fork and sent the utensil to the hardwood floor. She barely noticed, too busy watching her friend with a cheery look that suddenly hinted of confusion as she took a closer look at Kam.

"What is it?"

"I can't marry him El..." Kam raised her hand to stay Eliza's budding argument. "We haven't known each other long enough for that."

"Oh," Eliza mocked relief. "Because for a minute, I thought you were gonna say it was because he had a past that didn't compliment your present."

"Hell Eliza, I don't care about any of that old shit," Kam gave a dismissive wave. "There're things in my past that he may not be able to overlook either," she fidgeted with the frayed cuff of her chenille robe and shrugged. "I'm not sure I'd want him to."

Eliza shook her head once fast. "What the hell does *that* mean?"

"El..." Kam reached for her coffee, looking completely regretful that she'd shared so much. "It's just that we've *all* buried things- it's best for some of it to stay buried."

Bewildered, Eliza watched Kam guzzle her coffee. "And if all that burying robs you of the man you love? What then?" Eliza retrieved her fork from the floor, had a bite of a gooey cinnamon roll and then took the dirtied utensil to the dishwasher. She'd obviously decided not to insist on an answer to her question.

That was just as well since Kam didn't have one to give.

~15~

"As bad as that is, I think I have you beat. What was that you said about long past circling back to the present?" Huron queried while thumbing the metal tab off the beer bottle he'd taken from the ice chest.

Following his intentional run-in with Kam the night before, he'd left Rave and Nevil to pay the check and hit the road to Malibu. He was knocking on Cousteau's front door around 4a.m., ready to apologize to Cousteau and Eliza for the hour of the visit. To Huron's surprise and curiosity he found Cousteau awake, alone...and packing.

"So come with me and punish yourself the way I'm about to," Cousteau's lazy Bronx accent sounded even lazier after the four beers he'd downed.

"I already said I'd go-stupid as it is," Huron muttered.

"Ah...that resistance is just the city guy in you talkin'."

"Hmph, says the man from NYC."

Easy laughter rumbled between the friends. That, in spite of the several serious hours they'd spent recapping their individual dramas from the previous weeks. Cousteau had revealed that he couldn't take another day alone in his house, so he was taking his new bar partners up on their offer to join them on a hiking trip through Big Bear.

"Since when are cell phones not allowed on hiking trips?" Huron sighed, delighting in the cool breeze hitting the terrace from the Pacific.

"Jeez man, since it's a survivalist's trip," Cousteau explained in a tone of mock impatience.

Huron shifted to a more comfortable position in the deck chair and crossed his bare feet at the ankles. "Please tell me I'm not gonna wind up with a bullet in my back at the end of this trip. I can get one of those in my own neck of the woods, you know?"

"It's not a hunting trip," Cousteau grunted a laugh. "And the purpose of a survivalist's trip, is to survive."

A few seconds passed, marked only by the sounds of the ocean and the minute tap of beer bottles as they were retrieved and replaced upon the overturned tin tub that served as a makeshift table.

Huron introduced the swell of laughter as Cousteau's remark began to weave its comedic magic.

"We do this right and we might even survive going back to beg the women we love to forgive us." Cousteau predicted, and leaned over to clink his bottle to Huron's in toast.

"In your defense though, you really didn't do anything that needs forgiving." Huron declared.

"I could've kept my mouth shut."

"Why didn't you? She never would've known you're one of *the* Rileys."

Cousteau grinned, but the gesture didn't hold out for long. "I'm sure Jessica's got that recording."

"You know there's a chance she doesn't. You said there was another woman there."

Cousteau relished another swig of the flavorful domestic brew. "I just bet a life with Elly on it, so I'm praying I'm right."

"You could've let her rot," Huron took a long drag of the import he'd selected. "She never did anything to keep you and Eliza together."

"True- but she's her mother. Knowing I could do something to save her and didn't- didn't sit well with me."

Huron grinned. "You're a good man, Cous."

"So are you. Don't beat yourself up over what happened with Kam."

"I pushed her too hard," Huron clenched his jaw as memories of the night in question resurfaced. "I knew she didn't want to talk about it and I wouldn't let up."

"Give yourself a break. You love each other. Kam'll be ready to talk marriage soon enough."

"You didn't see how she looked when I kept at her about it." Huron looked as though he were envisioning Kam then. "She seemed terrified."

"You think there's more goin' on than just cold feet?"

"I don't know," Huron left the deck chair to stand at the terrace railing. "But I knew there was something she was determined to keep to herself. And how did I respond to it?" He laughed drily. "By practically raping her in the scariest room of my house."

"Don't do that, B," Cousteau straightened on his lounge. "I'm sure Kamari didn't see it that way."

"*I* saw it that way, dammit," Huron's voice was ragged, wounded. "Now she's afraid of me-"

"B-"

"No Cous, if there's one thing I know, it's when someone's afraid of me. I've damn well seen it enough times in my life."

"So what are you gonna do to change that?"

Huron paced the terrace for a time. Walking the perimeter of the wide space, he absently scratched the light beard that shaded his jaw. Sighing dejectedly, he reclaimed his chair and rested his elbows to his knees.

"So?" Cousteau persisted.

Huron managed a weak smile. "Whatever I can."

***

"You're just gonna make everybody else miserable if you come up in here."

"Thanks."

Tenille laughed when her boss' response croaked through the line. "It'll do me good to be on my own first day back and all."

Tenille and her husband Blake had just returned from their getaway. Kam wanted to take it as a sign that her assistant's first day back coincided with one where she felt about as useful as a bag of scraps. Still, she didn't want to take advantage of the situation by taking a sick day-something she very much wanted to do. She relayed that concern to Tenille.

"Let me think...when was the last time you took a sick day? Oh! I remember-never."

Kam forced out a laugh. "Point made."

"So you'll take the day? I promise to call if I come up against anything I can't handle."

"In other words, you won't be calling."

"It's so nice to be appreciated. Get some rest. Bye..." Tenille disconnected from the call.

Kam hated to be out for anything as flimsy as needing sick time. Having a trusty assistant did make her feel a lot better. Emotionally, at least. Physically, she still felt like a bag of scraps. Her head was pounding from what could be mistaken as nothing less than a migraine. She wasn't prone to such things, but diagnosed the sensitivity to light, nausea and dizziness as just that. She'd barely been able to lift her head off the pillow when the phone rang earlier. Not until she heard Tenille's voice through the message speaker, did she realize she was late getting to the office.

The monotonous beeping of the phone reminded Kam that she hadn't replaced the phone to its mount on the bed table. She winced when just the simple move of reaching out to set down the phone, sent ripples of pain spiraling between her temples.

A groan followed the wincing when she heard the doorbell. Kam groaned again, deciding the visitor could leave a message and she pulled the covers over her head.

The ringing continued and she could have sworn the sound grew louder with each passing second.

"Damn," she muttered and wrenched back the covers. Gingerly, she pushed herself up in the bed, wincing the entire time.

The ringing continued, despite her calling out to the ringer that she was coming. In the person's defense however, Kam realized they probably couldn't hear her since she could barely raise her voice above a low moan.

The uniformed gentleman gave a start when the door he stood before suddenly flew open and he saw the small, glowering woman on the other side.

"Apologies, ma'am," he tipped the dark blue cap he wore. "Pasko Deliveries."

"Pasko?" Kam weakly repeated the name.

"If I could get you to sign ma'am for your delivery." The thin Hispanic man produced an e-pad from a broad utility belt at the waistband of his navy trousers.

Kam accepted the stylus pen the man offered and leaned in to put her name to the block he indicated.

"Thank you ma'am. Apologies for the bother," again he tipped his cap and then turned away to reach for the basket he'd set to the floor while he rang the bell. He set the delivery just inside the door and straightened.

"Wait a sec," despite her aching head, she managed to remember to tip the man.

"Oh ma'am, no, no it's quite alright." He urged her not to go to the trouble. "It's already been well taken care of," he added while tipping his cap again. "Good day to you ma'am."

Kam observed the basket once she'd pushed the door shut behind the delivery man. The item was large and, as she peered through the cellophane wrapping, she could tell that it was stocked with all her favorite treats. Very thoughtful and very welcomed on a day when she felt like crap.

"Dan," she sighed, turning the basket and smiling when she saw one of her favorite herbal blends tucked in among other treats.

"Save it for when I solve this mystery of yours," she suggested to an absent Daniel Tate.

206

Silently, Kam noted that she wasn't surprised that Dan had followed up their dinner from the previous week with such a gesture. Such thoughtfulness was one of the things that had drawn her to him when they'd been linked romantically. Her admiration held out only a couple of minutes before the dizziness and sensitivity to light set in once more. Eyes half closed, Kam trudged back to her bedroom.

***

"This classic sex flick just might be your ticket to freedom," Paul Simmons usually grinning face showed distinct signs of frustration while he glared across the table at his client.

"It is not a sex flick." Jessica's expression clearly rivaled her lawyer's for coldness. "If you'd watched it, which I'm sure you have, you'd know that."

Paul stiffened, his plump hands rising in defense. "I apologize for being unsympathetic. It was a horrific thing but what that tape shows- combined with the assholes involved will get you out of this place with a pat on your back."

"Why do you think I'm still here, Paul?"

"Because you confessed to killing your nephew."

Jessica's mouth curved down in a cynical smile. "Those 'assholes' know where I am- they could come after me anytime. I *killed* a man," she leaned into the table to study Paul Simmons brown eyes with her blue ones. "If I suddenly traipse out of here, they're gonna know I put something pretty good on the table to make that happen." She leaned back in her chair. "That insanity defense is sounding better every day. It's the only way I can walk out of here with a chance of them not assuming I used that tape."

207

"You do realize that any kind of plea will result in some jail time," Paul noted.

"Even better."

"Jess-"

"My freedom isn't worth piss next to Eliza's safety," Jessica brought her fist down on the table. "I'm only even entertaining this insanity nonsense for Eliza's sake- she's beside herself worrying over me being in here." She gave Paul a cursory look. "You came highly recommended by my daughter's best friend, but if you won't go for this I'll find an attorney who will. I don't care how media savvy you are."

Paul appeared effectively tongue-whipped. "I'm not the enemy, you know?"

"Oh Paul…" Jessica bowed her forehead to her palm. "I know that, but the men on that tape are more than just public servants with mafia ties. They have the power to keep me in prison or under it. To me, sharing that tape with the so-called authorities is just like putting it in their sick hands only I'm putting my child's safety on the line with it."

"Jessica…" Paul left his chair to come around and perch on the table corner nearest his client. "Media savvy notwithstanding, I'm damn good at what I do for a living." He squeezed her shoulder. "You're gonna have to trust somebody, love. Can't it be me?"

Jessica's smile was grim. "My bitchiness notwithstanding Paul, but it's not you I don't trust."

"I got it," Paul nodded and glanced toward the camera in the ceiling. "But please don't dismiss the fact that there are people at all levels of law enforcement who do their jobs honorably. Those are the people I intend to plead your case to."

"Do you think we've got a chance in hell?"

Paul gave a soft chuckle that shook his meaty frame. "Folks who do their jobs honorably love the chance to take down the bastards who disgrace it. They're gonna salivate over the chance to strip Senator Ethan Errol and his friends of all the power they've abused over the years."

"Maybe they cleaned up their act." Jessica postured.

Paul shook his balding head. "People like that don't clean up 'specially when they've benefitted so long from being dirty," he leaned over to squeeze both Jessica's shoulders then.

"We're gonna get 'em Jess. Every stinkin' one of 'em and not one pretty blonde strand on Eliza's head will be touched."

**

A day home had done Kam good. The migraine and all its nasty effects began to ease around lunch time. She even felt well enough to help herself to a little hot broth and tea from the hefty stash inside her cupboards. She resisted tearing into the decadent basket, preferring to set it to the credenza in the living room for a centerpiece. She'd admire it there, until she could no longer resist the temptation it carried.

Feeling measurably better, she tried to get a little work done in her home office. It was the least she could do since her new clients had been sweet enough to favor her with such a lovely gift. Besides, Will Cormack's mystery had her too curious to spend much more time away from it.

Kam had spent a great deal of her previous afternoon trying to make connections with the leads she'd already compiled. She was an overachiever in the worst way and wanted to have more on hand to dazzle William Cormack.

Such was not to be, unfortunately, and Kam feared the day would turn out much the same with little to show for an afternoon of research.

Not much changed on that accord, until she played a hunch. She checked to see if any other corporate troubleshooters had ever been hired to investigate James Bolton. Kam wasn't surprised to discover they had. What did surprise her though was one of the newspaper stories she uncovered in the digital media archives of the open reference files one of her colleagues linked to.

"Hero Takes Deal"

"Hero," The word silenced on Kam's tongue just as her cell chimed. She smiled, noticing Dan Tate was the caller.

"Hello…" she greeted.

"Well, well, you sound chipper." Dan's voice carried on soft laughter. "That's good considering how agitated you seemed before you left the restaurant after our meeting."

"It'd been a rough day," Kam conceded, "but things are starting to shape up nicely now. I think I'm about to crack the James Bolton mystery."

Dan whistled. "What was that I said about calling you impressive?"

Kam's laughter was still rather weak, but it was there. "Don't go celebrating yet. All I uncovered is a news story that he's apparently mentioned in- could be nothing."

"Hmph, knowing you it won't be 'nothing' for long." Dan guessed. "So tell me about this story."

Kam jiggled the desktop's mouse to activate the monitor's flatscreen. "Hero Takes Deal," she read the headline.

"Hero." Dan sounded amused. "Hmph, Will would love to know more about that."

210

"I'll bet," Kam managed a bit more laughter than as well, "especially since Mr. Bolton is exhibiting less than heroic tendencies right now."

"I'll leave you to it then. Don't work too hard."

"You know me."

"Right- hence my order."

"Oh-" Kam ceased grinning over Dan's dig as she remembered the basket. "Thanks so much for being so thoughtful and please thank Will too. Tell him I said it was very sweet."

"Are you serious? I wouldn't call piling a new mystery on an already overworked mystery solver, thoughtful."

"Well...yeah, there is that. But I was talking about the basket."

"Basket?"

"Yeah, it came yesterday- had all my favorite things. After the other night, I guess you guys thought I could use it."

"Well yeah, that was a thoughtful idea. Whoever sent it was right. You did look like you could use a pick me up."

"*Whoever?*" Kam straightened at her desk and then went still.

"Mar?"

"You didn't send it?" She looked toward her office door.

"Sorry but...no, I-I wish I had. If you haven't noticed I'm really trying to get back into your good graces."

Dan's words made Kam smile even as she pushed out of the plum, suede desk chair. "You've never been in my bad graces."

"Says the woman who turned down my marriage proposal."

"Dan," the reminder halted Kam's steps to her office door. "That was all about me and *my* hangups about marriage."

"And how are you coming along in dealing with those hangups?" He asked.

Kam's smile was sad, yet she continued her trek towards the office door. "Remember what you said about me being a workaholic? That doesn't leave much time to cure marriage hangups."

"You're right...but now you're in love again. That changes things, doesn't it?"

"In love?!" She gave a stunned laugh.

"Don't even try it. What? Do you think no one can tell how in love you are with Huron Base or how in love he is with you?"

"Oh, I get it," Kam laughed again, but the gesture held a nervous chord, "you're referring to our little display in the restaurant a few weeks ago?"

"You can save it if you're gonna try and make me believe it was an act."

"No...no I won't do that," she spoke in a dazed fashion then. Her slow steps had carried her out to the living room to the elaborate basket set in the center of the shiny, maple credenza where she'd moved it that morning.

"Dan um...can I call you back?"

His laughter was soft, "Sure thing. Talk to you soon."

"Bye," the word was barely audible before Kam clicked off the phone and held it to her side. She stopped a few feet from the credenza and studied the basket for more than a few minutes. Then she was dropping the phone and rushing for the table.

212

She took the basket and settled to the floor with it. She was unmindful of the pristine cellophane wrapping securing the beckoning presentation. She ripped through the contents like a mad woman until she found what she was looking for.

Aside from the erratic beat of her heart, her moves seemed to cease when she located the card tucked between a box of her favorite cookies and chocolates. She brushed her fingertips across the envelope that carried her name scrawled in familiar handwriting. She was tearing into it seconds later. Her eyes raced across the words on the card. A tiny moan swelled amidst the emotion filling her throat.

Please Forgive Me- I Love You. H.

~16~

Between all the pacing she'd done at home and at her office, Kam felt as though she'd walked a million miles. Following a two day hiatus from work, she decided that making an attempt to be useful at the office would serve her much better than loafing around the house waiting on Huron to return one of her three calls.

She'd decided to stop at three calls, fearing she was beginning to look a little desperate.

After discovering who her elaborate basket had come from she'd scrambled across the floor to grab the phone from where she'd dropped it after hanging up with Dan Tate.

She'd held her breath while making the call, expelling it slowly when she realized Huron wasn't going to answer. She left a message.

And another, and another until it became clear to her that he wasn't ready to talk to her- or he never intended to talk to her again. The morning after the third call, she decided it'd be better to head back into the office. Either that or try to track down Huron until they talked. After all, his card had asked her to forgive him. They would have to talk if he expected her to do that, right?

Whatever the reason, the fact was he wasn't taking or returning her calls so she was off to the office in the hope of working off a wealth of nervous energy. Being at the office, helped to settle thoughts of Huron to the back of her mind, but that only made other issues glaringly apparent.

The migraines had returned and held on vengefully. Almost ten days had passed since their onset, but suffering at home was just too much. She had been granted *some* moments of relief to focus on various work related fires that only *she* could tend to.

Tenille couldn't wait to tell her all about the romantic getaway she'd enjoyed with her husband. Then, there was the unfolding mystery surrounding James Bolton.

It turned out that Bolton was more than just a mere mention in the story she'd uncovered- he *was* the story. Apparently, the man had made news earlier in his life when; at age eleven, he alone rid the city of Los Angeles of two high-profile crime figures and eight of their men.

Kam was thrown by that bit of information, that had only received a brief blurb in the 'Hero Takes Deal' story. Not surprising, she was like a hound with a scent in her endeavors to uncover more. Sadly for her, it seemed that the media outlets back then were thwarted in their efforts.

215

They were unsuccessful in their attempts to turn the young gunman into a sensationalized piece of news. The eleven year old Bolton and his mother had been taken into protective custody and the boy's records were sealed. The media hadn't even made out with a decent photo.

Kam uncovered the latter by calling on a few law enforcement acquaintances. They promised to do what they could to scrounge up a mug shot or any artwork that might have accompanied the story. All Kam had to go on was an old text file.

There was a knock to her office door. Kam didn't argue over the interruption when she saw Eliza peek inside.

"What's up?" Eliza called.

"Trying to solve a mystery," Kam waved her friend inside.

"Mystery?" Eliza seemed to perk up, a definite bounce to her pump-shod steps when she moved across the room. "What kind?"

"The kind where a man cuts a deal on drug charges nine years after killing two crime lords and their men."

"Uggg," Eliza made a face. "I was hoping you had happier plans in mind when you called about getting together."

"Sorry," Kam peppered the apology with a shrug, "still no word from Cousteau?"

Eliza's expression spoke volumes. "Guess he got tired of waiting on me to come to my senses and tell him none of what he told me was his fault." She stopped, giving Kam a sympathetic smile. "Have you heard from Huron?"

Kam shook her head and Eliza slapped her hands to her sides in reply.

"Can we *please* get on with the happy plans now?" Eliza groaned, stomping her feet like a petulant child.

216

"Listen El, my um...my apology was because I really had no 'happy plans' when I called before." Kam was slow to rise from her desk and slower to move around it.

"I need you here for this, El."

"This?"

Instead of answering her friend, Kam walked over to the full washroom on the other side of the office living area.

Eliza followed. The curiosity in her blue gaze transitioned into shock when she saw what Kam took from the counter and waved in the air.

"Oh...wow..." Eliza's eyes tracked the back and forth movement of a pregnancy test.

~~~

"Thanks Tenille," Kam was saying to her assistant when the woman escorted Will Cormack and Dan Tate into her office forty minutes later.

"Apologies for the unexpected visit," Will said after Kam's greeting.

"No apologies needed," Kam smiled while giving an airy wave.

"It's really my fault," Dan grinned sheepishly. "I told Will about your breakthrough. He's been out of town the last several days-"

"And I couldn't wait to find out more," Will finished.

Kam gave an easy laugh. "It's really fine, gentlemen. I mean that. Have a seat," she motioned toward the chairs before her desk.

While the men moved to claim their spots near the desk, Kam turned to Tenille who still waited at the office door.

"Where's El?"

"She said she'd call you later," Tenille responded in the same whisper-tone her boss used.

"Thanks Tenille," Kam watched the woman head off, but took a few minutes before she closed the door and returned to her clients.

Expectancy illuminated Will Cormack's thin face as he sat perched on the edge of his chair. "Dan says you found something on Bolton?" He asked when Kam made her way across the room.

"A lucky break," Kam sighed, tugging at the cuffs of her tanned blazer while reclaiming her place behind the desk. "Not much of a break I'm afraid, considering the real story occurred when the man was eleven. Not only were the records sealed, but the media could barely get any details. I've got some friends who may be able to help me fill in the blanks- at least provide me with a picture."

"Dan mentioned a story about the man making a deal- what were the details on that?"

"Bolton was a pretty nasty soul," Kam fixed Cormack with a dry look. "He was only brought up on possession with plans to distribute but he was suspected of an array of crimes including a string of assaults and carjackings. Whether murder could be added, depends on the facts behind what happened when he was eleven."

"Depends on the facts?" Surprise streaked Cormack's usually unreadable face. "Isn't murder a given in light of the man's list of transgressions- drug deals, assaults, carjackings?"

"The chances are high, but so are the chances that the system failed him as a child."

"You're not going to blame the system?" Cormack spat out incredulous laughter.

218

"I'm not blaming anyone," Kamari's smile was curious in light of the man's demeanor. "Kids aren't born bad, Mr. Cormack. I'd like more information before I cast him off as a...bad seed."

"So you're buying into this hero thing?" Cormack sounded hushed, disbelieving.

"Not until I have more information," Kam subtly reiterated.

"How will that help you determine what he's up to now? Draining money from my boss' accounts?" Dan asked.

"That remains to be seen," Kam leaned back to swivel her desk chair to and fro. "Part of why I'm so successful gentlemen is because I insist on having a full picture of the people and organizations I investigate before I put my theories into place."

"You are very good at what you do," Cormack nodded as though he'd just reminded himself. "I haven't met a person yet who doesn't think so. My apologies for flying off the handle."

"You did nothing of the sort," Kam smiled, shaking her head. "I'd be flying off the handle too if I were hemorrhaging money with nothing to go on but a faceless name I couldn't track down."

"I apologize anyway," Cormack pressed a hand to the front of the tailored beige suit he wore. "I've always been a little testy about being played." He gestured toward the crutches leaning against the desk.

"People see me and immediately assume I'm a fool-weak in body and mind."

"Well we're about to make whomever Bolton is, sorry for being so stupid in his thinking." Kam boasted with an equally boastful smile.

Cormack gave a curt, approving nod, "I thank you for seeing me on such short notice." He reached for his crutches and stood.

Kam rounded her desk. "I'll be in touch as soon as I have more to share. I'm confident that won't be long."

Dan approached to take Kamari's hands and squeeze. "How are the migraines?" He asked while Will Cormack made his way to the office doors.

Kam closed her eyes. "Still, kicking my ass."

Dan laughed. "Get some rest. You look like you can use it."

"I promise." Kam relished his hug and then waved the man out behind his boss. She returned to her desk chair when the door closed behind the men.

Dan was more right than he knew, she thought rubbing her stomach and focusing on the fact that she was now sleeping for two.

**

That evening found Kam at home in her bathroom. The mirror had become her preferred place for the last twenty minutes since she'd walked past the front door. She'd hurriedly changed clothes, stopping before her dresser mirror for observations and then making a beeline for the bathroom.

The lighting there was much higher wattage. She raised her T-shirt to reveal a relatively flat tummy in her estimation. Kam replaced the T-shirt, smoothing both hands across the material while twisting back and forth to observe her form at every angle possible.

Pregnant. The word weakened her legs as it had done each time it echoed through her head. She could beat herself up for not doing everything possible to ensure this didn't happen, but what would be the point. She and Huron had been active (boy was *that* an understatement) for months. She was on the pill, but clearly should have insisted he continue to wear a condom. He wouldn't have argued with her- much.

She'd been insatiable for him from the first time he'd taken her without one. The feel of his sex bare inside hers, stroking with a beautiful and savage abandonment... The experience was only rivaled by the ultimate sensation of him filling her with the liquid proof of his satisfaction. Both were equally riveting- treats she couldn't deny and remain sane.

Such decisions had consequences, however. Nausea stirred and Kam gave the toilet a longing glance. Relief weighed her eyelids when the need to rush for it had subsided. Yes, such decisions had consequences. What Kam wondered was how they could be beautiful and terrible in the same vein.

Kamari inclined her head toward the bathroom door when she thought she heard her cellphone. She gave a last look into the mirror and then hurried to take the call before it went to voicemail.

"Hey come on up!" She laughed into the phone when she caught it. "I'm on my way to the door now."

"That's good. I wasn't sure I still had an open invitation."

The gasp was forced out of her when the rumbling voice reached her ears. Kam snatched away the phone and saw Huron's name on the faceplate.

"I..." her grip tightened on the phone. "I um..."

"Ah..." His voice rumbled again. "The invite wasn't for me."

Despite it all, Kam couldn't resist smiling over the subtle amusement that seemed to always color his words.

Approaching her bed, she reached back to brace on the mattress as she settled to it.

"El's on her way over."

"I see."

"I called you," she blurted, thrilled and nervous to be talking to him.

"I know, babe," Huron expelled a remorseful sound. "I was out of town."

"Where no phones are allowed?" Her voice sounded small.

He laughed quietly. "I decided to punish myself by going to Big Bear on a survivalist's trip with Cousteau."

Kam was hit with the urge to smile again. "Was it fitting punishment?"

Huron seemed to shudder. "You might disagree, but I'd say 'hell yes'."

Silence held between them for several heavy moments.

"I'm sorry."

"I know. I got your basket and I loved it."

"I meant everything I said on that card."

"I know and you have nothing to apologize for."

"Don't do that, Kam." His voice carried annoyance then. "Don't let me off the hook for that. I should've never touched you- angry as I was. I'll apologize for as long as it takes."

"Okay...then you've already done it twice, three times if you count the card. Let's say that's enough."

He laughed then and Kam felt her heart warm over the sound.

"I love you," he said.

"I love you. When can I see you?"

"How about now?"

"Where are you?"

222

"Cafe around the corner. Meet me here?"

Kam looked back at her bed. "Why don't you just come on up here?"

He sighed. "You should come here."

"We'll have more fun if you come here."

"Yeah," he laughingly agreed, "that's why I want *you* to come *here*. We need to talk, babe."

"Right," Kam nodded, a good deal of her playfulness dissolving.

"So you'll meet me?"

"Give me ten minutes. I need to put some clothes on," she smiled at the tormented sound he replied with.

Kam shut off the phone and went to grab the jeans that lay over the back of the armchair when the phone rang again. She thought to check the faceplate that time and saw that it was Eliza calling.

"Sorry I left. Those guys there to see you looked pretty serious."

"It's okay- those were the clients about the Bolton case."

"So um, how are you doing? Has the news had time to set in yet?"

"Hmph," Kam settled to the armchair. "I don't see that happening anytime soon."

"Guess you haven't had the chance to talk to Huron yet, huh?"

"On my way now. He was on a trip with Cousteau, El. A survivalist thing- no phones."

"Oh?" Eliza's tone was hushed, yet anxious.

Kam grinned at her friend's reaction. "Why don't you go talk to *your* man while I talk to mine?"

Eliza laughed then. "Sounds like an excellent idea. Call you soon?"

"You bet." Kam studied the phone for a few seconds after Eliza disconnected.

~~~

"We're not that busy tonight, kid. Why not grab a booth?"

Huron smiled at the cafe owner he'd gotten to know pretty well since meeting Kam. "Things should liven up once Kamari's gets here. I um…" he studied the wood swirls in the oak bar's surface. "I screwed up pretty bad- haven't seen her in a while," he shrugged. "Thought this might be a safer place to meet and get a bead on her mood."

Tino Marconi chuckled. "Well obviously the girl knows a smart man when she meets one."

Huron's phone rang, interrupting the laughter Tino's comment instilled. The older man walked away to rub down the other end long bar. Meanwhile, Huron spoke a cheery greeting into the phone.

"Here's to the good life, eh Base? You've created quite an impressive one for yourself- obscene wealth, power, respect. I think what's most impressive though is that unbelievably smart and sexy beauty on your arm."

Huron moved the phone from his ear to check the faceplate. The call was listed as private.

"Have you ever thought about what became of all those people you fucked over to get where you are now? I wonder…"

Huron looked down the counter. Marconi was speaking with one of the cooks near the swing doors leading to the kitchen. Huron turned his focus back to the call.

"The only people I concern myself with are the ones stupid enough to cross me." He said.

Laughter rose from the man on the other end of the line. "Well lets just say you're about to know what it feels like to have part of your life ruined."

The caller abruptly disconnected and Huron resisted the urge to crush the phone inside his fist. He left the barstool, the muscle flexing wildly along his jaw as he moved. Dazedly, he reached inside his wallet to drop a few bills to the counter.

"Leavin', kid?" Marconi called. "Did she stand you up?"

"Something came up," Huron forced himself to smile. "We'll have to do this another time. See you, Tino."

"Huron," Tino Marconi tossed a wave.

Huron's forced smile vanished as he headed for the cafe's glass door. Outside, he put in a call to Rave.

"Find Nevil," he ordered the man once the connection had been made.

"B? What happened?"

Huron knew Rave could hear the animalistic chord that he'd spent years trying to rid himself of. Rave was well aware of the lethal acts that tone of voice usually foreshadowed.

"What happened, B?"

"Just do what I said, Rave, alright?"

"I understand, B. I'll find him. Where are you?"

"Meet me at the office. I'm on my way there now."

Huron disconnected without waiting on a response from Rave. Immediately, he scrolled for Kam's number, muttering a string of curses at the thought of having to cancel out on her. She'd been the only thing on his mind since his return from the all-too-real life threatening activities that comprised the survival trip.

Every evening, following a hearty meal and laughter around the campfire, he returned to his tent.

Thoughts of correcting the mistakes he'd made with Kam ran rampant.

Shaking off the thoughts that had nagged him all during the trip, Huron fixed himself on finding her number.

"Hey!"

The cozy street was quiet that time of night which allowed her voice to echo. Huron paused before hitting the phone's SEND button. Finding Kamari down the short block, made him smile and forget the unsettling call he'd just received.

Huron's focus was so fixed on Kam that he didn't notice the car moving at a snail's pace further down the road. The driver suddenly activated the high beam lights- too late for Huron to react- just in time to catch Kam off guard.

Aside from the quick turn she made in the direction of screeching tires, Kam was otherwise glued to her spot. The dark figure behind the wheel had the perfect target.

Huron realized he wasn't able to move either. Disbelief and terror churned through him and he looked on as the car practically mowed Kam down, fishtailing wildly until it righted itself. Tires screamed as the vehicle sped away.

~17~

Faint calls of alarm and sudden piercing cries jarred Huron from his horrified stupor.

"Kam?" His voice was beneath a whisper. His legs felt like lead but he forced them to move. At first, he trudged, stumbling down the brick sidewalk until he was running to where she had fallen. She appeared as a blur when he dropped to his knees beside her.

"Somebody call an ambulance!" a voice demanded, echoing into the night.

People scurried, gathering to form a wide, half-circle where Huron crouched near Kam. She was too still, and he couldn't tell whether she was breathing.

He knew then why she appeared as a blur. Swiping the back of his hand across his eyes, he gazed in horror and fascination at the moisture there- tears.

"God...Kam..." he needed to hold her.

"Sir, don't," a voice from above softly urged. "You could hurt her more if you move her."

He considered the words spoken in concern. *Hurt her more?* He had done quite enough of that.

You're about to know what it feels like to have part of your life ruined.

The unfamiliar voice on the line had promised him that. The son of a bitch had been aiming too low, Huron decided. Tenderly, he pulled limp coils of auburn hair from Kam's blood-smeared cheek. She lay on her stomach. Only one side of her face was visible and he felt sick letting her lie there, her lovely delicate skin flush with the ground.

Yes, the son of a bitch had aimed too low. Kamari wasn't a part of his life- she was *all* his life. Because of him, she was now fighting for hers.

~~~

Huron Base couldn't have looked more beaten down had he just been in a vicious prize fight- and lost. His eyes were bloodshot, swollen from all the crying he'd done that night. His clothes were a wrinkled mess- soiled with dirt...and blood.

So much blood... the emergency room attendants thought he needed to check himself in when the ambulance arrived with Kam. The time he spent answering their questions and responding to police inquiries about the ... incident all seemed like part of some bad dream. He hadn't even recalled taking a seat on one of the small uncomfortable chairs that filled the waiting room. He hadn't moved once in the last four hours. The only sign that

228

he wasn't completely paralyzed was his hypnotic squeezing of Kam's phone and keys. They were the only things she'd brought with her when she left the condo to meet him.

The phone began to chime. Huron watched it for a while looking as though he couldn't fathom what the sound meant. Absently, he read *Eliza B* on the faceplate and then in a mechanical fashion accepted the call and lifted the phone to his ear.

"Yeah?"

"Oh! Uh-Huron? It- it's Eliza. I- I'm sorry I was- sorry... I told Kam I'd call to check in."

"Eliza."

"I'm sorry to be calling so late, I couldn't sleep and I- I thought Kam might be up," she took a break from her rambling to laugh nervously over the irony. Kam was quite obviously... up, but surely not in the mood for a phone chat.

"Sorry Huron- just tell her I called-"

"Come to the hospital, El."

Silence met the command.

"Huron? I don't-"

"Come to the hospital. Kam's here-"

A tortured sound erupted from Eliza's throat.

"What? Why? Where- where's Kam? Is- is she alright? Huron what the hell are you saying?!"

"She..." Huron could feel his numbed emotions sparked faintly by Eliza's upset. "They tried to- Jesus... Eliza just get here, will you?!"

"Okay! Okay..." Eliza sighed the word seconds after she screamed it. "Oh my God," she gasped. "Huron- the baby- is the baby alright?"

His head had been swimming for over four hours. Eliza's question made his insides shift and he swayed on the waiting room seat. Somehow, he pushed to his feet, bracing a hand to the wall for support.

"What did you say?" The animalistic chord stirred in his voice for the second time that night.

Silence carried the line for a time. Gradually, Eliza's panicky breaths surged through the line. Huron's voice had gone from hollow and lifeless to grating and fierce- the effect was startling and wholly intimidating.

"I'm sorry Huron I- I thought you knew, I- dammit, idiot," she berated herself.

"Eliza-"

"Kam said she was on her way to talk to you I- I just assumed…"

Huron risked moving his hand off the wall in order to massage the nerves knotted in his neck. That did about as much good as sitting in the morose waiting room- none. He needed to walk until some of the night's senseless events began to right themselves.

"Eliza," he closed his eyes, relieved that his voice sounded less savage. "We're at St. Francis- just get here." He hung up, expelling an anguished sigh. He used the phone to give his forehead a few monotonous taps. His chest felt like it was constricting and he feared he'd explode if he didn't get out of there.

"Mr. Base?"

Huron heard the call before he'd gotten halfway down the hall outside the waiting room. Turning, he saw a young Asian man dressed in operating room scrubs. A lime green surgical mask hung around his neck.

Huron watched the man tug a matching cap from his head. Moving any further down the hall was out of the question then. His legs had gone to lead again.

"Mr. Base I'm Dr. Joseph Lau," the doctor gave a welcoming nod and advanced. "Would you like to sit down with me?" he asked.

"Just- just tell me," Huron breathed out loud, labored tufts of air. "Did I lose her?"

The doctor's face was unreadable for a second longer before a patient smile emerged. "You've got a fighter in there, Mr. Base. My prognosis is that Ms. Grade will make a full recovery."

The lead in his legs turned molten against the onset of relief. Huron slid down the wall until he sat right where he'd stood seconds before. Dr. Lau joined him there.

Still smiling, the smaller man crouched next to Huron and patted his shoulder reassuringly.

"She's alright?" Huron's voice and gaze held equal portions of disbelief.

Dr. Lau nodded, clapping Huron's shoulder again in the process.

"She's pretty banged up," the doctor shared. "She suffered a sprained wrist and ankle, two bruised ribs-one suffered a mild fracture. We feared it had punctured the lung, but that wasn't the case. There're a few cuts and bruises to her face, but those will heal in no time."

"She's pregnant." Huron swallowed noticeably once he'd shared the news. As stunned as he still was by the news however, he didn't miss the change in the other man's expression.

Dr. Lau bowed his head as though the checkered linoleum floor was suddenly demanding his attention.

Huron braced a hand on the floor and turned to face the man more fully.

Dr. Lau had raised his head. His dark, tilted stare harbored an edge instead of the ease it had earlier. "It took us a while to stop the bleeding when they brought her in.

231

We couldn't determine the source of the hemorrhage until we realized… she miscarried Mr. Base. I'm sorry."

Huron's big frame appeared to wilt as the full weight of the doctor's words hit him like an anvil. He went through a series of movements as though he wasn't sure if he wanted to wring his hands, clasp them atop his head, use one to massage the bridge of his nose or hold to his brow. Eventually, he braced one to the wall to use as leverage from the floor.

"Mr. Base?"

Huron shook his head, not sure of his reaction to hearing more devastation just then. He bolted away from the doctor as if the man were about to give chase to inflict more pain. His determined steps turned into a slight jog that gained speed until he'd made it outside to the parking lot nearest the hospital's emergency room wing.

He made it to a group of pruned bushes that were illuminated by the direct light of the street lamp they clustered around. There, he dry heaved until his ragged sobs took over.

***

"Eighty nine seventy Boulder Crest Way."

"Is that-?"

"That's Aspen." Eliza shared as the nursing assistant entered the contact info for Casper and Raven Grade.

Eliza had arrived at the hospital within forty five minutes of Huron's call. He was nowhere to be found when she got there. Luckily, it didn't take Eliza long to find someone to give her answers. Her heart skipped several beats when they told her Kam had been moved to a room in the Intensive Care Unit. She was assured it was only a precaution; the doctors wanted to monitor her following the surgery a few hours earlier.

Eliza spoke to Kam's parents once she'd obtained as much information as the hospital personnel were allowed to share. She told the couple as much as *she* felt comfortable sharing. All the while, she prayed she wouldn't devastate them too much. Casper Grade said that he and his wife would take the earliest flight out of Aspen.

The CNA at the desk thanked Eliza for the personal info she'd been able to provide and promised to let her know when Kam had been moved from the ICU. Like a lost soul, Eliza roamed the long hospital corridors which opened into an expansive soft lit lobby. The chairs there were far more cushiony and comfortable than those in the emergency wing- an area that only seemed to swell with the amount of patients to be treated or concerned parties hoping for just a word of encouragement about the condition of their loved ones.

She tried to eat, but just stared at the selections she'd made in the hospital cafeteria once they were on the plate before her. Sleep was also a hopeless wish, though she tried as best she could to nod off. The effort only resulted in tossing and turning for the better part of a few hours. Later that evening, Eliza found herself roaming the hospital again until she was standing before one of the mounted hospital directories. She stared, but read none of what the small, white block letters spelled out. Her jumbled thoughts drew to Cousteau and she considered calling him again. She was about to pull the phone from her back jeans' pocket when she saw Huron walking through the lobby's sliding glass doors. She broke into a run, enveloping Huron in a tight hug when she threw herself against him.

"Where have you been? How are you holding up?" She asked when he weakly embraced her.

"I did this, El," his voice was hoarse, dazed. "I did this to her. I-"

"Shh…" Eliza shook her head, lightly tapping her fingers against his cheek. "Don't do this-"

"She came to see me," Huron refused to be silenced. "I behaved like a jackass- worse than that- I was rough with her, El. I-I treated her like she meant nothing to me and then I told her to get out…"

"Shh…honey please don't do this to yourself," Eliza rocked him slow. "You don't need to do this- not tonight."

"I got her pregnant that night, El." The hunter green of his stare sparkled brilliantly thanks to a new sheen of unshed tears.

"Listen to me," Eliza cupped his face. "This wasn't your fault."

"It was, dammit," he rubbed the back of his hand across his eyes in a quick, agitated manner. "I got her pregnant while I fucked her against a wall in my house like she was trash!"

His voice boomed and Eliza feared they would capture the unwanted interest of hospital security. A few members of the detail had already thrown curious looks their way from the tall, maple desk across the spacious lobby.

"Huron," Eliza nudged him toward the lobby doors. "Honey you have to stop this. Kam doesn't blame you and she's all that matters right now."

"She didn't even tell me. Why didn't she tell me she was having my baby, El?"

"Oh honey…" Eliza pulled him close. "Sweetie, she only found out today- yesterday," she corrected given that they were into another dismal day. She felt him stiffen in their embrace and inched back. "Huron?"

234

"She found out yesterday?"

"Yes…she asked me to be with her while she took the test."

Misery beat him with a stronger whip then. "She found out about our child the same day she lost it?" He slumped against the wall.

Eliza shut her eyes then and mentally kicked herself. Once again, she'd shared too much of the wrong information. Helpless, she watched the powerful looking man before her, break down into a wave of sobs.

"Huron-"

"I got him, babe."

Eliza whirled around, bringing her hand to her mouth. She was ready to dissolve into her own mess of tears when she saw Cousteau.

"I-I'm so sorry, I-"

"Hey…shh…shh, shh…enough of that now," Cousteau tugged Eliza close. Squeezing her nape, he tucked her face into his neck.

With Eliza in tow, Cousteau reached out to grip Huron's elbow and draw him close as well.

"It's alright, man," Cousteau soothed his friend.

Huron accepted the calming words while his body shook beneath the weight of emotion.

~18~

"Ow…" Kam gave up on opening her eyes around eleven the next morning when the attempt sent pain lancing down one side of her face. Hearing what sounded like a giggle prompted her to try again.

The pain persisted, but it was worth the agony when she finally focused her eyes on Eliza's face.

"Hiya Blondie," Kam's greeting was a groggy one, but lovingly delivered.

Eliza giggled again. "Hey Red," she kissed Kamari's hand that was clutched between both of hers. "The friendship's over if you *ever* scare me like that again, do you hear?" She laughed amidst a thick sob.

Kam wanted to give in to a bit of laughter as well, but the gesture only elicited pain. "Understood," she managed to croak. "What happened to me?"

Eliza studied her friend curiously. "What do you remember?"

"I was," Kam closed her eyes, "that's right...I was talking to Huron. No...wait I- I only saw him. I...waved to him and I-maybe we *did* talk?" Confusion clouded her gaze when she looked up at Eliza. "Where is he?"

"I think he's off somewhere talking to Cousteau." Eliza stood to plump the pillows behind Kam's back. "I even talked to your folks. They should be here soon. The doctors are really impressed by how good you're doing. They'd planned to keep you in ICU another day instead of moving you a day early."

"Thanks," Kam motioned to the freshly plumped pillows. "And thanks for acting fast, calling my parents before they heard it elsewhere."

"You're welcome, but it's really Huron who acted fast. He was the one who got you here."

Kam rolled her head on the pillows and moaned. "Dammit, why can't I remember? Feels like I've been hit by a truck."

Eliza cringed. "You're close."

***

Eliza had gone above and beyond and she felt exhausted enough to prove it. When Kam woke earlier that day, Eliza remained with her friend until just before 2pm helping her to piece together the events of the accident.

While Kam was able to recall some of the aspects of the night in question, the majority of it remained a blur. Eliza couldn't say that she was too upset about that. Kam hadn't asked about the baby and Eliza hoped that'd be a question she'd save for Huron.

The flight Casper and Raven Grade hoped to take out of Colorado, had been delayed. They kept in constant contact with Eliza for status updates on their daughter's condition even though Eliza had given them the contact info for Kam's doctor. The Grades however were clearly not ready to hear from the man and have him deliver news from afar.

Huron had gone in to see Kam around four, so Eliza used the time for the cat nap she desperately needed. When her eyes opened again, she would have sworn she was still sleeping- or fantasizing that she was looking up into Cousteau's eyes.

"God, you're dreamy..." she swooned.

He laughed. "Right back at 'cha, babe," he leaned in to murmur the words against her brow.

Eliza blinked, stunned. She tried to sit up and realized he was really there and holding her.

Cousteau didn't want to relinquish his hold, but did allow her to sit up.

Eliza gawked at him. They'd had no time alone since his arrival in the lobby the night before. "Where's Huron?" She asked.

"Still in with Kam."

"Good," she relaxed a bit and shook her head as the hint of wonder crept into her gaze. "Wasn't so long ago that *I* was the one in the hospital, huh?" her attempts at lightheartedness didn't hold up and her eyes pooled with tears.

"Hey, shh..." Cousteau dropped a hard kiss to the top of her head and rocked her a bit.

"Sorry," she used the hem of her brown Henley top to dab at her eyes. "I really am sorry Cousteau," she looked at him then- her meaning clear.

"Stop," he kissed her head again. "You had every right to be upset by what I told you."

"No," the word held a defiant edge. "Takes things like what happened to Kam to make you see what's really important. If you hadn't told me, I wouldn't have had a leg to stand on convincing my mother to use that tape- to at least *try* to get herself out of trouble."

"You think she'll use it?"

Eliza shrugged, using the gesture to relay her uncertainty. "She already showed it to her lawyer. Hopefully it's just a matter of time before she can come home."

"I miss you, Elly," he stroked her hair, gave a tug to one lock. "I love you."

"I love *you*," Eliza reciprocated, going one better when she arched up to kiss him thoroughly.

~~~

Kam had drifted off to sleep, shortly before Eliza left her earlier that afternoon. Huron entered the private room she'd been moved to as though he expected to be hit. Eliza had told him about her talk with Kam and that she hadn't asked about the baby. Eliza wasn't sure Kam even remembered taking the pregnancy test, but felt it best that Huron hold that part of the discussion with her.

Finding her asleep, drew a relieved sigh from his chest. He pulled an armchair closer to the bed while she slumbered.

You could've lost her. The words had replayed in his mind like a loop for too long. He knew that a smart man would see this for what it was- a warning. A guarantee that he *could* lose her if he didn't let her go.

Yes, the smart man would let her go. A life with a man like him…it wasn't for her. Her world held too many unknowns- ones like the voice on his phone that night.

"Wake up, babe," he leaned against the bed and rested his elbows near her hip. He reached for her hand, squeezing it and brushing his mouth across her knuckles.

"Wake up and tell me to go to hell," he said. It would take nothing less than that for him to leave her be. Letting her go wasn't an option for him. He'd have to count on her ending it. That was something she was sure to do when he told her their child was dead because of him.

A ragged sound rushed from his throat when he felt her fingers move against his cheek. He looked up, uneasy expectancy shimmering in his stare as he waited.

Her fingers continued to flex and then she was subtly shifting her position beneath the covers. Huron couldn't resist moving up to capture her tongue in a gentle kiss when he saw the pink tip dart out to moisten her lips. Her tiny moan melted his heart and fueled his need, but he resisted deepening the kiss.

Instead, he brushed his mouth across her cheek and bruised forehead. "Kam?" He waited, noticing her lashes flutter until her eyes opened and fixed on his.

"Hey," he breathed the word which was caught up in a shaky relieved laugh. As much as he wanted her anger, in that moment, he prayed for her forgiveness.

"Feels like I've been hit by a truck, but El says it was only a car," her voice was laced with weak amusement.

"Yeah," Huron's shaky laughter returned. "That's what it looked like."

"You were there."

"Yeah…yeah, babe I was," he bowed his head expelling a slow unsteady breath. "I've never been more terrified in my life-I'm sorry."

"No," she cooed the word. "It's okay," she saw tears brim in his very long lashes before he lowered his head to swipe at them with the back of his hand.

"It's alright, Hon, it's not your fault."

"It is."

"Huron stop now, come on."

"Do you remember what happened?" He asked. "Anything? What about during your day yesterday?" He hoped she'd focus on her time at the office. "Do you recall anything about it?"

Kamari appeared to concentrate. Her voluminous brown eyes scanned the soft lit hospital room. "Oh yeah, I had a meeting with Danny. He came with his boss Will Cormack."

The grimace darkening Huron's face eased off when Kam mentioned Dan Tate's boss being in attendance.

"El was there…" Kam recalled, frowning as though she were working harder to grasp something just out of her reach.

"She…why…she left." Kam blinked, looking as though the matter was settled in her mind, but not quite certain that it was.

Kam pressed her lips together, putting forth greater effort to focus. "She left so I could take the meeting…"

"Why was she there?" Huron prompted. He hoped that getting Kam to remember the baby on her own would be easier than being told.

"I called her…to-to help me with something-"

Huron watched Kam's gaze circle back around to his before it drifted towards the bed covers- towards her middle.

241

"What?" he asked.

Kam only shook her head at his slight insistence.

"You asked her to help you with the pregnancy test."

Her stunned gaze flew to his face, remaining there only a second or two before skirting back to her middle. One hand rested low on her abdomen. "You know."

"Eliza thought you told me."

Kam sat quietly for more than two minutes, then her eyes were darting back to Huron's face. "What happened?"

"You were coming to meet me at the café when a car came out of nowhere-"

"No, Huron. Eliza told me that- every detail, but we never discussed the baby. Why-"

"She thought we should talk about it. We...we lost the baby, honey," his deep voice carried an unmistakably heartbroken tone.

Kam's quiet gasp still echoed across the room as her nails curved into the covers at her lower stomach. Her expression appeared sharper, more alert even as Huron's seemed to deflate under the weight of misery.

"I'm sorry Kam..."

"Huron-"

"You should get away from me now, Kam."

"I don't want that."

He expelled an incredulous breath. "How can that be after what I did? Do you remember that night at my house?"

She knew what he was referring to and nodded. "I do," she said.

"I don't even know how you could want the child considering how you got it."

"Huron?" She was horrified then, unable to get out more than his name. Clearly, he thought he'd forced her

242

into sex that night. Worse, he was holding himself responsible for the baby they'd lost and for the accident itself.

She didn't have time to bring Huron down from his latest wave of self-pity. Dr. Lau was knocking and walking into the room then.

"Well look at you! Awake and looking so alert." Dr. Lau celebrated after greeting his patient and the man at her bedside.

"I'm just getting all the details about my injuries," Kam squeezed Huron's hand, smiling when he squeezed back.

Dr. Lau's expression dimmed with sorrow. Reverently, he moved to take a seat in the empty chair on the other side of the bed.

"I'm sorry for your loss," genuine emotion reflected in the man's dark eyes as he looked from Kam to Huron.

"We've run extensive tests to determine any other injuries brought on by the accident," the doctor continued. "Of course you'll want to confirm my prognosis with your gynecologist but I've found nothing that makes me think you won't be able to carry another baby to term in the future."

"I only just found out I was pregnant," she gave a forlorn smile. "I haven't even had a chance to make an appointment with my gynecologist. Hmph...I don't even know how far along I was."

"Let's see," Dr. Lau checked the chart he'd taken from the end of the bed. "The fetus measured at seven weeks. We-"

"Seven weeks?" Huron straightened a bit in his chair.

Dr. Lau nodded, taking no offense to the interruption. "Kamari was in her first trimester. The first

243

three months are usually the most crucial. Many women often keep news of their pregnancy secret until their second trimester."

Kam felt Huron's hold on her hand becoming tighter. "Huron?"

"You didn't get pregnant that night." He sounded as though he were speaking to himself.

"Honey, it's okay-"

"No, Kam," he dismissed her soothing words with a wave. The fact that their child had been conceived during an act of love and not war was like dealing with the devastation of loss all over again.

"Huron?" Kam whispered that time.

"Will she be alright if I leave her for a few hours?" Huron was asking the doctor.

Dr. Lau smiled. "She'll be just fine. We're gonna take good care of her."

"Huron?" Kam was starting to feel like a scratched disc.

He stood abruptly, but took time to drop a hard kiss to Kam's forehead and then another to her mouth. "I'll be back soon- I promise," he nudged her nose with his and eased back. "I love you," he said.

"Huron?" Kam didn't try to mask her surprise or worry for the doctor's benefit. Huron left the room without a look back.

* * *

A bustle of activity surrounded Kamari for the next few hours. Eliza had made contacting Kam's office part of her duties. Grade employees dropped in throughout the evening to check on their boss before visiting hours had ended.

Tenille came with a flurry of flowers that filled the hospital room with splashes of color and fragrance. Kam was amused by how overboard her assistant had gone, but she had to admit how greatly the flowers boosted her mood.

Casper and Raven Grade arrived later that night. Their apprehensiveness eased tremendously when they found their daughter sitting up in bed and eating. Kam dissolved what remained of their apprehension when she complained about the food.

"I'll make you a deal Kam-Kam," Casper Grade was saying as he settled in behind his wife who had taken a seat facing Kamari on the edge of the bed. "I'll smuggle in some of those sloppy burgers you love, if you eat the rest of what you hate," he promised, a cunning smile on his handsome tanned face.

Kam gazed at her father longingly. "Isn't a spoonful enough?"

"No," the Grades spoke in unison.

Kam burst into laughter that sent slight discomfort through her chest. "I'm fine, I'm fine," she insisted. "At least it feels good to *want* to laugh."

Seriousness hovered in spite of Kam's tease and she squeezed her mother's hand when the woman expelled a heavy sigh. "Don't cry, Mommy," she urged, watching as Raven did that very thing.

Casper tugged his wife back against his broad chest and squeezed her close. "We could've lost you," he looked over Raven's head to Kam. Casper Grade smiled in a way that was equal parts miserable and encouraging. He and Raven then moved closer to their daughter and enveloped her in a tender hug.

The Grades were still embracing, when Eliza rushed into the room. Happy surprise illuminated her features when she saw the family.

245

"I didn't mean to interrupt," she still saw fit to apologize.

Casper waved a hand. "Don't start with that," he ordered as he and Raven left Kam to hug her friend.

"Has there been any word about the coward who did this, Hon?" Raven asked when the embrace ended. "To just drive away without stopping..."

Eliza squeezed the woman's arm. "From what I've heard, the witnesses can't seem to recall the color of the car, but they all agree it was some old sedan. They also agree that there was no license plate, but I think they just can't remember it."

Seriousness returned its heavy weight to the room until Eliza gave a quick, rejuvenating clap. "I'd say we're all due for some good news," she grabbed the remote control from the night table near Kam's bed.

The Grades watched as Eliza turned on the TV and surfed channels for a few seconds until she found what she was looking for. Eliza clasped the remote to her chest and watched the news broadcaster on screen. Happiness radiated through the tears in her eyes.

"...no details on the wording of the deal Mrs. Breck supposedly made with officials. Sources say key players in federal law enforcement are somehow involved. We will continue to follow this evolving story. Once again, Jessica Breck, previously arrested and charged with the murder of her nephew Simon Breck, may be on the verge of being a free woman after her surrender of sensitive material that has yet to be verified. More to come after this..."

Eliza muted the sound and turned. Her gaze locked with Kam's.

"Is she home?" Kam asked.

Some of Eliza's glee abated. "Doesn't look like she'll be going back there anytime soon. They're gonna have to keep her under wraps- especially once the details of that tape are revealed." Eliza seemed to shed more of her elation.

"Then, there's my family," she sighed. "Understandably, they want someone's head for Simon's death. They'll fight her release."

"But if this evidence is as good as she says…"

Eliza nodded at Kam's insight. "It is, from what I've been told."

"Is there anything we can do, love?" Casper asked Eliza and then smiled over at his daughter. "Looks like we're gonna be here a while."

"In that case," Eliza slapped her hands to her sides and regained some of her glee. "I could sure use one of Miss Ray's incredible suppers."

"Me too!" Kam clapped and then pushed away the thin, rectangular bed table that held the uninviting hospital meal.

Much needed laughter filled the room.

~19~

Las Vegas, Nevada~

"Gentlemen, I'm afraid you'll have to wait. Gentlemen? Sirs?! The woman's harried expression turned to one of sheer astonishment as three intimidating and impeccably dressed men stormed the hallway leading to her boss' office suite.

The small brunette almost stumbled from her chair in an attempt to round her desk and make it to the office doors before they got there. She must have realized the futility in attempting to beat their lengthy strides. That, combined with their sheer size and murderous expressions were clear indicators that any attempts to interrupt their plans could be foolish and possibly life threatening.

The admin maintained a steady pace behind the men. She left off trying to urge them to wait and be announced.

"Knock, knock," Huron called when he threw open the doors to the office Dutch Breslin shared with his wife.

The Breslins looked to be in the midst of a heated discussion if one took Sandra Breslin's expression as proof. The woman stood over her husband, her finger pointed inches away from his forehead. The couple stilled, looking from Huron to the men he'd arrived with.

"Mr. and Mrs. Breslin," the small brunette waved in an endeavor to be seen behind the men who dwarfed her. "I tried to get them to wait-"

"It's alright, Lisa. It's alright," Dutch waved to his admin.

Nevil, who stood to Huron's left, shook his head while making a tsking sound. "Hasn't anyone ever told you it's not nice to lie to your employees?"

Lisa gasped and backed toward the office doors.

Rave, who'd entered the office behind Huron and Nevil, smoothly blocked the woman's exit.

"Please stay," his appealing grin was more dangerous than inviting. "I insist," he added.

"Huron," Dutch nodded while standing behind his desk. "Nevil, Rave," he nodded toward the other men as well.

"Dutch," Sandra called when her husband stepped from behind his desk. She wasn't as convinced as he seemed that the unexpected visit was to be a cordial one.

"Drinks, fellas?"

"Son of a bitch," Huron growled, Dutch Breslin's offer was apparently the final straw or the *only* straw the man was to be allowed. Closing the distance between them, Huron yanked the man off the floor.

249

"Dutch!" Sandra rushed toward her husband. She'd only taken a few steps before Nevil's arm around her waist, stifled all movement.

"Dutch! Dutch!"

Nevil gave Sandra a rattling jerk. "Shut your mouth," he snarled against her ear.

"Listen to me, Base. Let's just talk-" Dutch Breslin's attempt to reason was useless once Huron's fist connected with his jaw and filled the man's mouth with the metallic flavor of blood. His eyes bulged, threatening to roll back in his head.

Fists bunched at Dutch's shirt collar, Huron gave Dutch a vicious jerk to keep him conscious. "Everyone keeps tellin' me what a bad guy I am," he seethed, lashes fluttering as his temper continued to elevate. "Guess all that reminding's finally kicked in." He savaged the man's jaw with another punch.

"Dutch…" Sandra moaned, her body limp in front of Nevil's.

"You thought you could just kill her?!" Huron raged, punctuating the question with another blow. "And I'd fall in line," he used his fist to backhand Dutch's cheek "I'd fall in line like a good nigga?!"

"We never-!"

"I said, shut it bitch!" Nevil shook Sandra until she cried out that time.

"Did you think you could just run her down in the street like a fuckin' dog and not have me come take it out of your ass?" Huron followed up the eerily quiet question with a succession of blows that split Dutch Breslin's lips, swelled his eye shut and produced a distinctive crunch in the vicinity of his cheek, shattering it.

The women cried and mewled as they watched the monstrous display.

250

"Please...please, he hasn't done anything."

"You want some of what he's getting?" Nevil growled the hollow threat into Sandra's ear.

"He didn't do it. I wouldn't let him." Sandra continued, too terrified for her husband to heed her captor's warning. "Please, he didn't do it. I wouldn't let him, please..."

Sandra's last words were effective in stilling Huron's fist which was mere seconds from connecting with Dutch's face again.

"Please, I can prove it..."

Nevil looked to Huron who, after the passing of a few creeping seconds, nodded to indicate he should release the woman.

Sandra scurried to her husband's desk, stumbling out of her high heels along the way. The chic pumps weren't made for such high, intensity moves. She gathered papers from the desk, clutching them to her chest when she returned.

Nevil stopped her before she could approach Huron. He snatched one of the pages while the rest cascaded to the floor. Nevil studied the sheet while Sandra knelt before him to collect what had fallen.

"What the fuck is this?" He demanded when she stood with the rest of the pages compiled in a messy stack.

"We thought we- we wanted to find something to use against Ms. Grade," Sandra hiccupped the words between sobs. "We were looking for some-something embarrassing that might...keep you in business with us," she looked fearfully toward Huron.

"Hell lady, you needed my man's backing *that* much?" Rave asked from his position near the office doors where he stood restraining the Breslins' trembling assistant.

251

"Some of our side deals haven't panned out the way we hoped and-" Sandra hiccupped another sob. "We owe people because of it. With Huron as part of our business," she took a few steadying breaths to slow the tumble of words from her lips. "No one dared to come after us for what we owed. When he- he cut ties with us, the way he did, word spread-"

"And your asses were left twistin' in the wind," Nevil sneered.

Huron stood. He used the front of Dutch Breslin's shirt to clean the blood from his hands and then let the man fall back to the floor as though he were discarded trash.

Sandra retreated, cowering behind Nevil when Huron approached. He extended a hand for the papers. Nevil handed over the one he held and then tugged the rest from Sandra Breslin's stiff hand.

Huron studied the papers and then rumbled out a curse that made the woman whimper. "What the fuck is this?" His snarl that time was directed at Sandra. He moved in another step. "What the hell are you doing with Raven Grade's medical records?"

***

Cousteau was blowing across the surface of the coffee he'd just taken from the hospital vending machine when he noticed Huron heading down the hall towards him.

"For a guy your size, you sure have a talent for disappearing," he teased his friend, taking note of the smile the man barely managed.

"Stop worrying, B. Kam's doctor is very impressed by how well she's doin'. He says she'll probably be able to do most of her recovery time at home."

Huron leaned against the wall opposite the vending machines. "She didn't get pregnant that night I-I thought I got her pregnant the night I had her in my house," he shook his head, lowering his gaze to the tops of his black suede hiking boots.

"The doctor told us she was seven weeks. Seven weeks, Cous," he looked up at his friend, not afraid to let the man see the emotion stirring in his gaze. "The baby was alive inside her almost two months. We made it in love."

"Where'd you go tonight, man?" Concern held Cousteau's gaze and question.

"I felt ready to pass out when I heard that." Huron massaged the bridge of his nose. "I had to get out of here- had to find someplace to put the rage."

"And where'd you finally settle on?"

Huron heard the skepticism in Cousteau's voice. "I went to see Dutch Breslin- took Nevil and Rave with me. That idiot Breslin thought killing Kam would bring me back into the foal."

Cousteau gave Huron a quick once over. "Where're your blood-stained clothes then?"

"Breslin claims he didn't do it."

"And you believed that?"

"Not even when his wife starting begging for his life."

Cousteau paled beneath the rich copper tone of his complexion. "Jesus B, please tell me you didn't kill the fucker?"

"No…" Huron rested his head back against the wall and closed his eyes for a while. "But it got bloody. I changed my clothes before we left Vegas."

"Did it help?"

Huron grimaced. "Didn't hurt."

Solemn nods passed between the men.

"Kam was asleep when I called to check in on her. Eliza answered, told me her folks were here?"

253

"Yeah, Kam made 'em go get some rest though. Nurses found 'em someplace to crash," Cousteau raised his chin. "Sure you're alright?"

Huron looked anything but. Agitated, he scratched at the whiskers darkening his cheek and winced. "I seriously underestimated how far those fools were willing to go to keep our partnership."

"You think they'll come after her again?" Cousteau sipped his coffee then turned to order a cup for Huron.

"They won't forget my visit anytime soon. Dutch will need recovery time of his own to nurse that shattered cheekbone of his."

Cousteau whistled.

Huron's expression reflected no pride when he accepted the coffee. "I thought I'd almost buried the guy I used to be."

"You haven't *almost* buried him. You *did* bury him—a long time ago."

"He doesn't feel buried. He feels like he's right beneath my skin."

"It's nothin' to beat yourself up over, man." Cousteau raised the thick paper cup in toast. "I feel like the guy I used to be is itching to rush back to the surface a lot. 'Specially when I'm stressed."

"She keeps me sane," Huron spoke the words quietly, keeping his eyes fixed on the black coffee. "I've never let anybody have that kind of control over me and she's got it," he snapped his fingers, "just like that."

"I hear that's to be expected when love happens."

Huron suddenly grinned. "You're right."

Cousteau frowned playfully. "So quit holdin' *my* ears hostage and go spill your guts to the woman you love."

Huron needed no further encouragement. He clapped Cousteau's shoulder and headed down the hall.

~~~

Kamari was sleeping when Huron looked inside her room. One lamp burned softly near the windows and the place was lit by a soothing glow. He hated to interrupt her much needed sleep, but he needed to be near her. Luckily, she didn't appear to be in a deep slumber for her eyes opened the moment he settled to the edge of the bed. Gently, he drew her against him.

"I was waiting up," she said.

He grinned at her drowsy tone. "I could tell."

Kam punched his chest, smiling when he faked injury. "You missed my sponge bath and everything."

"Damn...that good, huh?"

"Mmm...I'd say it had X-rated potential." Content, Kam settled deeper into his broad, hard torso.

"Was it a male or female nurse giving you the bath?" Huron inquired, his tone curiously playful.

"Female, why?"

"Sounds like my kind of flick, is all."

"Well..." Kam luxuriated in the feel of her nails grazing the silky whiskers of his close beard. "We could still add a few more scenes if you're up for it."

"Kam..."

She ignored his warning tone, her hand leaving his jaw to skim his neck and collarbone until she reached his torso defined under the black Oxford shirt he wore over a white T-shirt. She continued her downward stroke until she contacted his sex, thick and stiff beneath a pair of dark blue denims.

"Feels like you're definitely up for it."

Huron took her hand and squeezed gently. "No way are we doing that and definitely not here."

"No fair..."

255

"You *were* hit by a car yesterday, remember?"

"It wasn't yesterday," she argued, resuming her caress.

"Kam..." Huron, rested back into the pillows and closed his eyes. "No..."

She inched closer, feeling friskier by the minute as thoughts hit home of how long they had been apart. "Part of my recovery includes exercise, you know?"

"Kam..." Huron was quickly losing his ability to resist her none-too-subtle advances.

"My mouth could use a workout too," she was relentless and her heart flipped when he opened his eyes and gave her a thoughtful look.

"Alright then, let's talk."

"I had something else in mind," she palmed his semi-hard sex.

"Me first," he pulled her hand off his lap. "Do you want another child?"

She blinked, tugging her hand from his. "Where the hell did *that* come from?"

He shrugged. "I'd like to know. This all happened fast. We didn't have the chance to discuss how we felt about it."

Kam's lush mouth curved into a coy smile. "You want to talk about our feelings?"

"I want to know how you feel about this."

"Well," sighing she offered a flip shrug. "How do *you* feel about it?"

"I find it hard to believe you don't know the answer to that already," his riveting stare was fixed, unwavering on her face. "The thought of you having my child inside you...there *is* no better thought for me."

The admission struck Kam and the reaction reflected in her eyes. Quickly, she masked the emotion.

256

"Like you said, this all happened so fast. It's gonna take a minute to feel up to discussing it, you know?"

He gave her a slow nod. He didn't need her response. He'd gotten the reaction he'd dreaded, but expected.

The contents of the papers Sandra Breslin had handed over, hinted at a sinister reality. Still, there were too many variables for him to accept those hints as truth. Seeing the haunted look in her beckoning gaze, knowing he'd put it there made him feel lower than he'd felt all day and *that* was saying something.

"Consider the subject dropped," Huron saw the light return to her smoky stare.

Kam snuggled closer. "Is it my turn now?"

Huron gave her what she-what they both craved then. He whimpered, proudly acknowledging that the sound had indeed come from him. He nuzzled his tongue inside the sweet darkness of her mouth.

Kam wanted more fierceness, instead of the gentleness he was giving her. His touch was no less seductive, but she hungered for him too much. The languid tangling of their tongues merely teased until she claimed his mouth the way she wanted.

Her needy purrs and the way she rubbed her pliant, petite frame into his side sent Huron's hormones into a rage. He cupped her hip, intending to set her away but he tugged her closer instead. Her trembling moan of approval gave him pause. Another second and he'd have had her beneath him without a care for her injuries.

"Kam," he squeezed her hip, "honey wait-"

"Mmm mmm," she murmured amidst the kiss. Her tongue thrust insatiably inside his mouth while she cupped and fondled his arousal.

"Stop," he made no effort to physically encourage her compliance. "Kam…"

"Come on…" she urged, thrusting her tongue with an increased fervor. "My painkillers are amazing. You won't hurt me. You can do whatever you want…"

"I will," he promised, his voice a quiet agonizing tone. "When you're well enough to enjoy it."

"I *am* well enough to enjoy it…well enough to make *you* enjoy it too." Kam squeezed his sex and gasped into his mouth in response to the pronounced ridge straining his zipper. "You're really going to let all that go to waste?"

"Kam…" Huron indulged in a few more of her teasing caresses. "Babe, I've got no choice…"

Gently, so as not to jostle her too much, he left the bed. Kamari let loose another gasp, that one in disbelief. Her anguish faded though and she smiled when he moved to lay behind her on the other side of the bed.

"This is nice," Kam nudged her bottom to his easing erection.

He squeezed her thigh, holding her fast. "Stop moving or I'll find a waiting room to sleep in."

To prevent that, Kam took his hand in a surprisingly strong grasp. She tucked it between her breasts, trapping him there.

Huron sighed, content that he was giving her a break and that she was letting him.

"Huron?"

"Yeah?" he feared he'd spoken too soon.

"I love you," she murmured a tad drowsily.

His heart seized, and then felt as though it were melting. Huron tugged her closer. "I love you," he said, burrowing his handsome face in Kam's hair and using the beckoning fragrance to lull himself to sleep.

258

~20~

Kam's doctors came to check in on her early the following morning. While she was occupied, Huron figured it was as good a time as any to have the conversation with her parents. He'd already avoided it longer than he'd intended. The Grades were sitting down to breakfast in the hospital cafeteria when Huron found them.

"Ms. Raven, Mr. C," he greeted.

Casper Grade's handsome face carried an easy grin. "Huron, my man have a seat and some breakfast," he motioned to an empty chair at the table.

"I'm good." Huron accepted the seat, waving off the food. "Sorry for interrupting you guys. We need to talk."

The Grades seemed to freeze in motion. A look passed between them though. They attempted to draw strength from whatever they found in each other's faces.

"Is she alright?" Raven Grade's voice was a shudder, but resolve had hardened her light eyes.

"She's fine," Huron's words rushed out on a quiet sigh. He pulled the empty chair close to the woman and squeezed her hands. "She's fine. I'm sorry I upset you."

Raven searched the vivid gaze of the young man next to her and seemed eased by what she saw. Smiling, she waved toward the fruit and waffles on the table. "Are you sure you won't have something to eat, honey?"

"No ma'am," Huron gave a solemn shake of his head. "I don't think you guys are gonna be in the mood to eat soon either."

This time frowns were exchanged between the attractive, older couple.

"Maybe you should say what you came to say, son." Casper advised.

"I suspect Kam's accident was about me. Former business associates went after her to encourage me to stay in business with them."

"Are they dead?"

The cool query stunned Huron. He lost his train of thought and simply sat watching Raven.

Casper chuckled, forking up a morsel of cantaloupe. "My wife fully approves of bodily harm being inflicted on anyone who threatens our girl. We both do." He said, and helped himself to the cantaloupe.

Huron had to laugh then. "Uh-no, no Ms. Raven they aren't dead," he thumbed away a laugh tear and brought the seriousness back into his voice. "I think they planned this too well to ever be brought up on former charges but I *was* able to inflict some bodily harm of my

260

own, so there will be lingering pain for quite a while." He knew Dutch Breslin's injuries would bring his wife just as much misery while she nursed him back to health.

"Once they've recovered from the pain, I'll be back to inflict more." His shrug sent barely a wrinkle through the lightweight maroon hoody he wore. "Probably best if you guys don't know all the details."

"I like the way you operate, kid." Casper said, sharing an approving nod with his wife before they returned to their waffles and sausage.

"They denied having anything to do with what happened to Kam," Huron said after watching the Grades eat for the better part of a minute.

Casper laughed harshly around his mouthful of Belgian waffle. "I would too if I had to answer to you for it."

"They told me the plan was to find something to use against Kam- to embarrass her, threaten to expose it unless I stayed in business with them." Huron noticed the slightest hesitation in Raven's handling of her fork.

"They couldn't find anything against her," he said, "but they dug anyway until they got to you."

The Grades were fixed on Huron then. He stared at Raven.

"What did they tell you?" She asked, appearing ashen beneath her rich, honey complexion.

"They had hospital records and a few other documents. I came to my own conclusions," he closed his eyes for scarcely a moment. "I'm not here to ask you to confirm them, but I think you should discuss it with Kam."

"What did they say to her?" Panic loomed in Raven's eyes then.

"No one's said a thing to her," Huron squeezed Raven's hands again. "But I don't think I'm the only one

261

who's come to conclusions. Do you have any idea how she feels about marriage and family?" He asked her.

Intrigue mixed in among the confusion Raven expressed.

"The thought of having a child terrifies her," Huron continued, withdrawing into his own fears. "It's got nothing to do with lack of time or thinking she's not 'mommy material'. It goes deeper- the fear is at the heart of who she is."

Raven's confusion and intrigue gave way to something haunted.

"How do you know this?" Casper asked.

"I could see it in her eyes when I asked if she ever wanted to have kids," Huron took no offense to the man's question. "I um…" he mopped his face with both hands.

"I could see it in her eyes when I told her I knew she was pregnant with my child and I could see it there when I had to tell her it died in that accident."

Raven Grades's expression warped into something miserable and heartbroken. A wounded sound slipped past her lips and she put a fist to her mouth to prevent another outburst.

"She was pregnant?" Casper's voice was hushed. Tears welled in the striking depths of his gaze when he saw Huron nod.

"They don't think there's any lasting damage. Her doctor's sure she can have another baby whenever she wants." He turned back to Raven. "She doesn't want that. Not because she doesn't want to have a child or be a mother to it, but because she feels there's something wrong inside her. I don't think I can convince her that's not true."

"There's *nothing* wrong inside her." Raven sobbed. "She has to know that."

Huron took the woman's trembling hands into his own once more. "Ms. Raven, I don't think she does."

~~~

"What the devil are you doing?!"

Kam was attempting to leave her bed when Raven walked into the hospital room and gasped.

"Mommy I'm al-"

"Hush."

"I've gotta get out of bed some-"

"Would you just stop it?! Just stop and be quiet a minute and listen!"

"Mommy?"

The woman's uncharacteristic shortness had Kam attempting to leave the bed again. One look from Raven changed her mind.

"It's not every day a woman finds out she was on the verge of being a grandmother, you know?"

"Huron..." Kam groaned, slapping a palm to her forehead.

Raven ceased her pacing around the room. "Don't blame him. He loves you. He's scared for you."

"Scared for me?"

"Why don't you want to have kids?" Raven wilted when she read what flashed in Kam's eyes. She trudged to the bed, almost stumbling on the cuffs of her form-fitting gray yoga pants.

"It's true, isn't it?" She breathed, "that's what you think?"

Raven's reaction confused Kam but she wouldn't question the woman- not then. Leaving bed at that point was the last thing she wanted. Burrowing deep beneath the thin covers sounded best to her then.

Raven wouldn't allow it. She closed in on the distance to Kam's bed before she could move. "Why did you give that look when I mentioned having a baby?"

"Mommy?" Kam watched the woman as though she were a stranger. "You- you know why."

Raven sat down on the bed close to Kam and took her face between her palms. "Dear God, what's going through that head of yours?"

"Mommy, stop," Kam wrenched her face from her mother's hold.

"I won't. Not when this is killing you." Raven shook her head as though Kam were a stranger to her as well. "All the times we've talked and you never- why would you turn your back on one of the most wonderful gifts a woman could be blessed with?"

"Stop it Mommy, please," Kam wailed then, her voice distorted by emotion. "Why are you doing this?!"

"Honey what am I doing-"

"Jesus Mommy what do you think?! Don't you think I hate myself enough for this! I was dealing with it just fine- just fine and then, then Huron…" She used the back of her hand to wipe away a tear with a vicious swipe.

"God he came out of nowhere and I-I love him, Mama," Kam virtually cried out the words then. "I love him and it's killing me that I can't give him something he'll want one day- something I'll only want with him."

"Baby shh…" Raven cupped Kam's cheek. "Honey you can still have that with him-"

"Are you serious?!" Kam shrank away from her mother's touch. "How can you say that, Mommy? How could you encourage that for someone like me?"

"Someone like-like you?" Raven's voice dropped as though the answer she dreaded was at hand.

"For God's sake Mom, you had me from your own father!"

Raven closed her eyes, covering her mouth with the back of her hand when she heard Kam say the words. "All those times we talked…" Dazedly, she pushed off the bed resuming her pace around the room.

"Now that I think about it we- we never really got to the true issue, did we? You were never… never specific about what you really thought and I could understand why. I knew you had to remember the strangeness of that time- you were young but perceptive. When we left I just wanted to forget. Later when we did discuss it, I only wanted to convince you that we were fine and that *you* were fine even though you shied away time after time from every man who met you and inevitably fell head over heels. I wanted you to believe that none of that old drama would affect you- ever affect you again…"

Raven heard Kam crying softly and saw her drowning tears into the corner of a pillow. "How long have you thought that?" She asked with a coolness she couldn't quite believe was her own.

Kam didn't answer and Raven bolted back to the bed, snatching away the pillow and taking her daughter by the shoulders. "How long Kamari?!"

"Always! Since I was old enough to know having a baby when you're fourteen isn't a good thing. I was old enough to remember Poppy." Kam grimaced at the pet name for her grandfather. "I was old enough to remember you calling him daddy." She shivered when a chill skimmed her spine.

"Then all of a sudden we were leaving him and you were scared and I knew it was because of him." Kam sniffed profusely, using the corner of the sheet to wipe her nose. "You were scared for a long time and I knew it was

265

probably not best to ask questions about Poppy. Then you met Daddy…" A serene smile crept to Kam's mouth when she thought about Casper Grade.

"And you didn't seem scared anymore and I *definitely* didn't want to ask about Poppy. So I put it together myself and I dealt with it."

"Jesus," Raven released Kam's shoulder. She squeezed her eyes shut and let out a quiet breath. "Kam listen to me, honey. What you were dealing with was a lie."

Kam rolled her eyes. "I know why you have to say that."

Raven expelled a frustrated cry. "Dammit Kam… shut up! Contrary to what you might think, not even *you* are able to figure out every mystery in the world. Jonah Orvitz was not my father." She grimaced, feeling bile rise at the back of her throat. She had just uttered a name she'd sworn never to speak again.

"He wasn't even my step-father," she continued with a cold smile. "But my mother didn't think that little detail mattered when she left me with him and took off with her new flavor of the month.

Now your grandmother…" Raven snorted a laugh. "That was a bitch who never should have had a kid. But to her credit, she *did* keep your… Poppy away from me after we moved in with him. Hmph," Raven began to fidget with the pillow she'd taken from Kam. "She only did it because her ego couldn't stand not being *all* the woman any man needed.

We went to stay with him when I was twelve. My mother left three months after I turned thirteen." Raven reclined on the narrow bed, bracing her weight to her elbows.

"She said she named me after some fashion model she saw in a magazine from some remote village in East

266

Africa and I wondered if I'd ever have the nerve to get the hell out of there and run as far as *I* could- not for fortune or fame but just-just security. I was terrified when she picked up and left me. I wasn't so much scared of Orvitz as I was of what could happen to us. I had nowhere to go and he didn't miss a chance to tell me that.

I believed him and I stayed." Raven pushed herself back into a sitting position. "After I got pregnant he started...taking precautions to make sure it didn't happen again. I took his bullshit for four years and then I got the hell out of there."

Kam studied her mother and was able to see traces of the young, frightened girl she'd once been. "Why did you take me?" She asked in a small voice.

"Because you were mine," Raven's response was matter-of-fact, the look in her gaze proved how horrified she was by the question. "That son of a bitch took everything from me. I damn well wasn't going to let him take the most beautiful thing." She scooted close to cup Kam's face and put a tender kiss on her mouth.

"I'm sorry I made you think of this Mommy. Think of him..."

"Shh..." Raven kissed her daughter again. "We should've talked about this-*really* talked about this a long, long time ago."

"I guess you think about him every time you see me, huh?"

"Shh..." Raven soothed the word across Kam's brow where her lips feathered kisses. "That man's face... my hate for him gets weaker every year of your life. Every year that you've become more stunning, smart and accomplished."

She pulled back to look at Kam. "I hate what happened to me, but I adore the gift I received in the

267

process." Regret intervened. "Forgive me for not telling you the truth, baby. I was so young when we left and then we met Casper and we've had such a happy life with him. I told myself that none of it had touched you- none of the ugliness would ever touch you. I was wrong to keep it."

"You were right to keep it." Kam fingered a lock of her mother's dark hair. "If you hadn't, I might not be with Huron right now."

Raven's smile reflected renewing strength. "Is he really the one, baby?"

"I hope so," Kam sighed, her warm eyes sparkling, "because I really love him."

Raven's eyes narrowed, she smoothed the back of her hand across Kam's cheek. "What's that look for?"

Kamari scooted back on the bed and let Raven help her get settled beneath the covers. "He doesn't think he's good enough for me."

"But that's crazy!" Raven looked astounded. "He's gorgeous! And smart, compassionate, strong-in mind *and* body. Did I already say he's gorgeous?"

"But he's damaged too, Mom," Kam shared once the need to laugh had eased. "There's... something. He doesn't want me to know-thinks he can clean it all up and we won't have to deal with it."

"Does he know you'll love him regardless?"

"I've told him enough." Kam stared out across the room as though she were envisioning him then. "As bad as we had it, Huron came from an even tougher place. The only way to ensure something didn't come back to bite him was to take it out of the equation."

"Just make sure he knows that love is part of the equation."

There were a few seconds of silence and then Kam gushed laughter. "That was just a bit corny, you know?"

268

Raven shrugged. "I thought it was pretty poetic."

Laughter flooded inside the room. The exuberance was partly due to the corny statement, but more to the lifting of the unimaginable weight of the past. Kamari was secure in her mother's embrace when the laughter softened once more.

"Do you think he'll still love me once he finds out how damaged I am?"

"It's guaranteed," Raven dropped a stern kiss into Kam's curls. "'Specially since he's the one who came to us- told us what he suspected you were thinking."

"How?" Kam breathed the question.

"Come on, girl," Raven squeezed her daughter tightly. "You don't think you're the only one capable of this troubleshooting thing, do you?"

Quiet laughter livened the room again.

*****

Kam was finishing the last of another unimpressive hospital meal when the door opened and Huron peeked inside. Her heart thudded with a happy intensity as she studied the uncertainty of his expression.

Huron took more time than necessary closing the room door. He sighed and finally turned with his hands raised defensively. "Anywhere but the face when you hit me," he said.

"Hmm…" Kam set down her fork and pretended to ponder the request. "The face is the best part, you know?"

He appeared playfully dubious then. "I can think of a much better one, but I ask that you not hit me there either."

She laughed and pushed away the sliding table that supported her food tray. "Come 'ere," she waved and then patted a spot near her hip on the bed.

269

"I didn't go looking for it, babe," he was explaining the moment he sat next to her. "Dutch and Sandra Breslin dug for it- thought they'd use it to embarrass you unless I agreed not to cut ties with them."

"How'd you find out?"

"I went to Vegas yesterday. When the doc told us about the baby I-" he waited for the muscle to cease its wicked jig along his jaw. "I snapped. Knowing that accident took our child-one created in love and not… something dark and depraved- it was too much Kam."

"I won't try to convince you *again* that it was never that. And besides," she tapped a silent absent tune along the back of his hand. "I've got my own explaining to do. I should've told you why I felt the way I did."

"Are you stupid?" His gorgeous features contracted fiercely. "Who'd want to talk to anyone about something like that?"

"I was wrong," she raked all ten fingers through her curls. "He wasn't my mother's father."

Huron leaned close to brace her chin on the curve of his fist. "Did you think I'd give a damn if he was?"

"You want kids," she wanted to bow her head, his fist prevented it. "I wouldn't have felt comfortable giving them to you."

He cupped her face then, practically smothering it inside two large palms. "I want *you*. Having kids would be the cherries on top of an already amazing cake," he kissed her.

It was intended to be a sweet peck, but immediately turned into something naughty when Kam took advantage and chased his tongue with hers.

"Kam," Huron tensed, murmuring her name in a manner that hinted of resistance.

"Kiss me," she ignored his reluctance.

270

He squeezed her elbows, gently urging her back. "Baby, we can't-"

She interrupted him with a lengthy thrust of her tongue followed by a thorough suckling of his. Huron groaned something obscene and gave in. He devoured her tongue while pressing her flat to the bed in the process.

Kam sighed her approval and draped her bowed legs over his lean hips. She squirmed and shifted impatiently until she felt what she most wanted nudging the middle of her panties. Desperate to be pleasured, Kam immediately began to grind on Huron whimpering into his mouth as sensation flared like wildfire. Her trembling moans did nothing to cool the arousal throbbing through Huron. His dick was painfully erect and felt fully capable of splitting the zipper of his jeans. Somehow, he managed to resist taking her every way he could. He could feel her hips, rocking, arching and rotating with greater urgency.

Mindless to have her, Huron squeezed the supple length of her thighs and ample bottom. Impatiently, he hooked his thumbs around the sides of her panties and yanked until the sound of ripping fabric jerked him from his sex haze.

"No…" Kam's voice was a whiny sob when he hesitated.

Huron held fast to his refusal, fisting his hands on either side of her. "I already promised to make this up to you later."

"Make it up to me now," she scratched his whiskers beneath her nails, repeated the move with her nose.

"Kam-"

"Come on…Just a little bit…I'm in absolutely no pain, I promise you," she imprisoned his wrist and worked his hand into her panties even as she tugged them off her hips.

271

Exercising greater strength and far greater will, Huron resisted her hold. He smiled when she glared up at him. "Not even a little bit," he said, kissing her cheek when she punched his side.

~21~

To Kam's dismay, the doctors opted to keep her another two weeks for observation. Given the extent of her injuries, most of all the miscarriage, no one except Kam scoffed over the medical staff's reasoning. Her release the following week was due in part to the fact that the Grades had decided to remain in San Francisco until their daughter had made a full recovery.

Huron decided that everyone would be more comfortable at his home in Marin County. The place had ample space to house an in-home nurse to give Casper and Raven downtime from caring for their daughter. The fact that Huron's place also boasted a fully equipped workout room; where Kam could work with a physical therapist if need be, satisfied the doctors that their patient would be released into quality care.

Kam was ecstatic to finally be leaving the four walls of the hospital room which had witnessed way too much drama. She was up and dressed a full two hours before her scheduled release time. She would discover however, that being released to the care of loved ones could provide its own set of…challenges..

~~~

Marin County, CA~

"But you've got *two* studies."

"And you won't be using either of them."

Kamari fixed the man she loved with a look that should have reduced him to a puddling mess. Huron's expression remained closed.

"I can't just spend weeks here without getting anything done. Where am I supposed to work from?"

Huron smiled then, his vivid jade eyes caressing the California King bed that was to be hers for the duration of her stay.

Kam didn't appear impressed by the decadent bed or the plush comfortable mauve and mocha room suite. "The doctor didn't say I had to be on bed rest."

"No he didn't. I did."

Too exasperated to challenge his declaration, Kam slid her glare from Huron to the other people in the room. One look at her parents, told her she'd get no sympathy from them.

Casper Grade stood wearing a broad grin across his attractively weather-beaten face which he directed toward Huron. "Does my heart good to know my girl has a man who can handle her."

"Daddy!"

Casper walked over to clap Huron's shoulder. Then, without a care for his daughter's sense of betrayal, he lifted Kam off her feet, kissed her cheek, set her back down and whistled a lively tune as he strode out of the room.

Raven Grade was less vocal about her approval, but the dreamy look in her eyes was approving enough. She walked past Huron and squeezed his arm on her way out the door. Disgusted, Kam rolled her eyes and looked to the other two people in the room.

Cousteau raised his hands defensively while crossing over to Kam. "Sorry sweetheart," he dropped a kiss to her temple and then made a pretense of whispering. "She'll hurt me bad if I don't go along with her," he glanced back to where Eliza stood near the foot of the bed.

"How's pizza sound for dinner tonight?" Eliza asked, not waiting on an answer before she left the room behind Cousteau.

Huron sighed satisfactorily once the room cleared. He drew Kam up high against his chest and kept her there. "We can't wait to have you back as the workaholic we all love and admire."

"That's bullshit, but it seems I'm outvoted," she pouted, crossing her arms over the baby doll T-shirt she wore and stubbornly refused to loop them around Huron's neck.

He grinned. "Let's get you in bed," he suggested.

"Just me?"

"For now?"

"For how long?"

He appeared playfully stressed. "Come on, babe… we got a house full of people."

She threw him a sharp look. "This house is as big as a castle."

275

"And you get pretty loud when I do things to you."

"Hmm…" Kam looked up at the high ceiling as though pondering the idea. "It's been so long, I've forgotten and since you're not in the mood to remind me…" She wriggled in his hold until he set her to her feet.

She stalked to the bed and began unpacking her things. "Close the door on your way out."

Undaunted, Huron walked up behind Kam and brushed a kiss across her nape. "I'll be back," he spoke the words against her skin.

"I won't wait up."

He grinned. "You will."

He was right and she resented having to admit the fact. When the door closed behind him, she reached for one of the smaller chocolate satin bed pillows and threw it out of protest.

***

Huron had arranged for a full house while Kam stayed with him to recuperate. The Grades as well as Cousteau and Eliza had suites in opposing wings on the other side of the house. As promised, Eliza had ordered pizza for dinner. Casper and Raven wouldn't be taking part in the meal that evening. Huron had arranged for them to have a night out on the town and the couple wasn't expected to return until the following morning.

As ordered, Kam kept close to her bed for much of the day. That evening, she was propped against the pillows lining the long cushioned headboard and reviewing her notes on the Cormack job.

Cousteau and Eliza relaxed on the lounge chairs they'd pulled to the foot of the California King. Two extra extra-large pizzas were set out along the bottom edge of the huge bed for all to enjoy. The large plasma screen was tuned to one of the 24 hour news channels. No one had been more surprised than Eliza to discover that her mother's story was getting national coverage. Cousteau and Eliza chatted idly about the various stories being covered during the broadcast while they ate.

Kam was reaching for her water glass, when she noticed her companions simultaneously lean closer to the wall mounted television. The split picture above the broadcaster's shoulder, showed Jessica Breck to one side and an older, vaguely familiar man on the other.

~~~

"A stunning development in the case of California socialite Jessica Breck-Mrs. Breck, in jail on charges of the murder, of her nephew Simon Breck. Mrs. Breck's nephew had allegedly threatened to reveal her past as an adult film star for a Las Vegas film studio. Mrs. Breck was recently cleared of those charges, following a plea arrangement contingent on evidence Mrs. Breck claims reveals the perpetrators in a rape case.

While the alleged rape is decades old," the broadcaster continued, "it's the perpetrators of this brutal crime who now have officials at some of the highest levels of law enforcement in an uproar."

Lead In News has learned that the key assailant in this crime is allegedly Republican Senator Ethan Errol of Pennsylvania. You may recall that Senator Errol was recently named to lead a national task force charged with the investigation and apprehension of those suspected in the sale and distribution of weapons to Middle Eastern and West African regimes…"

Cousteau's low whistle of amazement gained a few decibels when Eliza lowered the TV volume.

"*These* are the people I encouraged my mother to take a stand against for her freedom?" Eliza breathed, her tone one of disbelief…and fear.

Neither Kamari nor Cousteau offered up a response but they were both thinking similarly to Eliza. Jessica Breck may have been safer tucked away behind bars.

***

Kam continued to work after Cousteau and Eliza retired to their own wing of the house. The three of them had chatted long after the airing of the latest development in Jessica's case. Afterwards, Kam worked to catch up on what she'd missed out on being absent from the daily operations of her company.

Around midnight, she was satisfied that she'd done enough. Instead of returning her files and notes to the large oak desk in the room's spacious alcove, she just set them to the other side of the bed on the floor. She was setting the last of the paperwork to the floor when the door opened. It was Huron.

Sighing, she kneeled near the head of the bed. "Don't have a cow, I'm about to go to sleep."

"Hold off on that," he shut the door, twisted the lock.

"So…are we gonna talk or watch TV?" Kam refused to let any other hopes work themselves in. She slapped her hands to her bare thighs and gave a defeated shrug. "What side of the bed do you want?"

When he stood before her and stripped, her mouth went dry. Her eyes followed the descent of his shirt until it hit the floor.

"We'll just play it by ear, see where we wind up afterward."

278

"Afterward? After what?" She still refused to let her hopes rise, yet her eyes faltered to his hands at the belt around his jeans. She cleared her throat and forced her eyes to his, realizing he was intentionally taking his time dropping the jeans once he'd unbuckled the belt and loosened the button fly.

"Women don't like to be teased either," she told him.

Huron let the jeans fall. "I'll remember that."

She made quick work of pulling her T-shirt above her head when he stood before her in nothing but his boxers. The garment tented at the middle where he sported an impressive erection. Kam was nothing beneath her T-shirt, but a pair of pink, cotton boy shorts.

"Tell me if I get too rough," he said.

"I wouldn't dream of it," she returned his smirk.

Huron reached across the bed, linking one arm about Kam's waist. He brought her up high against his sleek chest. Despite her eagerness, the substantial pects flexing beneath her fingertips held Kam in a state of awe. Hesitantly, she tested the firmness of the muscular slabs. Her fingertips applied the slightest pressure as they dug into his taut flesh.

She shivered when his erection nudged her belly and lifted herself so that the crown of his cock was nudging her clit instead. They were both still covered by their respective undergarments, but the friction generated when she moved against him, was supremely appreciated.

Huron clearly appreciated it as well. His generous palms curved about her bottom, cradling the full globes while plying her middle with faint, mocking thrusts.

Kamari moaned, taking his earlobe between her teeth and pampering it with a dry suckle. All the while, her thumbnail grazed a male nipple which instantly pebbled

279

beneath the manipulation. She had become so used to him holding out on her, that she was content with the subtle grinding he used to pleasure her. Huron realized that, knowing she was seeking release through the heated yet mediocre act.

She cried out suddenly in surprise and disappointment when he tugged her away, letting her gently tumble back against the bed. Delight glimmered through her when she saw him follow her halfway down. Crouching above, he focused on removing her panties.

Kam helped, lifting her butt until the garment hugged her thighs. They held there briefly until Huron had completely removed them. She bit her lip, concentrating on helping with the removal of his boxers. Huron, it seemed, wasn't seeking such assistance just then. Instead, he knelt to the floor, tugging Kam downward until the plump swell of her bottom was touching the edge of the bed. Spreading her thighs, he pleasured her slit with faint, delightful caresses using the tip of his nose.

Kam's resulting cry provided a wondrous massage to Huron's ego. He glanced up to find her cupping her perfect breasts as she arched her body toward him in a show of complete submission. He had to squeeze his eyes closed to block the sight. He was sure to cream his shorts soon enough without the added stimuli of her fondling herself.

He outlined her clit with the tip of his nose until tasting her became paramount. His tongue flicked the nub until an erotic rhythm ensured. Each time he bathed the sensitive mound of flesh, a breathy cry wisped past her beautiful mouth.

She pleaded with him then, motivating him with soft choruses of 'yes' when Huron used his thumbs to spread the silken caramel toned folds of her sex. Her hips left the bed when he finally took her with his tongue, plunging the organ deep. He didn't break contact when her hips lifted, merely set his palm to her tummy and eased her down.

Huron penetrated deep, rotating with an expertise that had Kam moaning as she shamelessly rode his tongue. He withdrew following only a half dozen impassioned thrusts before returning to nibble her puckered and needy clit.

Kam bucked her hips again and he cupped them keeping her virtually immobile then. Spasms of pleasure radiated in response to being restrained and subjected to such erotic torment. There was no escape with his broad torso lodged between her thighs.

Of course, she had no intentions or hopes for escape especially when he ruthlessly suckled her clit instead of merely nibbling on it. He eased one hand beneath her butt and used his thumb to stimulate her anus.

Kamari didn't know whether to use her limited movement to arch into the attention he gave her clit or to ride on his thumb where it probed her ass.

The decision became moot when he straightened over her. Cupping her thighs, Huron pushed her higher on the bed where she lay parallel to the headboard. He followed her up, tugging at the waistband of his boxers until his dick was free of the material. He was so erect, so hard for her, that he didn't need to use his hand to guide himself inside her lithe body. He eased home the second the wide, flawless head of his sex met her entrance.

"Yeah…mmm…" Kam stammered out the words when he breached her core, stretching her with a merciless delicious intent.

"Kam…God…" he fisted his hands to either side of her on the bed until he was buried deep inside her.

For purchase, Kamari clutched his powerfully chorded forearms, squeezing him there as she worked her hips in clockwise and counter moves that drew sultry moans from them both. Her thighs caressed his hips, the curve of his ass and she used her small feet to move the boxers on down his thighs until he kicked them off once they slid to his ankles. She locked her legs about his waist then, in case he had any plans for depriving her of what she'd been denied for too long.

Huron knew their encounter wouldn't be a lengthy one, but he wanted to make it good while it lasted. Buried to the hilt as he was would have him coming in seconds-she felt just that incredible. The way her inner muscles squeezed his shaft had him gasping her name as he mindlessly pumped his hips. He was obsessed with losing himself inside the tight, moist well of her sex.

"I could get you pregnant again," he panted over an erect nipple.

"'Kay," she panted back, lost in the sensation stirred by the languid advance and retreat of his thick endowment.

Huron's low chuckle, curbed on a sound of sheer satisfaction. He tensed inside her a split second before he was drenching her walls with his semen. He moved just slightly to his knees, taking Kam's hips and securing himself in the vee of her thighs. The position made him come more freely and he was sure he'd pass out any minute.

His unforgettable stare roamed the little beauty who gave herself to him so completely, so trustingly. "Tell me you're mine," he said.

"I'm yours," there was no hesitation. She didn't need to think about it when it was so very accurate.

He closed his eyes, hands tightening like a vice on her hips. Directing her moves, he eased her back and forth on his ejaculating cock, believing he'd soon be flooding her with his seed. When he was thoroughly spent, he gently returned her to the bed. He labored to still his breathing while bracing his weight between the fists he'd planted on either side of Kam.

She looked depleted and Huron feared he may have pushed her too far until he spied the contentment glowing on her lovely face.

"Please tell me we can do that again," she sighed.

He settled over her, careful not to give her the brunt of his weight. He dropped a kiss to her cheek. "Anything for you," he said and nuzzled his face into the crook of her neck.

~~~

Huron was first to awaken after he and Kam had collapsed following a third love session. He frowned, not quite sure where she was on the mammoth bed which they'd had sex over every square inch of.

He smiled, finding her sprawled on her back near the foot of the mattress. He watched her for a long while, loving the way her mouth parted and the rise and fall of her bare breasts as she slumbered. Her legs were parted- one knee raised slightly above the other.

His dick twitched, sending a message to his brain that it wanted more of what his eyes were then fixed on. He didn't have the heart to wake her, but moved over to partly cover her with the corner of the comforter. It would be best to remove the temptation just the same, he decided.

They hadn't bothered with turning off any lights beforehand, so Huron decided to take care of that while he was half awake, he'd been asleep near the head of the bed. Once his vision cleared, he noticed the files and pads on the floor.

To avoid them, he began to ease towards the bottom of the mattress. That was when he spotted the news clippings that had slid from one of the folders. Curious, he bent to retrieve one of the clippings and was reduced instantly to a weakened mass. It took some time before he regained more control over the hand that clutched the clipping.

Huron reminded himself to breathe. He looked towards Kamari then, his expression one of disbelief and devastation.

~22~

Kamari smiled when she woke, feeling more content than she'd felt in what seemed like years to her. Her smile deepened as she snuggled into the pillow, wanting sleep to carry her back into oblivion. It seemed she'd had her fill of the treat however. Instead of her lashes drifting shut to shield her gaze, her eyes scanned the room where she rested.

Kam slid her hand from beneath the cool pillow to where she knew Huron would be resting. She didn't feel him next to her, but thought nothing of it considering how insanely huge the bed was. Languidly, she eased to her other side. Her contented smile adopted a curious element when she saw that he wasn't in bed, but sitting in the armchair next to it. Her head lifted from the pillow when she saw he was already dressed.

"Hey…" she added a lazy wave to the greeting. "Early meeting?"

"Not exactly," Huron directed a fleeting glance toward his worn jeans and T-shirt emblazoned with the logo of his favorite football team. One of his bare feet was propped on the edge of the bed.

Kam shrugged. "I figured that," she scanned the length of him. "So? Why are you up?"

"I thought you'd want to get back to work," he offered a thin smile, "looks like you've got a lot of it here."

Kam took note of the work she'd transferred to the floor the night before. Huron had set it to the bed where it waited in four neat stacks. "Thanks," she fixed the work with a stale look, "but I'm in no hurry to get back to it."

"Really?" his eyes narrowed curiously. "Looks interesting…will you tell me about it?"

Her smile turned wicked. "Come back to bed and I will."

"Looks dangerous," he glanced toward the stacks of paperwork. "I couldn't help but notice when I took it all from the floor."

Kam saw him wave a folder of the news clippings. "Yeah," she sighed then as some of the wickedness fled her eyes. "It's not the 'feel good' case of the year."

"Case," he nodded, tapping the folder to a raised knee. "So it's for an investigation."

"Looks like some embezzlement scheme," Kam pushed up a bit on the bed.

Mild amusement along with something more subtle lurked in Huron's stare. "Embezzlement. And you think this guy-"

"James Bolton," Kam supplied.

His stare narrowed further. "James Bolton...and you think he's responsible?"

Kam got comfortable against a few pillows she'd bunched together. "That's what my client wants to know," she said.

"Someone hired you to find out about him?"

"Dan Tate's boss is losing money," Kam closed her eyes, relishing the pillows beneath her back. "He can't account for it and all roads seem to be leading toward that guy," she nodded toward the clippings.

"All roads?" Huron queried.

"I've found accounts set up under phony names with Mr. Bolton's being the only one I can get a bead on."

Huron set the folder to the bed. "What kind of... bead?" he asked.

The case intrigued Kamari so, that she didn't think to question Huron's interest. It'd been some time since she'd had anyone to spout her theories to.

"That guy's got a pretty colorful past," she gave the folder an engaged look. "I found an array of charges to prove it- carjackings, assaults, illegal weapons..."

"Hmph, not the kind of guy you'd want to meet in a dark alley."

"I don't think he's the kind of guy I'd want to meet anywhere."

Kam didn't notice Huron averting his face to hide the stricken look there. Her expression mellowed, adopting a contemplative gleam.

"I think there's more to his story, though," she said.
"How so?"

"Those clippings paint a picture of a pretty scary guy, but when he was eleven he was labeled a hero."

"Kam," Huron grimaced, "this guy's far from a hero."

"Agreed," she shrugged half-heartedly, "but I couldn't help but think that the system failed him somehow."

"Is this all you found?" he waved toward the array of folders and pads on the bed.

"Pretty much," she fixed her compiled work with a hopeful look. "I just refuse to believe it's the sum total of the man's life."

"Maybe it is."

"I doubt that."

"So take it on faith, then."

Kam yawned. "Maybe I could if it wasn't my job to find out more."

"What does finding out more have to do with proving whether he embezzled money?"

She smiled, cuddling deeper into the pillows. "It's just part of the quirky way I do my job-helps me to gain a clearer picture of the people I go after before I make judgments based on the client's observations."

"Like you did with me."

"Like I did with you," she smiled. "You're not as scary as I originally thought," her smile gave way to a short laugh that hinted of a deeper meaning.

"What?" Huron questioned the gesture.

"I was just thinking about how I *still* don't have your full story."

His was an ill-humored laugh when it emerged. "You've got more of it than you realize."

"Really?" She almost giggled then. "And what about the stuff you asked me not to go looking for until you'd *handled* things?"

288

"Well…there's that," he smiled, "but it's nothing compared to what you already know."

"But I don't know anything," she did giggle then, "certainly nothing that hints of you being this deep, dark monster you insist on making yourself out to be-"

"Kamari…"

"What?" At last, she took note of his torment. "Baby what? What's wrong with you?"

Huron took a moment, then forced himself to look at her. "James Bolton, Kamari…Honey, he's me."

~~~

The conversation came to an abrupt halt when a knock sounded on the bedroom door shortly after Kam had quickly changed into a comfy sleep set. Lukas Moyers had arrived with Kam's breakfast. Not only was eating the last thing on Kam's mind, it was something she felt ill-prepared to accomplish given the ceaseless jarring of her stomach muscles.

"Eat," Huron decided, once his houseman left them to dine alone.

"Huron-"

"I talk- you eat," he bartered from his chair near the bed.

Kam obliged albeit slowly while anticipating how hard it would be to swallow the inviting breakfast.

"I don't understand," her voice held an equally lost tone as she unrolled the silverware from a thick navy and green plaid napkin which she draped over her lap.

"I don't understand either, babe. I never expected to hear the name James Bolton again."

"Why'd you change it?" She broke off a corner of cinnamon raisin toast and popped it in her mouth when Huron looked pointedly at her plate.

"My life changed in ways I never saw coming after that night. The um- the night it happened," he swallowed with effort. "My mother always said she wanted to get me out of California before the place had the chance to spoil me the way it had spoiled her. She planned to take me back to Bay City, Michigan. That's where she was from."

Huron folded his arms over his chest, shifting in the chair as memories stirred. "Her father- his name was James- he was a fishing guide up there. Mama said her parents' quiet life just wasn't for her- she wanted more excitement to show for it. She told me that later on she hated that it took her so long to understand how blessed she was back then. 'You should see Lake Huron, Jamie,'" a poignant light softened his gaze then and he smiled. "She always used to tell me that. She named me for my grandfather."

"I saw you in a picture with a woman-you were a kid in a baseball uniform. Was that your mom?" Kam probed.

Huron squeezed his eyes closed for just a moment. "Yeah...yeah that was her."

"She was really beautiful."

He nodded. "Yeah, she was...very...Hmph, baseball...she could've never afforded for me to play on her salary. Hmph, salary," he seemed amused by the word, but sobered quickly. "You're right," he sighed, "she was a real beauty.

She could've had any man she wanted. She had two that I remembered. Just her rotten luck that they were two of the worst."

"Crime bosses," Kam put that together based on the stories she'd read.

Huron chuckled. "If a pimp and a drug dealer pass for crime bosses, then I guess that's what they were."

He leaned over in the chair, bracing his elbows to his knees and studying the life lines in his hands. "The pimp started out as her boss and then a trick," he expelled a heavy breath and rubbed the bridge of his nose when pressure built there.

"After that, her pimp decided she was just too special to be a whore- a whore to anyone other than himself that is. Up until I was nine, I thought the son of a bitch was my father. He had a lot of money-gave us whatever we wanted or needed. But he also had a helluva temper."

Kam noticed the clench of his jaw when she looked up from cutting into one of the thick beef sausage medallions on her plate.

"It was nothing for him to grab her, knock her around…he didn't want her turning tricks, but he still treated her same as the other girls who worked for him. All the time, she talked about getting us out of there so she could take me to Michigan. 'I'm gonna show you Lake Huron, Jamie…'" he spoke softly to mimic his mother and then held a fist to his mouth.

Kam had noticed his bottom lip trembling and knew he was attempting to hide it. She listened intently, but kept her eyes on her food.

"As bad as he got- his name was Esteban Orroyo- that didn't stop her from betraying him. When she met Carl Ives, she forgot all about taking me to Michigan."

"Was that the drug dealer?" Kam asked, while cutting into the second sausage medallion.

"Yeah," Huron's mouth thinned. "He was worse than Orroyo ever was. Ives was new on the scene, but he

291

had a lot of juice- a lot of people ready to do his bidding and even more who were afraid of him. But he was smart too. He went to Orroyo asking to use his girls as drug mules and the man was all too ready to profit."

Kam's fork paused over her food. "How do you know all this?"

Huron's smile held a reminiscent flare. "Folks are always willing to share war stories especially with someone they thought had saved their life." He gave a weary shrug. "Like I said, Ives was smart; his clientele was robust but not as diverse as he wanted.

He and Orroyo met up somewhere and he thought the man might be able to help him break into a more mainstream market. Orroyo ran high end call girls that serviced everyone from businessmen to pro athletes."

"So it was a match made in heaven," Kam noted, idly munching on a crunchy white grape.

Huron straightened, shifting his big body in the chair when he relaxed back into it. "It could've been just that, had Ives not been at the house one night when Mama was there and discovered that Orroyo was the 'complicated relationship' she'd told him she couldn't get out of."

"That's what she told him?" Riveted on the story, Kam absently reached for another grape.

"That's what I heard when they were all arguing downstairs. I was in my room when I heard the voices- the yelling," he sighed. "I got downstairs in time to see Orroyo hit her and she…she um-hit her head- they didn't even notice her- Orroyo and Ives- they just kept arguing over her. I held her until she died." Huron tried to swallow down emotion, but it was useless. He didn't try to wipe away the tears that pooled his eyes and streamed his cheeks.

"They each had bodyguards there. I don't remember how many I…I knew where Esteban kept his guns. I was um...big for my age and I-I got two of the biggest I could handle and ran down the stairs blastin'. When it was over I called 911 for my mom even though I knew she was gone," he smiled weakly thinking of the simplistic outlook of his eleven year old mind.

"At first, they thought it was a deal gone bad but then they discovered the truth and there I was- in the system and fucked."

"No one tried to argue self-defense?" Kam asked.

Genuine amusement flashed on Huron's face. "Not for me, they didn't."

"Your mom's family?" Kam asked.

Huron shook his head. "Her folks were dead and they couldn't find any other relatives so...I went into the system- met some good people but...that didn't stop me from adding to my already colorful list of indiscretions. I left Cali and changed my name when I turned eighteen."

"Where'd Base come from?"

He smirked then and leaned forward to swipe one of the strawberries from her plate. "I thought it sounded powerful. Hmph...I made almost the same idiot moves as Huron Base as James Bolton, but then you know all that." He studied her coolly.

"After a while, I came back to California- didn't have a plan but it turned out I didn't need one. I was welcomed like a fucking hero. A lot of people benefitted from Orroyo's and Ives' deaths. A lot of important people...my street cred," he smiled over the phrase, "it was established for life."

Regret rimmed his brilliant gaze though. "I didn't want to be the man I was, but I wasn't above using the advantages my rep granted me. I reasoned it all out using the fact that some parts of the past could never be erased.

I've done questionable things as Huron Base, Kam," he said when she looked over at him again. "It's amazing what you can get away with when you've got a rep admired by villains and a talent for making money for everybody else including yourself. I discovered the last thanks to a really good man who took me under his wing and tried to teach me the benefits of doing business legally."

"Huron," Kam shook her head in wonder over the complexity of his story. "Baby, you've got nothing to be ashamed of now-you've paid for those mistakes."

Huron looked as though he wanted to believe her. "I don't feel half as much shame as I do regret that my mother didn't get me out of that hell."

"I guess she did what she thought was best," Kam smiled. "She'd be proud of you now."

He gave a playful cringe. "I don't think she'd buy that the ends justified the means. For better or for worse though, I am who I am and I um…I've become pretty fond of my name."

"That's good," Kam laughed. "Because I like *it* and who *you* are."

"I never wanted you to know any of this," his tone was hushed, "James Bolton may have been a hero at eleven, but he did far more heinous things down the road. That's a past I tried to bury deep under a new and powerful life."

Kam pushed back the wood grained bed table she'd eaten from. "What was that you said about parts of the past never being erased?"

"I know, right?" He agreed, a measure of ease having resumed. "Some folks who knew me when- would never let me forget-"

"Huron?" Kam noticed the sudden change in his expression when he moved forward on his chair.

"I need to go check on something," he spoke as though dazed and then seemed to snap out it and looked at Kam. "Will you be okay?"

She nodded slowly, still watching him with concern pooling her smoky stare. "Mom or El should be in to check on me soon."

"'Kay," Huron moved in to kiss Kam's cheek. "I'll be back for lunch. I love you." He spoke into her skin and then eased back to search her eyes before he left the room.

~23~

The hunch Huron played was shaky at best, but it was one that made perfect sense. Kam's curiosity had been insatiable when she demanded answers on his disappearing act following their revealing discussion. When he told her to give him a little more time and then topped it off by saying; if it panned out she might be able to tell her client she'd solved his case, she was too intrigued to argue.

Now, a week later, Huron realized his curiosity still hadn't outweighed his anger- anger at himself for underestimating who he'd considered a friend.

~~~

"B?" Theo Sturgess sounded happily surprised when he discovered who waited inside his office that afternoon. He hurried into the room, apparently taking no offence at finding Huron seated behind his desk.

"Good to see you, man! Wasn't sure when I would after our last talk."

"Right…you told me I'd never be more than who I am," Huron pushed up from the desk.

"Aw B, don't be like that," Theo drawled, laughter mixed with his words. "You took what I said the wrong way. I just don't think it does anyone any good to not be true to themselves."

"Like you? Upstanding to a fault, huh?"

Theo tensed, the fine material of his cream double breasted suit coat growing taut across his barrel chest. "We all make mistakes, B."

"You're damn right we do," Huron's smile was grim, his gaze like jadestone. "Some of my biggest were believing I'd never find a woman to love me for who I am and who I was and thinking that who I was defined me. But my biggest mistake of all was probably believing that you had interest in being as much a friend to me as your father was."

Theo raised his beefy hands, "Now hold up, B, we-"

"You were ever only interested in what I could do for you- who I could scare the shit out of for you."

Theo was incredulous. "B, man where the fuck is this shit comin' from?"

"It's coming from James Bolton. Or is that *you* now?"

Theo turned ashen beneath his light complexion. He laughed after a moment, but the gesture held a decided edge. "Huron what-"

"Do you know why your dad never wanted to give you the run of his business?" Huron paced the office, hands shoved deep inside honey beige trousers to hide fists clenched so tightly they ached.

"Because you never surprised him by doing the right thing," he went on, his voice menacingly soft. "He always predicted you'd fuck up and you never let him down."

"Oh and you just knew the old man so well, huh?!" Theo finally snapped.

Huron's smile was quick but genuine. "I knew you were an idiot to steal from him. I knew he didn't give you the top spot in his business because you were predictable and impatient and money is an unpredictable and patient game."

"Fuck you, B," Theo sneered, shaking his head as though he pitied Huron's opinions. "You want to know what *I* know? My father was a bastard who would've kissed a dog's ass before giving me one syllable of encouragement!" He spread his arms wide in a deceptively welcoming gesture.

"He rolled out the red carpet for you though, didn't he? Taught you all his secrets of success. You! The son of some twenty dollar hooker!"

"So you decided to get back at him by embezzling money from a string of companies including your own father's- funneling the money into an account you started with *my* former name and social security number?"

Theo staggered back a bit on the pretense of confusion.

"Was it just my identity you used for this scam or others?"

"What are you doin' here, B?" Theo Sturgess sounded as if he already knew.

"I'm here to tell you to resign your position here. Your dad built a good company for you to sit up in here and dishonor it with deceit."

"Who the fuck do you think you are?" Theo leaned over his desk, bracing his fists to the gleaming wood surface.

"I'm the one who's hired a team of accountants to start tracing that money in hopes of getting it back to its rightful owners." Huron reclined against the office door. "They've already proven that the phony accounts link back to you, tsk, tsk, the smart thing to do would've been to build a phony ID for yourself but well...predictable and impatient..."

"Get out," Theo turned, strolled behind his desk.

"Happy too, but I won't be going far," Huron braced off the door. "If I can try to clean up my act, so can you." The grin he gave held no amusement. "Me being the son of a twenty dollar hooker and all...should be easy for you given where you come from."

"Mighty Huron Base..." Theo relaxed in his desk chair. "You got no power over me."

"None I ever thought I'd use. But I owe your dad way too much, and since I'm trying to clean up my act," Huron shrugged, "I can't look the other way anymore, Thee."

"What are you-" Theo's eyes widened with sudden realization. "You son of a bitch. You can't-"

"Actually, I can." It was Huron's turn to shake his head at his old friend. "All those years ago... You were so fixed on getting revenge on that poor guy who really only told the truth about you that you didn't think twice about signing away over half of what your father built for you."

Theo seemed to wilt in the big chair supporting him. "You-you can't-"

299

"Again, I can. The board seemed satisfied by the transfer of papers you signed back then especially since it came with a rider signed by your father."

"My-" Stricken, Theo couldn't even breathe out the rest of his question. "He-he knew I-I gave you..."

"That gave them all the confidence they needed to vote you out." Huron stroked his whiskered jaw and pretended to be most interested in the design of the carpeting beneath his feet. "You never wondered why Mr. Frank gave you the run of things when he took the early retirement for his health? He trusted me to keep you on the straight and narrow which was like the blind leading the blind since I was way off the straight and narrow my damned self.

I owe him more than that and I plan on repaying in full. We'd appreciate it if you didn't take any files on your way out of here, Thee. Security guys won't like it much when they frisk you."

Theodore Sturgess watched his oldest friend leave the room without another word. He stood motionless for the greater part of two minutes. Hands finally fisting at his sides, he let out a pained sigh that sounded closer to a wheeze.

***

"Kam?" Huron looked into the bedroom later that evening. He'd been told that she'd asked to have a 'normal' dinner that night with everyone seated around the table.

He saw that the TV was off. Kam was on her side and he was happy to find her getting a little sleep before the meal.

Huron stepped into the room. Closing the door, he leaned against it out of the hope to steady his suddenly choppy breathing. Half a minute passed, before he accepted that it would probably not calm until he told her what he'd come to say.

"Kam?" Slowly, he crossed the room and eased onto the bed where he settled down behind her. "Babe?" He smiled when she gave a little moan and he grazed the shell of her ear beneath his mouth.

"Huron?" Kam wiggled onto her other side.

Adoration filled his eyes while he watched her give into a yawn. Then, she was looking up at him with a sleepy smile.

"Can I tell my client I solved his case?"

"You can."

"Yaaay…"

Huron's adoration intensified as he took great delight in her appearing every bit the happy little girl.

"Can I tell him how I did it?" She asked.

"Sure."

"Well?"

"Later. There's something else I need to tell you first."

"Okay…"

"I want to marry you."

Kamari's eyes stretched in sync with her mouth opening, but no sound emerged.

"I don't expect an answer yet," Mild dismay crossed his gorgeous face as he sighed. "I guess we can wait a little while for you to make up your mind."

"We?"

"Oh," he reached into the back pocket of his trousers and removed a tiny, black suede box. He thumbed it open to reveal a dazzling square diamond perched in the center of a platinum band. "Me and this guy," he watched the shock intensify her surprise. "He'll just wait in here 'till you're ready to have us lay claim to you," he added.

301

Dazed, Kam reached out to trace the ring beneath her nail. "So um…he's just gonna stay in there torturing me with his beauty until I give an answer?"

"He's a diva like that," Huron shrugged. "Besides, he guesses it's only fair."

"Fair?" Curiosity narrowed her lush brown gaze.

Huron nuzzled his nose to hers. "You torture me with your beauty every time I see you."

"Torture, huh? And now you're asking for something that'll pretty much guarantee constant torture for years?"

"Forever," he clarified.

"Huron, are you sure?"

"Completely," his response came without hesitation- his voice unwavering. "Just say you'll think about it."

"I don't need to think about it."

His breathing staggered at the sound of her words and he readied himself for her refusal. Then, he noticed that she was extending her left hand toward him, fingers stretched apart. Huron shifted his weight transferring the box to his other hand.

"He's possessive," he told her, "it'll be impossible to get rid of him once he'd attached," he tugged the ring from its cushiony perch.

"That's good to hear," Kam whispered, a nervous eagerness clinging to her voice and expression. "I hope he won't get tired of being attached to me." She bit her lip while Huron eased the jewelry into place.

"Impossible," he whispered back. "You're his lifeline. And mine," he cupped her chin until she was looking at him. "I love you," he said.

Kam scooted closer, "I love you," she spoke the sentiment against his mouth.

302

Huron initiated a deeper kiss, driving the phrase home with every thrust of his tongue. Kamari moaned the words back into his mouth. The sensuous, meaningful wordplay blended into hushed, happy laughter until the unmistakable sounds of lovemaking flooded the air.

Dear Reader,

It's not easy to craft stories such as this one. Layers of the Past was my intention from the original release of Layers. I knew, however, that what I had; at that time, simply envisioned, would not be possible were it not for the laying of a gripping foundation and the characters that would support it.

Huron Base and Kamari Grade are those characters, but not simply because of their chemistry. Anyone who reads my work, knows how much I adore flawed, complex, dark characters. Again, Huron and Kam were those people. I knew though, that they would require a platform where the complexities that gave birth to their flaws and darkness could be thoroughly exposed.

The secondary characters are who made that possible. From Cousteau and Eliza to Theo Sturgess and the Breslins, the secondary characters allowed for this story to deepen as layers of revelations were peeled away.

Thanks for coming along on this journey and for sharing your thoughts on the experience.

Email Me: altonya@lovealtonya.com

Be Blessed,
AlTonya

ALTONYA EXCLUSIVE TITLES

Soul's Desire
Through It All
Truth In Sensuality
Ruler of Perfection
Layers
Another Love
Expectation of Beauty
Dancing With Destiny
Pleasure's Powerhouse
What the Heart Wants
Taboo Tree
Mixed Signals
Model Intentions
TimeChange
Ravenous: Ruler of Perfection II
When Ice Melts

FIND ALTONYA ON THE WEB

www.lovealtonya.com
www.alsreaders.com
www.facebook.com/altonyaw
www.goodreads.com
www.twitter.com/#!/ramseysgirl

An AlTonya Exclusive